Cinderella Boy

A NOVEL BY
Kristina Meister

TRITON BOOKS

Triton Books
PO Box 1537
Burnsville, NC 28714
www.Tritonya.com
Triton Books is an imprint of Riptide Publishing.
www.RiptidePublishing.com

Cinderella Boy

Cover art: Shayne Leighton, parliamentbookdesign.wordpress.com
Editor: May Peterson
Layout: L.C. Chase, lcchase.com/design.htm

ISBN: 978-1-62649-799-3

First edition
July, 2018

Also available in ebook:
ISBN: 978-1-62649-798-6

Cinderella Boy

A NOVEL BY
Kristina Meister

TRITON
BOOKS

For my husband and partner. Thank you for seeing what I could be and helping me to realize it.

Table
of Contents

Chapter 1
The Moment

Suitcases built a little fort on the front step, and an Uber idled in the driveway.

"Don't give your sister trouble," Declan's mother said to him, as if it wouldn't be the other way around. She pushed the curly hair from his face, clearly thinking it a loving gesture. To him it was like being unmasked. He dodged.

Dad hugged Delia and snuck a look at his lock screen. Then his parents were off on their second honeymoon, looking as if they desperately needed it. Declan watched them leave, feeling the pressure build like a creeping mass in his chest.

Delia waited all of ten seconds before diving into her messenger. "I've got to go to the store."

"Mom already bought us groceries."

She rolled her eyes. "It's for the party, Dex."

His stomach lurched, as the thought of being overrun by a stampede of ridiculous teenagers crashed through his mind. He pushed up his glasses. "We can't have a party here!"

She slid her bare feet into sparkling sandals and grabbed her purse from the table. "Duh. It's at Carter's house."

Declan looked away, just as his face started to burn. Carter Aadenson, always first on the roll sheet, first in line, first place, first in mind. First.

"I thought he dumped you," he mumbled, poking his fingers through the hole in his ancient, secondhand jeans. He hated them, but they were perfectly ugly. When Declan wore them, no one saw him, or the smooth skin beneath.

"*We* broke up. *Mutually.*" She scowled at her face in the hall mirror. Her lipstick was too dark for her. It looked better on him.

Declan glanced at the stairs. "How long will you be gone?"

"I'm fine like I am. I'll probably go right over. His parties usually end around midnight, because he makes amnesty bargains with the neighbors."

"You still like him, don't you?"

The bite in his voice must have been obvious.

"What's not to like? But we're just friends. Don't worry. He's not going to break your dear sister's heart."

Declan pictured Carter as he had been that snowy day over Christmas break. Never had an ugly sweater been so sexy. He'd had his perfect hair, his perfect face, his perfect blue eyes, and without a second thought, he'd folded up his perfect long legs and played *Minecraft* beside Declan, their arms brushing at least ten times. He was an athlete, which meant he gave off enough body heat to melt Antarctica, and Declan had felt it radiating off of him. Watching Carter's fingers grasp the controller, he'd counted breaths and fought for self-control. And when Carter got up, a perfect hand had tousled Declan's mop of hair. To Carter, Declan was "A pretty cool dude."

At once, the greatest compliment and blackest insult Declan had ever received.

Delia threw kissy faces at the mirror. "It's probably going to be a big party, this close to the start of the year. Not sure how many people will be there, but because of me, you know half the—"

"I'm not going."

"I know Mila is going to be there, and Priah too."

He looked back at the stairs longingly, feeling the itch. "Whatever. Have a G-D blast."

"That time of the month?"

"Fuck off."

"You know, if you pulled your head out of your games for like five seconds, you might think high school was fun, not the seventh circle of hell."

"That's the one for Instagrammers, right?"

She seemed to avoid looking him in the eye as she scrawled out a shopping list. "Look, you left Saint Catherine's for a reason. This is a chance to do things differently. My friends aren't like those prep-school assholes! If we cleaned you up, Priah might be willing to be seen with you."

He gagged involuntarily and ducked away from her outstretched hand. "Leave me alone. I don't want to date your bitchy friends."

Delia stared at him. She had to be confused, worried. Saint Catherine's had taken a huge toll on him, and with every confrontation, black eye, and night spent crying himself to sleep, he'd shut her out. It was because she was too smart, and he had spent a long time as her shadow, idolizing her. If anyone would see his secret, it would be her, and so she became the first enemy. It was unavoidable.

But that night was especially bad, because the *moment* was waiting.

Declan gazed fixedly at the ground, and Delia gave up.

"Fine. Stay in your room and be a dick. Enjoy jerking yourself off for the rest of your life."

She slammed the door on the way out. He waited until her bright-red Beetle pulled away, feeling the pain in his chest more acutely than ever. Switching schools was supposed to have fixed their relationship, but it was possible that he had forgotten how to be a brother.

He swallowed down his anxiety as he locked the dead bolt. He could forget about everything when he sat down at her dressing table. Taking a deep, cleansing breath, Declan pushed his hair back from his face and shed his glasses on the way up.

A pile of shoes and coats blocked her door. He stepped over them carefully, glad that her messy ways concealed his invasion of her privacy to a large degree. The dress was where she'd left it, hooked over her desk chair like a dirty towel, the tags still on it. He ran his fingers over the ruching and winked back the sting.

It was so effortless and inborn for her that she could toss her femininity around like nothing. She left her castoffs in her wake, giving him only a few stolen moments of peace. It was unfair. But nobody ever said life was fair.

He pulled his shirt over his head and caught sight of a skinny torso in her dressing mirror. If he didn't look, it would be okay, he told himself. Away went the jeans. He tugged the dress over his head and into place. Delia was curvy. Tailoring darts made it hang on his chest.

He considered socks stuffed into a bra, but a bra would show through the sheer back. He wandered into her closet to dig out her strappy stilettos from the winter formal and found the silver bangle bracelet on the way.

He was one dress size smaller, and one shoe size larger, but for the *moment*, he could deal with these discrepancies.

Brushing his tangle of hair back with some water, he pretended not to notice how boyish it looked. Pinterest told him that to do the eyes right, he had to find a makeup brush. Her makeup tools were always scattered around her pigsty of a bathroom, caked in cosmetics. He dug out the mascara there too, but she must have taken the dark lipstick with her. Declan settled for the pink gloss. The YouTube vids always said it was better to have either a dramatic eye *or* a dramatic lip, and his eyes were a saving grace.

"Carter Aadenson," he whispered. The sort of boy put on this earth to torment, and he had unwittingly tormented Declan for two years. Kissing his sister on the porch, cuddling her on the couch, sharing his private jokes in the hollow of her ear.

One day, when he could escape, Declan would do it right. He would be himself at last, not who they always thought he was. Maybe then, he could walk up to Carter, or some blessed angel like him, and buy him a drink.

"It gets better."

The old armor was a wrinkled husk on the bed. The shoes' straps cut into his skin but made him feel more powerful than ever before. He tipped the mirror and turned in profile.

So strange to think that the real person had to be drawn out like poison, bled out from inside. Who that real person was, he didn't know, but he knew he was a little closer to them.

He spotted the movement behind him much too late. In the span of a gasp, she appeared in the mirror and dropped her purse. Her mouth hung open in a hideous O as his legs, those gangly things, went weak.

Not a word was spoken. Cold burned through Declan and was replaced with fire. Like a newborn foal, his gallop to the safety of the closet ended in a haphazard pile on the floor. One of the chic strappy shoes had snapped, and a livid mark appeared on his ankle.

But Declan could not focus on that. He folded himself up into a pile of her laundry and did not have the strength to lift his head.

"Dex?" she choked out finally.

That he had a voice amazed him, and before Declan could stop it, it was sobbing out horrifying pleas. Balled up, buried, he hid. He wept until every last tear, saved for this rainy day over his supposedly formative years, was squeezed out. His body had gone numb. The room was an abyss beyond the warmth of his shameful little cocoon, and he lacked the courage to stand and flee.

"It's okay. Dex . . . It's okay."

Shivers tore through him like little lightning bolts. Her hand impeded an arc and sent it bouncing over his naked arms. He could hear her picking her whispers, feel her hesitate as each new phrase was discarded before it could be uttered. This was an unthinkable occasion, for which no person could ever be prepared, but he loved her even more for the attempt.

"I'm sorry."

"Don't." Her forehead pressed to his neck. "Is this . . . is this why?"

His face, covered with snot, stuck to her denim jacket. "Why what?"

"Why you're so . . . you know, upset all the time. I thought you were, like, on drugs or something! I thought you hated me, and I couldn't figure out what I'd done."

Sniffling and shifting, Declan surfaced. He couldn't yet look at her, but she had always been his second mother, when the real one stopped understanding him. She hooked his chin and forced the smeared face up to the light.

"God, you look terrible!" A kiss landed on his brow, and before he knew it, he was bundled up in her lap like the basket case he was. Her fingers worked through the tiny belts on the broken shoes and tugged them off. "Come on, get up. Go take a hot shower. Let's do this right."

"What?"

She smiled, and even though there were little black dribbles beneath her eyes, she had never looked more lovely.

"Clean yourself up, and let's try again."

Delia helped him to his feet. The ankle was sore but undamaged. He hobbled to the bathroom and pressed his face into the towel that landed on his head.

"We'll talk when you're finished, okay?"

Declan shut the door without thanking her. He didn't know how. He didn't even have the wisdom to put a situation like this to words. If he could have done that, explaining why they had slowly drifted apart would be easy. Telling her that every time he watched her get ready for a date, he hated her a little more would have been a walk in the park. He stared at the clown in the mirror in humiliation.

"Why didn't you tell me?" she said through the door. "I would have understood! You're my brother! Plus I've seen every episode of *RuPaul's Drag Race*!"

Declan stood under the water and went through his logic again and again. She hung out with the kind of kids who usually made a sport of harassing the uncomfortable and awkward, and it didn't matter that she was the nicest among them. The idea that she might in *any* way ridicule him or leak his secret to her cronies had been enough. That feeling had combined with his greater self-loathing and become hard fact: Delia would not understand, because Declan himself could not.

If she was bothered by his lack of response, she didn't seem it. "Make sure you use that face wash. It'll take all the makeup off. You have on *way* too much eyeliner."

A fresh bevy of sobs assailed him, but they ended in a laugh.

"That dress was all *wrong*. I'm going to pick you out a new outfit, okay? I'll be right back."

Away she went. He had ten minutes of scrubbing to himself before she opened the door and stuck her head inside.

"Okay, so I've *totes* got this. *I* am a fucking genius."

Relief was slowly taking hold, twisting through doubt and flourishing. He wasn't alone anymore. He didn't have to spend the evening by himself in a borrowed skin, scanning forums for transgender teenagers, deciphering which posts were real and which were traps laid by sexual predators.

"I can even deal with the hair! Hurry up and get out here."

And she was gone again.

He stepped out and toweled off, wondering if she'd spent time working through the decision to dress him up like a doll, or if it came to her like the rest of her spontaneously good-natured ideas. If anyone could make a profession of being spunky and conspiratorial, it was Delia. She was a born event planner and/or crisis-management specialist.

Declan emerged, sheepishly wrapped up in her purple bathrobe. "Dee, I—"

"Don't!" She sat on the bed, digging through her treasure trove of nail varnish. "You tell me what you want, when you want. For now, I'm just going to absorb the idea that you like wearing dresses, and run with my Barbie fetish."

His laugh shook, but she shored up all his crumbling resolve with yet another hug.

"Okay, I lied. Let me ask some questions that are strictly yes or no."

"Okay."

"Do you want to *be* a girl?"

He pursed his lips and looked around. "I . . . don't know. I know I feel . . . better . . . when I'm . . . not this."

Delia's gaze was as focused as it was when she was doing her French homework. "Right. I think I get it."

"I like being in between." He shifted from foot to foot. "It's called being nonbinary or gender-fluid, I think. I . . . I'm not sure if that makes sense. I don't know if I make sense . . ."

She made a dismissive noise. "As long as you make sense to you, what's it to me? Do we need to talk about pronouns?"

"I . . . No, leave it. It's . . . I don't—"

"Do you like girls or boys, or like both, or maybe none?"

That was, strangely enough, an even more difficult issue, but the fact that she asked it so matter-of-factly made it easier to finally whisper out loud, "Boys."

"So . . . you're basically a straight tomboy trapped in a boy's body?"

The translation was as good as any he was likely to mumble; he gave up trying to improve on it. "I really thought you'd hate me if you knew."

Her face crumpled up on itself. "Is that the kind of person you think I am?"

"No, but—"

"Fear makes people way too cautious."

"Yeah."

"Did you ever *try* to tell me?"

"A couple times. I finally quit when I heard your friend Nick make a gay joke at your birthday party. You laughed, so . . ."

She sighed and took his hand. "I'm so sorry if I ever did anything that made you feel bad. *I* don't think like that. I promise you. I shouldn't have laughed. It wasn't cool."

Declan nodded and glanced over the clothing items spread out on the bed. She was right; she *was* a genius. He picked up a self-adhesive silicone bra and shook his head. "So—"

"I figured we stick this to you. It makes the shape right. And then you wear my other push-up bra over the top, see? Instant cleavage." She nested the two together and grinned. "I'm not an expert in dangly parts, though. What do you think? I have these Spanx shorts and these . . ."

Declan ran his hands over his face and was amazed. Had she sat around nights trying to put him in her shoes, or had this all come to her in the twenty minutes since she'd found him?

"Delia, you're . . ."

"Awesome?"

"Yeah."

"We're lucky you're a waif, because this would be so much harder if you were built like a football player. I have zero garments in that size range." She threw the undergarments at him and shoved him into the closet. "Put these on and then come back out."

Before an hour had passed, they were in each other's confidence in a way they never had been, and Declan was sitting in a new, elastic suit of armor, having his face and nails expertly painted. The mirrors were covered, so that the great reveal could have its full effect, but Delia would lean back every so often with a wide smile and shake her head as if pleased with herself. She'd forced him to put in his colored contact lenses, plucked his eyebrows, concealed his birthmark, and glued on false eyelashes. She'd even managed to work with his overgrown mop of curly hair, flat-ironing, spraying, and pinning it back so that one of her old cheerleading hairpieces could be fitted. And as if that weren't enough, she explained everything as she went, boggling his mind with how much knowledge of fashion she actually had. His image of her changed from a carelessly beautiful girl who could be unwittingly cruel to a meticulously self-made diva.

"This is *the* dress," she affirmed, tossing out a royal-blue garment. "The peplum will create the illusion of a curvy hip, and it's sexy without showing off cleavage. We don't want to draw attention to the fake stuff. We want to augment the natural, like your legs, which by the way, make me want to punch you. Did you use my razor?"

"No. I wax them."

She tugged the dress over his head and zipped him up, then wedged his feet into a pair of black ankle boots. Last but not least, she strapped a leather cuff onto his left wrist and stood back to admire her handiwork. The perusal ended in a squeal and jazz hands.

"Okay, okay! Now, you'd better prepare yourself, because this is gonna blow you away!"

The curtain was lifted from the full-length mirror, and a gorgeous young lady stood looking back at him. She had dramatic soulful eyes and long legs, a messy bun and beauty mark, a punk-rock look and sporty curves. Declan's jaw dropped, and her luscious mouth fell open.

This was *the* moment. More momentous than any previous moment had ever been, and his heart soared in jubilation and pride. The costume was finally gone, and the true soul set free.

"So what shall we call this gorgeous bitch?" Delia snaked her arms around his girlish waist.

"Layla," he replied, without a thought.

"Like the Eric Clapton song?"

The beauty in the mirror nodded, her eyes glittering.

"Oh! You need a purse!" She vanished into the clothing cave and emerged with a sparkling black clutch.

"Why do I need that?"

"For the party!"

And the moment passed in a sensation of intense vertigo.

Chapter 2
The Party

C arter stood on his coffee table and whistled. Half the crowded living room covered its ears. The other half hooted like a barn full of drunken owls.

"Welcome to my annual 'Screw School' *soiree*!"

They cheered and toasted, tossing Cheetos he'd have to vacuum up later, and raising Solo cups that would end up in a pile of molten plastic in the fire pit. He kept the loose grin on his face, regardless. These little inconveniences were how the politics of high school worked.

"As always, no touching any buttons, knobs, or locks! No fighting over the Apple TV; everyone's music gets played! No putting things down drains! No tossing of fellow partygoers into the pool; this means you, Goat! iPhones are expensive, people!" A group of juniors booed, but were silenced by the angry shouts of those who'd been dunked in the past. "And, Toby, what's the last rule?"

The quarterback sniffed and dipped his face into his rum and Coke.

"No sexual contact in my bedroom! That's what your cars are for!"

Toby was buried in an avalanche of high fives and fist bumps from his herd of friends. Carter rolled his eyes surreptitiously and hopped down. The music started back up, and someone shoved a congratulatory beer into his hand.

He rescued a vase he'd overlooked, and stowed it in the locked cupboard of his mother's knickknacks, just as a wrestling match began nearby. He'd had to bribe five neighborhood families with bottles of wine, front the money for the cleaning crew out of his college fund, and ready the entire property himself, but if it bought him a year of hassle-free popularity, it was worth it. The teenage wasteland would be traversed eventually, but one only made it through unscathed if one had an adventurous spirit and did a shitload of planning.

A heavy arm fell across his shoulders. "Carter, the fucking trampoline, dude! Genius! Like, for reals. No shit."

He grinned up at the vacant face and extricated himself with a slap to the back. "Hey! You enjoy, man! And try not to break anything when you dismount!"

Yeah, that would be a marsh of puke by the end of the evening, if he was any judge of high school revelry. He'd have to hose it down with the pressure washer.

He wedged himself into a corner to catch his breath, downing the beer in a few sips. The cliques were mingling in predictable patterns. Liquid audacity flowed like water. The table of junk food was slowly being worked over by those too nervous to talk to others. The stack of board games were being appropriately turned into vehicles of sexual gratification and degradation. Outside, partly naked adolescents floated around the pool on an ark of inflatable animals. It was the perfect party: a well-calibrated machine for projecting his image into the upcoming year.

Finally, he could pause and get the lay of the land.

Summer was just long enough to make old grudges wear thin, just hot enough to melt cold shoulders, just brief enough to leave strong alliances standing. New couples had formed and new obsessions had come into being. Teams were coalescing for preseason practices and the girls were all roaming the malls in droves, picking out the newest fashion trends. Carter had not been the first teenager to figure out that a party was the best way to gain footing in a new school year, but he liked to think he'd done it best.

He greeted some friends. Bambi had descended on the event, fashionably late as usual, and was eyeing him lasciviously. He escaped across the room and broke up a group of sophomores trying to turn his staircase into a slide. Chloe and her girlfriend showed off their matching tattoos, while the debate team reconvened in his dining room and plowed through rudimentary politics. Carter wandered through the house aimlessly, glad this would be the last time he'd ever do this.

The music dropped from Sia to Hozier, just as the front door opened. Delia waved at him over the heads of the partygoers, and he breathed a sigh of relief. It was probably weird to have a female best friend, but he didn't really care. She had been the one to comfort him through his parents' divorce, the kiss that felt easy, the girl who could play touch football and didn't read into it when he got all philosophical. It was really kind of shitty that they didn't have more chemistry, but it had ended amicably, much to the chagrin of the rumor mill.

She was carrying her purse and a bag of snacks in one hand, and dragging someone through the door behind her with the other. Carter wondered if she'd found a date, as Delia had a whispered conversation through the portal. Couldn't be too comforting to escort your girlfriend to the house of her ex while he was busy earning his Homecoming crown.

Then Delia disappeared into the dining room, leaving the door to swing on its hinges.

A thump of deep bass masked his sudden tachycardia, and the wail of a guitar snaked up his spine. As it was happening, he knew. This was a *moment*.

A goddess in a blue dress glanced around, her arms down at her sides instead of wrapped around her body like the rest of her self-conscious kin. She wasn't going to wilt in a corner. She was going to fight through, tooth and nail, if necessary. Austere, smoky eyes ticked from group to group, clearly assessing the social dynamics of every clique within seconds, daring anyone to challenge her. She tilted her head back and her hair fell across her face, just so. Her shoulder shrugged, just so. Her hip tilted, just so. And Carter's whole body responded.

He lurched away from the wall instantly, but met another as the track team crashed through the door and displaced the angel from her stoop. Swearing, he gave a few obligatory chest thumps and handshakes, and maneuvered through the kitchen. Delia was arranging food on the breakfast bar.

"Who the hell is that?" he hissed in her ear.

"Who?"

"Come on! 'Who?' The . . . *stunning* girl you dragged through my front door!"

Delia's glance sparkled in mischief. "Caught your eye, huh?"

"Among other things. Seriously."

"My cousin, Layla. She's visiting before school starts."

Carter blinked. "I didn't know you had a cousin."

Delia shrugged and went back to her task. "Well, she's sort of not related to me. She's my dad's best friend from college's stepkid."

"So . . . it wouldn't be weird if I—"

She patted his chest distractedly. "Good luck, Romeo."

"Why, she stuck-up or something?"

"What? Oh, god no! She's super-awesome! It's . . . Well, let me talk to her before you pounce, okay? She's here to chill, not get pawed by lustful boys."

Carter gave her a wry look. "If that's what she was going for, she should have worn a sack."

"Trust me, she would *kill* in a sack."

The image was an enticing one. "Point taken. Let me know when she's prepped?"

"I'm *so* the best wing man." She swatted at his hand as he reached to pick up an empty bottle. "Let me manage the party. You go back to your people-watching."

They shared a knowing glance, and he was once again glad to have her on his team.

He wove through the house, participating in all of it with cursory enjoyment, his eye peeled for Layla in her drop-dead dress. Near the back door, he spotted her, standing off to one side of what was quickly proving to be an altercation.

Bambi and her gaggle of mean girls had cornered one of the free spirits and were dissing her avant-garde ensemble, their voices laden with sarcasm. Carter hung back, his attention focused on the hard disdain on Layla's face. As her green eyes flicked from bully to victim, they began to glow with rage. He knew at once that she had been bullied herself, and hated it to her core—another point in her favor. When at last she'd had enough, his heart danced to watch her swagger into the fray and shut the shit down.

"Did you get that in Harajuku?" Her voice was as he'd imagined, low and sultry, and completely calm in the face of aggression, like that elf queen in that movie.

The unfortunate target, a sophomore he thought he remembered transferring from Saint Cat's, looked close to tears. "I went to Tokyo with my *obā-chan* this summer."

"*Watashi wa sōda to omoimashita. Goth-Loli desu ne?*"

Carter's head bolted upright, and every voice in the immediate vicinity was silenced by the enthusiastic fluidity of Layla's tongue.

"*H . . . hai.*" The grateful girl smiled. "*Suki desu ka?*"

"*Ee, suteki desu ne! Urayamashī! Onamae wa nan desu ka?*"

"*Yuki desu. Yoroshiku onegai shimasu.*"

"*Layla desu. Yoroshiku.*"

Their polite bow was a welcome change of pace, and when Layla turned an imperious eye on the listeners, it became clear that *they* were the ignorant savages.

"I'm sure I don't have to tell you ladies that Harajuku is the place where fashion goes to be reinvented. Clothing is so expensive in Tokyo, that outfit probably cost Yuki more than a computer. Unlike your getup from Express. It's basically wearable art."

Bambi sucked in a breath to unleash a tirade. "Who cares how much it costs if it's fucking ugly? She looks like a dead French maid."

"And you look like every other rich girl on the planet. Well done with blending in, despite your personality."

Bambi was always high-strung, but when she made to suddenly slap Layla, Carter's smile slid off his face. If there was one thing the party couldn't absorb, it was a catfight. But Layla didn't seem bothered. She caught the raised hand easily and squeezed.

"It's not bad enough you have to tear people down to make yourself feel better, you also have to hit the person pointing that out? What are you, five? Grow up."

And the hand was discarded for one of Yuki's. Layla pulled her outside, giggling and carrying on in Japanese as they left a stricken bully behind them. Bambi looked around at her former backers and found him. In that moment, Carter made a calculated, if risky political decision.

"Don't look at me, Bambi. She said it. In *two* languages."

Bambi stormed away. He'd pay for it later, but damn that felt good. He made the rounds in considerably better spirits, and when he got the nod from Delia, did a circuit looking for trouble. It was a bitch to find her. She had snuck off the back deck, over the expansive lawn, and found the darkened fire pit. She had her exquisite legs tucked up beneath her on a bench swing and was texting furiously, completely ignoring the party he'd worked so hard to craft.

"What a girl," he whispered to himself.

He skirted the pool carefully, ignoring a dozen conversations that could suck him in. Hugging the shadows of the garage, he came around behind her and considered the approach. A girl like this wouldn't fall for flattery, but she would also know that any guy who talked to her had only one thing on his mind.

He dropped his upper body over the back of the swing beside her with a loud noise of relief. She jumped, and he had his in.

"Hi, I'm Carter. This is my party."

She blinked at him, unmoved and more stunning close-up.

"You're Layla, Delia's guest." When she still said nothing, he waved his beer expressively, and as the words "She's my ex-girlfriend" came out of his mouth, he kicked himself.

The dark head turned away, concealing a face that was even lovely when unimpressed. "I know who you are."

"Um . . ." For the first time in his life, he had no idea what to say. "You want the fire on?"

"That'll certainly make for an interesting evening when the football team finds it through the bottom of a vodka bottle."

He snickered and looked at the back of her neck, finally understanding what *swanlike* meant. His mouth dried up, and his brain ground to a noisy halt. If Delia were here, she'd make fun of him, and he'd laugh and feel like a human being again, instead of a robot with a gear loose.

"Can we start over?"

She examined him. Her eyes were unreadable, depthless, and when he couldn't tear free of them, they vanished in a fanning of long lashes.

"Give it a shot."

"Hi, I'm Carter. It's nice to meet you, and normally I'm not a giant douche."

"Good to hear. Have a seat."

"I hope Delia has only said good things."

"It's a double standard, right?"

"What do you mean?"

Her brow lifted. "What women say about a man matters, while a girl could be a complete bitch, and guys would line up."

"Men don't have trust issues."

Layla laughed out loud and shook her head. "You are so full of shit, Carter Who-is-not-usually-a-giant-douche."

He grinned and recalibrated. This was *not* going to be a normal conversation. Layla was a different breed.

"Okay, you got me. We just think with our dicks. But that is genetic and can't be helped! It's as embarrassing and inexplicable to us as it should be, I promise! It's like when we hit twelve, we lose our minds."

She leaned back and eyed him. "Is that when you start pulling girls' hair?"

"Yes. We have no idea why we do it! It's like this bizarre compulsion that controls our hands. And when they get mad at us, we hate ourselves, but we still can't stop." He squeezed the air and made a face that she seemed to find amusing.

"So when do you *stop* being idiots?"

"I'll let you know."

She took a sip of her hard lemonade. "See, this is one reason why Disney is so bad for young minds."

"Oh?" He leaned back and relaxed. How he could do that with so many butterflies swarming in his gut, he had no idea, but she somehow managed to inspire both.

"Disney says the prince is supposed to just ride around on his white horse scanning the horizon for a poor shoeless damsel who fits. That all that matters is meeting a pretty princess and spawning a bunch of dukes. And the damsel is supposed to wait to be found. What he's actually doing is riding around tugging on braids, violating the personal space bubble, until he meets the girl who breaks his nose and puts him in the Friend-zone. He doesn't give a good god damn what shoe size she is. And she probably doesn't care about her shoes at all."

"You're not wearing shoes," he pointed out helpfully.

"True."

"But if I pull your hair, will you sock me?"

"Right in the face."

"And the Friend-zone is a real place?"

"Yup."

"Glad we skipped all that. I was getting tired of being an aimless, if utterly charming, prince."

She pressed her mouth down on a wry smile. "No, you'd prefer to get ahead of yourself."

"Do you have a boyfriend?"

She looked away coolly. He'd touched a nerve, and if he weren't so eager to know the answer, he'd have felt bad about it.

Chapter 3
The Politician

Declan took a deep breath and clutched the bottle for dear life, Delia's advice echoing. He had to be who he wanted to be.

The ruse had gone over people's heads like a charm. He'd been hit on by at least a dozen guys. The girls thought his outfit was chic, and he'd managed to ease through conversations with them by attaching himself to Yuki, his closest friend, who *also* didn't recognize him. He felt like Superman in glasses. Just because the guy he was *actually* crushing on had taken the bait did not mean it was time to back down. If anything, it was a major win. And it was only one night, right?

"You don't want to mess with me, Carter."

"Why not?"

God, he was sexy. The crooked grin and dark-brown hair eroded every last nerve. Declan shifted in his seat uncomfortably. "You'll be disappointed."

"Someone told me once that youth was a wasteland of disappointment designed to prepare us all for bleak adulthood."

"You don't wanna grow up that fast, sweetie."

He gave a husky laugh and laid his arm along the back of the bench. He still radiated warmth like a furnace, and Declan could feel beads of sweat trickle down his spine.

"Give me some credit. My life isn't perfect."

Declan felt the sting again, that little pain when people unknowingly said hurtful things that rubbed salt into wounds they couldn't even perceive.

"Like hell."

Carter's smile vanished, and Declan knew he'd picked a fight. Best to finish it, and ward him off before he asked for Layla's phone number.

"Not sure I get what you mean."

"Here you are . . . smart, funny, attractive, in your nice house, with your pool and your fire pit. You don't walk down the hall at school feeling like a joke. You're Mr. Popular."

His head was ticking in a constant nod, but the blue eyes were far away. "Thanks for enumerating my finer traits. Saves me the trouble of advertising them. Sorry they aren't more impressive."

Declan sighed. "Putting reality into perspective for you."

"It's all an act."

He blinked at Carter, whose face was stony, but whose eyes blazed in the dim light. "Is it?"

"You know how when you go to work on a jigsaw puzzle, you have the picture to guide you? Yeah, well . . . I put the puzzle together into the picture I want to see. Every piece has to be carefully cut and fitted into the others. I hate this crap. It's never-ending hard work."

"But you do it."

"Yeah. So I can get through this bullshit and out into the real world."

Softening his voice, Declan now understood why Delia had been so encouraging. Carter was full of surprises. "Why isn't high school a part of the real world, is maybe what I'm asking."

"Because teenagers are irrational fucking lunatics."

"We're not. Us two, I mean."

Carter sagged back with a knowing smile. "Yeah. That's what I'm saying. So do you have a boyfriend?"

Declan felt the tension ease and was grateful. "No. I have trust issues."

"How bad are they?"

"Bad enough to send me to the outskirts of the party. Not bad enough to stop talking to you."

"So then, you won't go completely ballistic if I say that you look very lovely this evening and compliment your bilingual throw-down with Miss Bambi Weatherton?"

Declan sniffed. "Didn't anyone tell her that Bambi was a boy?"

"So was Flower."

"It was a whole movie about androgynous animals."

"Fucking cartoons. But seriously, where'd you learn Japanese?"

"Anime."

Carter nearly spit out his mouthful of beer. "No shit."

Declan looked down. Carter's muscular thigh was brushing his knees, and the arm across his back was sending a tingle over his skin. "You've been so forthcoming, this evening, Carter. Can I tell you a huge secret?"

The face dipped closer, and Declan's heart skipped. "Please."

"If I didn't have anonymity and the supreme confidence that none of these assholes are ever going to see me again, I would be hiding in some corner, stuffing my face with chips and debating which Star Trek captain was best for the Federation."

"Kirk. Hands down."

Declan broke into a laugh before he could stop himself. "Kirk Classic, or Kirk from the altered timeline?"

The blue eyes were sparkling. "Meh. Kirk is Kirk, in any timeline. Hashtag Kobayashi-Maru. Hashtag winning."

"Debatable. Anyway . . . I'm a huge nerd. I don't actually ever go to parties. I borrowed this dress from Dee."

"Well, I appreciate being the exception, and as I said, you look great. So tell me, what's your favorite anime?"

Declan examined the wicked glint in Carter's eye and gambled. "*Ouran High School Host Club.*"

When the boy looked away, nodding slowly, Declan wondered if he'd won their little flirtatious standoff.

"That's the one about the girl who gets mistaken for a boy, right?"

Declan blinked in awe. His heart did a happy little dance in his chest as he considered that Carter could be his soul mate, if only they occupied compatible sexualities. "You're probably the first guy I've ever met who knows what the hell that is."

"Again, that's because I'm amazing. But, really, nothing beats a good Mecha."

Grinning slyly, Declan looked at him from the corner of his eye. "Yeah, but *Escaflowne*, *Evangelion*, or *Gundam*?"

"*Escaflowne*, for real."

Unable to contain it any longer, Declan clapped his hands, keeping his laugh as girlish as possible. "I would have thought *Gundam*."

"Nah. *Esca* has swashbuckling, winged heroes, romance, science, magic, Atlantis, crazy villains, and Isaac Newton. Nothing beats Isaac Newton, except Neil deGrasse Tyson in a rap battle."

"Oh. My. God." Declan performed a breathing exercise and dabbed the corners of his eyes. "I did *not* know you were a closet nerd."

Carter turned away, his cheer faltering. "I'm not. I'm a huge faker, a con artist, a politician. I know a little bit about everything, so that I can talk to anyone. So I don't have to go through hell."

"Like Yuki, who fights to be who she wants to be?"

He took a deep breath. "Yeah. Exactly."

"So you're a coward."

Carter's eyes darted to his face and stuck. The mouth pressed down on a sardonic smile but said nothing.

The silence stretched, until Declan felt the ache of embarrassment build. "Can we start over?"

The perfect face turned and the perfect smile dawned, ever so lovely and bittersweet. "Turnabout is fair play."

"Hi. I'm Layla Who-is-not-normally-a-huge-jerk, and this is a lovely party you are so very generous to have hosted."

Carter made a humble bow and leaned a little closer, his breath tickling Declan's ear. "It's really a pleasure to meet you. How long will you be in town?"

He cleared his throat, controlling his voice though his throat ached. "Until Delia's parents get back from their vacation, since they don't know I'm here."

"And when is that?"

"The fifteenth."

"The day before school starts."

"I guess so."

"May I offer you my services as a guide? There are many fine attractions in our humble little suburb, such as the Sonic, the bowling alley, a statue of a man on a horse. The list goes on."

"I'll think about it."

"Well, let's exchange numbers so that we can arrange said outing when you're done thinking."

"How do you know I'll say yes?"

He pointed at his muscled chest, bound by a masculine-patterned button-up. "Remember? Charming. Also . . . exceptionally modest."

Declan looked down at the phone in his hand and wondered if it was a good idea. No, it was a terrible idea, but if it was so bad, then why on earth did it feel like the only option that wouldn't result in him eating an entire tub of ice cream and binge-playing *Skyrim* until he ached all over?

Carter pulled out his phone and snapped a picture before Declan could say no. On a feckless whim, he snatched the young man's phone away. Typing in his number, he was happy to see that his real name didn't pop up as a contact linked to it. He texted himself from it and heard his own phone buzz in alert.

Carter got to his feet and accepted the device with a deep bow.

"And now, because you seemed so content enjoying the solitude, I will stop insinuating myself into your company, and bid you a good evening. I do hope you'll say goodbye when you and Delia depart."

"Suddenly we're in the 1800s?"

He shrugged, and it was the kind of casually handsome gesture that melted underpants. "In my mind, you're kind of regal, so it seemed appropriate." He turned and waved over his head. "Catch you later, Princess."

Declan watched him slowly saunter across the grass, and felt every fiber of his being react with more violence as the distance increased. Finally, he couldn't stand the thrashing in his chest anymore.

"Carter?" he called.

The young man turned and cocked his head.

Declan couldn't shout, or the voice would sound too boyish. He lifted his phone and texted, *You got any marshmallows?*

Knew you'd want s'more, was the reply.

Declan rolled his head on his shoulders and went back to his bottle of hard lemonade, giddy and enchanted. When Carter vanished into the house, he called his fairy godmother.

"Well?" Delia demanded.

"What am I doing?"

"You're being yourself."

"I know, but fuck! I just lied to Carter Aadenson!"

"Yeah, but soon he'll get involved in the new school year and his presidency and be over you by September."

"Wow, sis, thanks for that."

"I'm sorry, Dex! You know what I mean! Wait, he just came in here. What's he doing in here?"

"Looking for marshmallows."

Declan hung up when he heard Carter's drawl in the background, his mind returning again and again to the central difficulty. It didn't matter if Carter got over Layla, because Layla would still have to deal with him. Every day. As his junior year played out, Declan would have to watch Carter strut down the halls like he had the world by the tail, and try hard to forget what it had been like to sit that close.

"I can't do it."

He shoved his feet back into the boots and snuck toward the house. Waiting until Carter exited, Declan slid in behind him and tracked down his sister. Delia was leaning against the living room wall, wrapped up in a conversation with Mila and Priah.

"We have to leave!"

She jumped up and took hold of his arm. "What happened?"

"Nothing. We have to go right now, before he sees I'm gone."

"But—"

"Please!"

It took only a few seconds for Delia to read the urgency in his face and understand. She managed a curt nod and led the way to the front door, without so much as a goodbye to the girls. They waded through the crowd and made it to the porch. Outside, the sun had dipped below the horizon and the air was cool, but Declan's skin was on fire. Delia hit the key fob button as a shape came hurtling out the front door.

"Shit!" she swore.

Declan turned. There was Carter, bag of marshmallows still in hand, and suddenly Declan couldn't get his fingers to do anything but fumble with the door handle. The look on Carter's face was the most pathetic thing he'd ever seen: a shadow of a self-reproving smile beneath a pair of forlorn blue eyes.

Carter stopped a few feet away and gestured with the bag of marshmallows. The silence stretched. Delia got into the car and left him to his fate.

"Trust issues, huh?" Carter said quietly.

"I'm sorry. I—"

"Fuck it."

In a single step, Carter cleared the distance and cupped his face. Caught off guard, Declan managed only a squeak as Carter's mouth found his. There was no tongue, no fumbling teenaged hormones, just a tender goodbye kiss that sent a shockwave from the base of Declan's skull to the tips of his toes and back again. Before he could push him away, Carter was gone, and Declan was left beside the car with weak legs and an intense pain in his groin where their improvised gender-swap failed miserably.

He collapsed silently into the passenger seat.

"You okay?"

"Please," he whispered. "Get me home."

Chapter 4
The Crown

"He wants to know if he freaked you out," Delia said, looking at her phone.

The den was warm despite the air-conditioning. They languished over the huge sectional like a couple of marooned polar bears. Declan watched the blades of the ceiling fan circle, his smooth legs stretched out over her lap. She had lent him one of her tank tops and a pair of denim shorts so that he would feel comfortable during his mental breakdown.

"Gee, I don't know. Is it customary for your first kiss to make you feel simultaneously amazing and like the shittiest person on earth?"

"So . . . I'll tell him it's not him, it's you?"

Declan covered his face with a pillow. "I can't go out with him on a date. Number one, it's wrong. Number two, we don't have enough prop versatility."

Dee threw his legs off and slid over so that they were wedged side by side. She had her eBay app open and was scrolling through several listings for his benefit.

"I can have these overnighted," she whispered in his ear.

"You're totally instigating." But the thought stuck, and unconsciously, he began picking through the search. "Wow, they're really reasonably priced."

She giggled softly. "I'm *so* buying them. Call them an early birthday present. It's the perfect time, because we won't have to worry about Mom taking the delivery."

He managed a smile, and then her phone beeped and the message from Carter scrolled across the top of the screen.

"I'm not some horny goof-off. Please don't Friend-zone me for a thank-you kiss."

They shared a glance.

"He's not, you know. He's extremely focused. He's in the running for valedictorian. He's class president. He's on the swim and track team. And, just in case you were wondering, he's a really good—"

"No! Do not finish that sentence."

"We didn't have sex."

He gasped. "You dated for two years!"

She shrugged. "Didn't say we didn't fool around."

"Gaaahhh!"

Delia brought up the keyboard. *She. Got. The. Message. Calm. The. Eff. Down.*

Seconds later, Carter's reply arrived, laden with exclamation marks and a squinty face. Declan read it and smothered himself with the pillow.

"I ran away because I had second thoughts about dragging him into my life."

"He says he's texted your phone like fifty times and he's sorry if he's coming off like a stalker, but he *got a feeling about you*. Ohhh! A feeling. Those are so complicated with him."

"Gah!"

"There's really only one way to solve this problem."

Peeking out, Declan eyed her suspiciously. "What's that?"

"Carter's mom only lets him throw these parties because he works his ass off to keep her house in one piece."

"Okay."

"Usually, I go over and help. Then the maid service comes in the afternoon."

"Uh-huh."

She made a face. "Let me work my magic on you." She tackled him as he pulled the pillow back over his head, and unmasked him. "Let me dress you casually. We'll see what he thinks of you in full sunlight, and if he still shows interest, we deal with it. If he thinks better of his new obsession, then there's no sitch."

Declan screwed up his face in metaphysical anguish, but he knew he couldn't say no.

She tipped forward and narrowed her gaze. "I'll let you wear my espadrilles."

He squeaked. "The purple ones?"

"Mm-hmm." She pulled him upright. "They'll go great with the shirt I bought last weekend."

By the time they pulled up in front of Carter's house, Declan was almost convinced that Delia really was magical. Layla was truly a real person. He checked her hair and makeup in the visor mirror.

"You're sure the scarf plays? I feel a little *I Love Lucy*."

She tugged on her own bandana and made the "duh" face. "We're here to clean. And it hides the slight color difference between the hairpiece and your real hair. It wasn't obvious in twilight, but it will be now. If you keep this up, we'll have to get you a haircut, or something."

He slipped out of the car as if sneaking into a club and took the bucket Dee handed him. "Did you tell him we were coming?"

"Nope."

Declan made a series of sounds that perfectly expressed his discomfort.

"Words, babe. Use 'em."

"What if he figures it out?"

"He won't! He's seen Declan all of about ten times. Saggy, ugly clothes, hair in your face, glasses too big for your nose; you looked like a flipping zombie. Couldn't even see your eyeballs! Layla is swank and svelte and has a million-mile stare."

She poked his nose.

"Okay, so maybe he won't know it's *me*, but what if he figures out Layla is a *boy*?" Declan whispered the offending word as if about to be attacked by Death Eaters for saying *Voldemort*.

"He won't."

"He will if he kisses me again. And *leans in*!"

"Simmer down. I'll buy you some foundational garments."

"They don't make 'em to do that, Dee."

"Then you'll have to master Zen, okay?"

She dragged him up to the door unsympathetically, and didn't bother to knock. The scene beyond was a shady nightmare, and Declan's mouth fell open involuntarily. There was trash and food everywhere. The table of board games had been overturned. The coffee table was buried in a pile of food and paper goods. The kitchen and dining room looked like a bomb had gone off—a bomb that contained nacho cheese. Declan wandered to the back doors and surveyed the pool; a giant bowl of soggy Chex mix was floating around in a slow circle, and he could see the necks of several bottles on the steps.

"He does this *every year*? I'm pretty sure I'd rather set myself on fire! Now I know why you really brought me here, you bitch!"

Her laugh echoed through the kitchen. "I told you! We're here to clean, not make out!"

"Well," said a low voice behind him, "we *could* make out instead, but my mother would back over me with her car. It might be worth it, though."

Declan spun and clamped his mouth shut. Carter emerged stoically from the basement door, inspecting him with an unreadable gaze.

Managing a swallow, Declan finally shrugged out a hello. "I was teasing. I really would be happy to help."

"I'm sorry about last night," Carter blurted out. "I didn't mean to offend you, so—"

"You didn't! I..." Declan glanced around at the horrible mess and grimaced. "Like I said, I'm not used to parties. I kind of got carried away, and then realized I had stepped out on a tightrope, you know?"

Carter smiled, and it was somehow different from any expression Declan had seen on his face. It was relaxed, real. He took a deep breath and ran his fingers through his hair. "Makes sense to me. Thanks for helping. You don't have to. It's really nice of you."

Delia appeared with her hands on her hips. "Hey, asswipe, I'm here too!"

"Dee," he tossed over his shoulder.

"Wow, what a welcome."

The blue eyes slid shut and the mouth drew into an indulgent line. "Delia Elliott, I am very pleased to see you."

"Much better. Now, how do you want us to proceed?"

Carter spared one last seductive grin for Layla, and then presented her with a box of garbage bags. Before long, Delia was elbow-deep in cleaning fluids, and Declan was combing the backyard for rubbish. Confronted with the pool, however, he was stumped. There was no way he would stick so much as a toe in the water wearing as much makeup as he was. He walked over to the trampoline instead, but immediately recoiled.

"Hell to the no!"

When he turned around, Carter was sitting on the edge of the pool in his swim trunks, laughing. Declan shaded his face, glad that he'd already gotten enough sun to conceal his blush. He watched as the young man slipped easily into the water and sank to the bottom, little bubbles tracing tantalizing paths over his many sculpted planes and curves. Whimpering, Declan squatted down and waited beside the pile of debris slowly being raised from the depths. Carter's head popped up like a buoy beside him. He hooked an arm over the side and twitched his chin in Declan's direction.

"Here."

Something caught the light and sparkled. Declan stretched out a hand. "Who wore a tiara?"

"Someone with ambition."

Tan skin rippled as he pulled himself out of the water in a flourish of strength that made Declan glad he was already balled up. Perched on the edge, Carter lifted the tiara over Layla's head. Cringing as the damp diadem was positioned, Declan waited for some piece of costumery to fall off and require an explanation, but nothing did. Dee had apparently pinned him well enough to set off metal detectors at fifty paces. He reached up and ran his hand over the accessory.

"I don't think it goes with my bandana."

"Better than a glass slipper. Who makes slippers out of glass, I ask you? You know how many times I've stubbed my toe in the dark? I mean that's begging for blood loss!" And in a flash of teeth, he was back in the water with minimal splash. Pacing along the rim, Declan followed him with the garbage bag, occasionally reaching up to tap his little crown.

Delia had made major headway in the kitchen when Declan retreated from the task of pressure washing the vomit-oline. Four black trash bags sat beside the back door. All the food that could be saved was wrapped in plastic. Dishes were loaded into the machine, and she had scraped half the surfaces clean of cheese.

"Holy shit, Dee! Why don't you clean like this at home?"

"Because I thrive in chaos." She glanced up. "What's with the tiara?"

"Queen for a day," he said, accepting the last cookie from a proffered package.

Her smirk was contagious. "It was a good idea to come. Trust me. Relax. I know Carter. You don't."

Declan drifted into the living room and righted the game table, lost in thought. Did that mean that this meeting would cure Carter of wanting to have anything to do with Layla, or did it mean that Dee was happy he would have more occasion to borrow her clothes? He had tried to read Carter's features for signs, but all they said was "handsome." Screamed it, in fact. Until Declan's brain turned to quivering mush.

Monopoly money was sorted as Declan took an accounting of Layla. She was *his* truth, but could only exist amidst a host of lies. If he indulged, if somehow he could work up the courage to go out on a date *alone* with Carter . . . could a convincing cover story be spun? One good enough to pass muster, but forgettable enough to pass from memory as soon as school started?

He wasn't sure.

Then his conscience smacked him upside the proverbial head. It didn't matter if he *could* get away with it! He shouldn't! It was completely unfair to Carter. So it gave him a few moments of what life might actually be like on the other side of this "wasteland." So what? It would break Carter's heart.

But only if he found out. If he didn't . . . well, then it was just a summer fling. It was *Grease*, except the blonde ended up being a gangly teenage boy who never broke into the fateful song at the fair. If he could *pass*, then Carter could date a girl he actually dug, and . . .

What the fuck was he thinking? Talk about ego! How could he assume someone like Carter Aadenson would *dig* him? It was simply newness. The most popular boy in school saw a girl he'd never met. Of course he was going to be intrigued. Layla could have been picking her nose and sporting BO, and Carter would still have approached her out of politeness.

Tiny rainbows played over the wood floor. Declan turned his head and watched them dance. The word *regal* skittered through his mind a few times. It had to have been flattery, surely. Carter Aadenson would not find Layla attractive. But that was Declan's self-confidence talking, *his* mistakes, *his* experiences. It was possible Layla was pretty enough, charming enough, self-assured enough to make an impression *that* favorable.

He stacked the games and stood to his full height in front of the large mirror leaning against the wall. It was graffitied with dry-erase score tallies and penises, but he ignored them. If he stared, he could find himself, but that wasn't what he was looking for.

She had an earnest face with thoughtful eyes and flattering makeup. Her neck was graceful, and her limbs willowy. She was more porcelain than pasty. Her hips were narrow, but that was largely concealed by the drape of the blouse she wore. She could be a model, but there was something forlorn about her eyes. The scarf *did* work, but the tiara?

There was a knock at the door. Carter waved in the maids with a bluster of gratitude. They went to work almost immediately, and the teens were exiled outdoors. Delia had come prepared. She stripped down to her swimsuit with an apologetic smile and dove in. Carter threw an inflatable unicorn at her and took a seat on the stairs. "Didn't bring a suit?"

"Don't swim," Declan said. He set out over the grass and back to the peaceful fire pit. It was such a nice spot: a ring of wooden frames strung with little twinkle lights, supporting the weight of four swinging benches, all cushioned and shaded. The copper cauldron of fire rocks caught the light and appeared to glow. Cicadas buzzed in their little rhythm, lulling his mind into alpha waves. He stretched out on his swing and let his thoughts run loose.

It really wouldn't be fair to Carter. That was a fact, and if he actually cared about him, which he was quickly realizing he did, then Declan was obligated to be kind. He repeated it, again and again, each time feeling more sick that it had gotten this far.

The decision was made. Layla would return home early, leave a goodbye text, and then vanish. But how would he remove his phone number from Carter's phone? He had to, because he couldn't very well go to his mother and beg to have the number changed. How would he justify that?

"Hey, Mom, can you do battle with the phone company because I'm being stalked by Delia's ex-boyfriend who thinks I'm a chick?" he muttered. Nope. Didn't work.

Declan swung an arm over his eyes and let the other one dangle. Maybe if he ignored Carter, the guy would take a hint?

He felt the warmth before he heard the voice. "A sleeping princess? Lucky day!"

Declan couldn't help the smile. "And what exactly is so lucky about it? I think I have chocolate syrup under my fingernails, and I'm sure I stepped in vomit."

"Upon reflection, the trampoline was a bad idea."

Giggling, he uncovered his face. Carter was draped over the back of the bench. His hair was wet and skewed at a funny angle. Thoughtlessly, Declan reached up and brushed it aside. The young man blinked and then vanished, reappearing a few moments later with a cold bottle of water and a bowl. Without asking for permission, he scooped a hand behind Declan's neck and slid onto the bench.

"Best pillow ever."

"Think you can live up to such high praise?"

"Name one other pillow that will feed you berries." He dangled a strawberry above Declan's face and waggled his eyebrows.

"I cannot."

Visibly proud of himself, Carter plopped the berry into Declan's mouth, highjacking the silence. "Dee says your life back in Chicago is 'complicated.' Says you came here to escape."

Chicago? Well, okay, then, Chicago. He knew the city well enough. Their grandmother had been born and raised there. "You cannot imagine."

"She says you could really use a diversion."

"Does she, now?"

Carter stifled him with another berry. "Practically insisted I ask you out on a date, and that I not take no for an answer."

"Well, I *was* quite intrigued by the statue of a man on a horse."

"We have minigolf."

"That seals it, then, doesn't it?" Declan laughed.

Another berry found its way to his lips followed by the electric brush of a fingertip.

"So when can I pick you up?"

Declan blinked. Had he just agreed to a date without realizing it? Shit. Goddamn witty banter! He swallowed the berry whole to stammer out a refusal. Carter caught him as he attempted to sit up, and wrapped an iron arm around his waist.

His chin rested on Declan's exposed shoulder. "I know what I did wrong last night."

Declan swallowed hard and tried to pull free of the embrace, but the will wasn't there. Carter nuzzled Declan's ear and dropped his voice even lower.

"The first kiss matters. Any guy paying attention knows that. But what do you do when the girl is running away, because she can't believe that sometimes, one moment is all it takes?"

Declan's chest ached painfully. Twisted up as he was, he didn't have the strength to keep upright, but if he went limp, he'd be skin to skin. That could end in disaster.

"I wasn't pulling your hair," Carter whispered. "Serious thought went into that."

"Your sneak-attack kiss? That took serious thought? Was it your dick doing the thinking?"

A sculpted shoulder shrugged. "No. It was my brain. I'm not really known for being spontaneous."

"No, I guess that doesn't make for good politics."

The arms around him tightened. Suddenly, he was sitting sideways in Carter's lap, and the young man was looking up at him intently. "Let's hit pause on our real lives and hang out in the intermission together. Can we do that?"

Declan's spine melted. He let go and rested his head on Carter. Carter didn't seem to mind. Fingers played from the nape of his neck to his shoulder blades. He barely held back the shiver as blood rose in his cheeks and coursed through him.

"Don't blame me when the spell breaks at midnight, okay?"

Chapter 5
The Date

Carter fished his keys from the dish beside the front door. "Mom, I'm out."

She looked up from the dining room table and smiled. "First date in a while. You look handsome."

"Thanks, but you know, that's not really so difficult for me."

She shook her head tolerantly. "Three things: Who is she? Where are you taking her? And please remember my rules about grandchildren."

He saluted. "Her name is Layla, she's Dee's sixteen-year-old cousin from Chicago. I have a spectacular itinerary planned featuring all our major landmarks. And, finally, you aren't getting any grandchildren. I'm still in high school."

"I met your father in high school."

"Look how well that turned out."

The good humor drained. "You're never too young to see the *potential* for a lifetime."

"Then why did you guys divorce?"

"Because we were cowards."

As he reached for the doorknob, Layla's words echoed in his head. He froze. "What do you mean?"

"We never set out on our own. We stopped talking about regrets, stopped caring what the other one was thinking. We never *worked*, so . . . we never worked."

He stared down at his shoes and wondered, "How do you keep that from happening?"

"Find a girl who won't ever let you get lazy."

"Layla is definitely an iceberg."

Her glance was a question.

"I feel like there's a lot she doesn't want to talk about."

"Trust has to be earned."

"So how do you earn a girl's trust?"

She rose from her chair and brought her wine to her lips. "Well, it'll help that she's leaving. She'll be more open than she normally would. But the most important part of trust is that it's not on your terms. That's why it's so difficult to give, because once it's gone, it's in their hands, and they can hurt you. But that's how it works, and when it goes well, it's worth it. If you want that from her, you really need to make her feel safe."

"When did you get so wise?"

Her laugh sounded almost like her old self. "Right? Someone ought to nominate me for Mom of the Year or some shit."

She gave him a hug.

"I'll be back around midnight."

"Stay safe."

He pulled open the door.

"And Carter?"

"Yeah?"

"You'll know. Deep down. It's a pit-of-the-stomach feeling."

He blinked at her wistful smile. As he got into the Charger, he made himself the promise he'd uttered a thousand times, that he would never follow in their footsteps. Never. No matter how much planning had to be done. No matter how many times he had to back off, apologize, see professionals—he would never be hurt by or hurt another the way his parents had.

He thought of Layla's deep-green eyes, staring guardedly at him, summing up all his assets as if they needed more work. What had she gone through in her life to have such a serious, contemplative expression at such a young age? It couldn't be good, whatever it was. So how could he make her feel safe, if he didn't know? It was a catch-22.

Carter parked in Dee's driveway and trotted up to the porch, texting through the final details with his date night minions as he went. The door opened before he could even gain the steps. A breathtaking woman stepped out and immediately dropped her keys. He watched, his tongue suddenly numb, as Layla bent down in her backless dress and retrieved them. Her hair was different, a kind of textured bob, and she had on a pair of dangling earrings that perfectly traced the line of her neck. She looked like a modern take on something from *The Great Gatsby* and moved like she'd been wearing spike heels her whole life.

When she let out a string of whispered cuss words and fumbled to fit her phone in her impractically tiny purse, he lost it.

She was too perfect.

"I didn't think you could top the blue dress, but . . . damn."

She swiveled in place as if she'd been caught singing to her hairbrush. "What?"

"Is it possible to feel both over- *and* underdressed at the same time?"

The eyes blinked at him steadily. "I—"

"I'm teasing!"

She bit her lip and glanced around. "I didn't realize you'd come up."

"That's how dates work, generally."

"Yeah?"

"Well, I'm not going to honk at you like a carpool."

He held out a hand and watched her work through the mental barriers. She had no trouble calling him a coward, but every time he touched her, she flinched as if burned. His mind picked at the tangle of impressions as his fingers laced through hers.

She was silent as he drove through the residential neighborhoods toward downtown. He glanced her way and found her staring out the window like the world outside was a foreign planet she was trying to memorize. Any clever joke he thought to make seemed stupid, hollow enough to be crushed by the weight of the tension in the air. But he couldn't leave her in her solitude. That just wasn't good etiquette.

"You all right?"

Jolted from her thoughts, she looked around the car. "Sorry."

"I had this speech planned on the merits of dating me, but it's cool. Another time."

Her laugh shook loose, as silent and breathy as ever, like she was sneaking through her life, trying not to wake anyone.

He parked the car with a grin on his face. "Okay, so since the date technically hasn't started yet, let's get the rules out of the way."

Layla's brow rose in that imperious way, as good as picking a fight. "So it didn't start at my door?"

"Nope. Starts at the first location. The car ride is like stretching, or something."

"I'm humoring you."

He got out of the car and walked around to her side. She was already out, undermining his second attempt at chivalry. He made a mental note: he could not gain ground with the usual tricks. This date was going to be complicated.

"So, the rules are as follows: No bullshit. No small talk. No hair pulling."

Her arms were crossed, but she nodded. "Works for me."

"And just so that we don't have it as a fallback, let's get all the compliments out of the way at the get-go, yeah?" He welcomed hers with a hand.

"You're a very focused driver."

"Now, now! Clearly you have trouble with the concept, so I'll go first." He ignored her open-mouthed head shake. "Your ensemble is amazing. The haircut is extremely flattering. The shoes make your legs look gorgeous, but I am concerned about how they'll work into this date. Your presence fills me with a deep sense of inadequacy. Your turn."

She chewed it over with a suppressed grin. "Okay. You look very handsome."

"That's what my mom said! You can do better than that!"

He was pushing through the wall, and though she wasn't looking at him, she clearly wanted to.

"I like you better in color, but the black will do."

Carter put on a laborious sigh. "We'll have to work on it, I guess."

She took his arm, but remained stoic. "I didn't ask for compliments. You barely know me."

"Isn't that why girls dress like that?"

She glanced askance at him. "Maybe, but it's just building fortifications in familiar territory."

He led her through the dimly lit square, listening attentively to each note in her voice. "So why do you do it?"

"To shed my skin."

He drew up short and let her go. Damn, she was smart. He was going to have to work double-time to keep her attention.

Well, okay then.

"Allow me to point out the first stop on our tour, as promised."

Seemingly caught off guard, she blinked around and finally latched her gaze on the huge concrete plinth. The bronze stallion stared down at her. Giggling, she applauded him.

"The man on a horse! I cannot tell you how much I was looking forward to this."

"I know right? It's just—"

"So anatomical," she marveled, staring at its exposed stomach.

"Yeah, they didn't know when to quit."

"Well, Carter, it's *historical*!"

He chuckled and waved a hand through the air. "Take it in, I mean from all angles. It blows the mind."

She clasped her hands behind her back as if at a gallery and meandered around the head of the statue. He listened for the gasp and then came around the foot. She was gazing down at the tiny table set for two and ignoring his face.

Exactly the reaction he'd hoped for. "I know, it's a ridiculously old-fashioned thing, when a guy plans a unique date, but hear out my justification before you cross me off your list in the name of feminism."

He pulled the chair away from the table and was pleased to see her sit down without so much as a word of protest.

"You're not from around here, but we have the same chain restaurants as everywhere else. Figured this was the only way you'd ever remember you'd been here."

She was blinking furiously, a fixed smile on her face. "It's a very nice gesture."

"And I'm just that amazing."

She laughed out loud, finally onto his game. "That's a unique approach: self-aggrandizement as self-deprecation."

"Yeah, I like it."

"You're trying to get me to mock you and break the hair pulling rule."

Carter opened the picnic basket with a careless shrug. "I wisely did not tell you what the punishment would be."

Looking out over the parkland, she leaned back and crossed her long legs. "I noticed."

Though his nerves were increasingly shaky, he held the silence, setting out the food.

Layla leaned over the table and pressed her lips together. "Did you make all this?"

"Yup." Cooking was his hobby ever since the class he'd taken with his mom as a way of cementing their postdivorce relationship. He'd learned a lot more than culinary technique in that class, and it gave him confidence.

"You're working hard!"

"I can't tell if you're complimenting me, or breaking the rules."

"It's a fine line, I suppose," she murmured.

That stung. He sat back and crossed his arms. The salad sat there invitingly, and the soup sent steam into the air. "I like cooking."

"So you aren't trying to impress me."

"I wouldn't dream of it."

"Because I'd consider that *bullshit* at this stage."

"And I am working very hard to figure out why that is." He laid his napkin in his lap and took a sip of his water. The electric current in the air didn't dissipate. "I'm not allowed to demonstrate any talents? That's a little unfair. I can't help feeling at a disadvantage almost from the start."

Her expression was unreadable, but yet again, those depthless eyes were probing his face.

"Let's be honest," she said finally. "You wouldn't have spoken to me if I weren't pretty. If I'd been wearing jeans and a geeky T-shirt, and hid in the corner closest to the Risk board, you wouldn't have looked twice."

It was the paradox of the female: they dressed to look their best and then agonized over whether or not the affection was for their personality. Thankfully, Carter had been the only boy in a cooking class full of mature women, right as he'd been trying to court Delia. He could see it coming a mile away, but as he took Layla's measure, he felt uncertain. Something was missing. She wasn't like anyone else he'd ever met.

"You're right. I wouldn't have, but not for the reason you probably think."

"No?"

"The girl I noticed, the girl I approached . . . she was the one who shed her skin to come to my party. She looked confident and immune to stupid crap. She's the one who defended someone she didn't know in a language not even related to hers, that she learned by watching *cartoons*. And then, she had enough spunk to make yours truly feel like a complete asshole."

The stern look broke for a forgiving smile. "That's impressive."

"Yes, I have a tremendous ego. It really is astonishing."

The test passed, Layla picked up her fork and dug in. "That's why you're a Captain Kirk."

Chuckling, he poked his spoon at her. "True. Would this date have ended prematurely if I had answered any other way?"

"Yes."

He wondered briefly if she got tired of men not taking her seriously. "What's wrong with finding you attractive?"

Layla looked up from her food with eyes as hard as emeralds. "It's fine. It's just not romantic."

"No?"

"No."

"I would really love it if you would explain that to me." He was walking a very loosely strung rope, and if he wasn't careful, he'd hang by it. "Firstly, because it's just a good idea to learn as much as I can, and secondly . . . because your opinion on the subject is the only one I'm currently interested in knowing."

She had a bedroom stare—that was what it was called—the gaze that looked sleepy but dangerous at the same time. He nodded subtly and refreshed her drink. Definitely the most interesting girl he'd ever met.

"There's love, and there's chemistry. And then there's both. You can love someone without wanting to sleep with them, and you can lust after someone but think they're a complete asshole. If you have both love and chemistry, you're set. If not, you might as well quit, because it can only end badly."

"Okay. I will absolutely agree to that. Seems, though, like you're suggesting the chemistry shouldn't come first."

"Do you think it should?"

"We can't walk around blindfolded." He smiled. "Would you have bothered to let me talk to you if I weren't drop-dead handsome?"

She pointed the knife at him. "There you go again. Bad form!"

"Question stands."

"I suppose what I'm saying is, that it should be treated as skeptically as it deserves. Chemistry is separate from love, and it's a lot easier and more common. If you want romance, both have to exist apart from one another and then weave together as a relationship forms."

Carter wiped his mouth. "You . . . uh . . . think through all of this in between writing out your married title and drawing big hearts around my name? Mrs. Layla Aadenson. Mrs. Carter Aadenson . . ."

Layla tipped back and fixed him with a laser-stare. "I think you just broke the rules."

"Nope. That was affection couched in mocking terms, not the opposite. And I think that this whole conversation counts as you breaking the rules by implying I do not have a grasp of what constitutes a good relationship."

"It's not mockery, it's a challenge. You're the one who dated a girl for two years when you knew you had no chemistry with her."

"Touché." He leaned his elbows on the table and braced his chin with a fist, watching her eat. "I was going through a pretty hard time. I didn't have a lot of room in my head for romance, I guess."

"She told me your parents had a bad breakup."

He gave a perfunctory smile. "They loved each other. At least, I think they did. My mom loved him, maybe, but I don't know about him. What's stupid is that even though they had all these memories together, they still fought like children. I guess it's true what they say, that the ones who love you can hurt you the worst."

"That's wrong," she whispered. "That's so unbelievably wrong I can't form words to say how wrong it is."

His glance approached her face in a series of skips up her outstretched arm. Something greater than his routine life story had to be weighing on her, because there was no way she could be sad for him. And yet her eyes had turned to pools of deep jade.

Layla seemed to choose her words carefully. "It's true that love can be hard on a person—the *act* of loving someone the way they need to be loved instead of how you want to love them, I mean. It takes a lot of effort to make someone else's desires and troubles your own. You have to *want* it more than anything. And you have to want it whether they notice or not." Her voice caught, and a tear was hastily wiped away. "Because that's the nature of the thing: to care so much that it doesn't matter if they ever reciprocate. If you really feel that way, you can't hurt them. You just can't. And when they hurt you, you forget it right away."

Carter's throat had gone scratchy. Initially, that kind of love seemed like a curse, but the more he thought about it, the more he realized she was right. It was a selfless purpose that asked nothing in return. And even if the person you loved really was being an unbelievable prick, if you loved them, you knew what to expect. If they loved you, then the idea of causing harm wouldn't occur to them.

What the hell had his parents been doing all that time?

What, they'd met right as they'd become adults and *settled*? Maybe they hadn't realized they didn't actually love each other. Or they got caught up in the chemistry and failed to be skeptical of their emotions.

He recalled his mother's words and knew that she had loved his dad. She had put up with hell for him, but in the end, it hadn't mattered. And maybe after being rebuffed and slighted for months, she'd lost her stamina and given up.

Layla was right, and she was a kid.

He could bring up ten or twelve quotes about love with a google search, but Layla's wisdom cut right through them like a shaft of light, and showed them all bitter or confused. But if all those important people didn't know what they were talking about, it suggested that true love was a thing very seldom seen, indeed.

He pondered how rare it actually was, and if it was one in a thousand, ten thousand, how anyone ever found it.

If Layla really believed what she was saying, then she wasn't about to be seduced by a bumbling teenager, getting caught up in a whirlwind of sexual desire. She would remain aloof, cautious, objective. And if she ever did meet someone worthy of it, that person would get her everything.

And then he felt it, just as his mother had predicted. Right in the pit of his stomach.

Chapter 6
The Kiss

Carter was quiet for the rest of dinner, the bravado forgotten. Declan watched his face and, had it not boded ill, would have found the solemn expression irresistible. Anxiety growing, he ate every bite on his plate without realizing it and sat twisting his napkin.

Suddenly, Carter furrowed his brow. "Are you having fun? I feel like we've had a pretty heavy conversation for a first date. I want to make sure you're enjoying yourself."

Declan shifted in his chair. His stomach was warm and happy; Carter was a surprisingly great cook. He felt like he was getting to know the young man, perhaps in a way not too many other people knew him. The setting was secluded but charming. In reality, he had been thinking how much better this date seemed than any of the typical ones he'd seen in fiction. Better than a movie.

"Yes."

"You're sure?"

Declan shrugged and attempted a smile. "I guess I'm just not interested in wasting time."

"Well, we could cut right to the good-night kiss if you're that eager."

Declan choked down a sip of water and patted his mouth dry. Good-night kiss? That was one thing he'd completely pushed from his mind so that he could get through the evening without having a nervous breakdown. "I meant wasting time while getting to know someone! I like *engaging* the person I'm with, not distracting myself *from* them."

"Me too. I mean, I only have another seven days."

"You're counting?"

Carter's humor was replaced by an intense stare. "I'm conscientious that way."

Declan examined the coat of metallic polish on his nails, warmth rising in his cheeks. "And I'm sorry, by the way."

"For what?"

"For implying that your mom and dad didn't ever love each other. I was just trying to say that maybe they—"

He held up a hand. "No, you're right. I don't think they really did, in that sense. And knowing that doesn't bother me. In fact, it's kind of instructive."

"Learning by counterexample, right?"

"Sometimes it's the best way."

Declan withered beneath the constant scrutiny. It was impossible to be sure what Carter was thinking, what he was noticing about the "girl" across from him. Was he enjoying the date, or had Declan already fucked it up? It wasn't as if he knew what to do. He'd never been on one before, and Dee's advice was cursory at best.

In a flourish, Carter tossed down his napkin and stood up. "I'd say we've thoroughly exhausted this location."

"What about the food?"

"I have an elf coming by for it. On to the next."

Declan took his outstretched hand in something like surprise. "Where's that?"

"Well, you have options." He pointed down at Declan's shoes. "You can try to golf in those shoes, or bowl in that dress. Up to you."

Declan's mouth dried up. For some inexplicable reason, it hadn't occurred to him that Carter had been serious about the "sights." He followed the boy back to the Charger, in a daze.

"Do we have to do either?"

Carter glanced down at him with veiled eyes. "I find that friendly competition on a date really helps break the ice. Unless, of course, you're one of those girls I'm told likes it when the guy loses on purpose, because I don't mess around."

Declan swallowed down a flutter and curved his fingers around Carter's forearm. He could hear danger in those words, but would be damned if he'd back down from the challenge.

"I wouldn't know. I've never needed it. They sort of lose naturally."

Carter laughed. "Oh, now you're talking shit."

"Keep thinking that. See what happens."

As if he didn't want to let go of Declan's hand, Carter shifted his feet and finally leaned against the car door. "We could drive, but then we'd get there in like two minutes."

"Well, speed is generally a motive to drive, it's true."

Carter tugged, and in a stumble, Declan fell against him, his heart jumping.

"Or we could walk." Carter dipped his head, and his mouth brushed Declan's ear. "Slowly. Since you're wearing clogs, I mean."

Fighting to get words out, Declan felt his whole back tingle as fingers followed along his spine. "That's very thoughtful of you."

"Uh-huh."

"Or selfish. I can't decide."

There was a pause, a skip in the progress of Carter's hand as it slid down his flesh. "It's only selfish if you don't enjoy my company."

"How could I not? You're God's gift to women," Declan murmured, uncertain he'd managed to come off as humorous. But Carter's low chuckle thrummed in his ear.

"There you go. You're starting to get the hang of this."

Declan had only a moment to slip free and end the chain reaction already unfolding in his body. He danced backward, but kept hold of Carter's hand.

"Bowling." The decision was a simple one, in that there'd be fewer kids his own age there. There'd be rented shoes, and a bunch of sportsmen, and a distractingly ancient sport. And it didn't hurt that Declan was so good at bowling, he'd once rolled a Wii-strike from the bathroom.

"I was *really* hoping you'd say that." Carter grinned mischievously, slipping a finger straight up Declan's spine from the small of his back to his recently shaved neck.

Declan cursed Dee and her fashion sense. She'd gotten excited because of the new costume "appliances" and picked a dress she herself would have fasted a week to wear, insisting that a boy had a better chance of "achieving the look" than did a girl with enough body fat to have a real bustline. He was really going to have to learn how to dress himself in the future.

They meandered to the bowling alley, not that far away, Carter talking about what he imagined the new school year would be like. He spoke like he was looking forward to being the head of the student council, in that all the words were there, but his voice had an edge to it. In fact, the whole subject of school seemed to make him uncomfortable. That was unexpected. To Declan, Carter had always been the consummate "doer": in every club, in every yearbook photo, invited to every event, friends with everyone. To hear him sound so unenthusiastic set Declan to wondering.

"You don't really want to be president, do you?"

"No," Carter replied, before Declan could feel ashamed for being so carelessly direct. "It's a bullshit position. You don't do anything but look like you're organizing stuff that the school board outlines for you, fundraise for events, and show up at games. But it looks good on a college application, and the program I want to get into in California is very competitive."

"And with all the sports teams and the clubs and the grades, you're basically covering all your bases. If you don't get into a college, I'll bet it's because you just didn't go the full distance and summon a crossroads demon."

Carter made a noise in his throat. "There it is again . . ."

"What?"

"The sense that you aren't the least bit impressed by me."

And Declan made a decision. If no one else would tell Carter the truth, he would. At least, about the things that would make him better than he'd been when Declan found him.

"It's not that, Carter. I'd rather see you do something you want to do, no matter what the reaction from everyone else. If you did something the least bit difficult or spontaneous, that would be impressive, and I know inside you, there's someone who can do that. I mean, you're on a date with me."

They had reached their destination, but Carter turned into an anchor. With a strong yank, he captured Declan up in a tight embrace. There was just enough time to become accustomed to the coziness before he was set loose. Carter wouldn't turn to look at Declan as he shuffled them inside. He got them a lane and shoes without as much as a word. While he excused himself to the bathroom, Declan sat on the plastic bench and looked painfully out of place.

Declan picked out a neon-pink ball and wondered how well this date was going. It didn't bother him to discover that the boy he'd idolized because he'd been so untouchable was as scared as everyone else. Some part of him had always known that, or hoped it, at least. In a sick way, it made him feel better about the universe, to find that beautiful creatures like Carter had their own burdens.

With that steel rod of confidence strapped to his spine, Declan checked his phone and sent Dee a thumbs-up.

She replied by calling him. "What happened?"

"What do you mean?"

"I just texted Carter and he asked what planet you were from."

"I—"

"Why isn't he with you?"

"Chill! He went to the bathroom."

"He's fragile," she said quietly. "I know he doesn't seem it, but he really is. There's this thing to him I could never figure out."

Declan smiled. "Is that why you didn't break up sooner?"

Delia didn't answer for a long moment. "Yeah."

"You're a really nice person, you know that?"

Her laugh tickled his neck. "I would've pulled the trigger if I'd known about your crush, sib."

Carter appeared at the entrance to the lanes. Declan made a rude noise and hung up. By the time the young man reached their seating area, Declan had picked up his ball and was leaning casually beside the ball washer.

"I'm from Earth."

Carter blinked, and the sodas in his hands drooped. Declan suddenly knew why boys were always struggling to understand their girlfriends. Girls were echo-chambers, and boys were constantly dealing not just with the girl at hand, but all her friends too.

Declan squared his shoulders. "You ready to get schooled?"

To his immense relief, the crooked grin came out of hiding. "Go easy on me, Princess. I'm fragile."

Rolling his eyes, Declan lined up his shot, and only considered how the dress and various other accessories would do when he was halfway through his follow-through. The ball skidded in an exquisite arc to the left, hooking the front pin and sending it smashing through the phalanx.

After performing a curtsy, Declan slinked back and leaned alluringly over the console. "Why don't we make it interesting?"

Carter looked up at the score monitor and whistled. "What did ya have in mind?"

"Hmm. I don't know."

"How about..." Carter picked up his ball and made a face. "Three out of five. Loser tells the winner a secret, like a deep, meaningful secret."

Declan blinked. "Okay."

Turning to the lane, Carter appeared to be settling in. He switched balls twice before picking one, and dried his hands. Then he did a little hip dance to loosen up.

Declan shook his head. There was no way Carter would win. Bowling was in his blood, as proved by the trophies from his dad's college years. He could bowl before he could walk, practically. His dad had bought him his own ball when he was five. And to top it all off, he'd gotten plenty of practice since the St. Cat's anime club met at the bowling alley every Saturday. He was unbeatable.

And then Carter rolled a strike, and Declan wished he'd insisted on mini-golf, where there was at least an arcade.

Carter sauntered down from the lane, grinning. "Probably should have let me bowl before you got all cocky."

Declan tried to smile, to be amicable, to exchange meaningful conversation, but as the game progressed, he found his focus latched to the score. Carter would make a joke, and it would take a full thirty seconds for him to react. His palms began to sweat, his arm was getting sore, and each tiny error in form put him further behind. When he won his second game, he breathed a sigh of relief, until Carter tied it back up with a Turkey.

When he wasn't taking his turn, Declan's mind was racing. If Carter won, he wouldn't settle for a cast-off secret like *I'm not really from Chicago*. It would have to be significant. He pictured that solemn face and knew he could never spin a lie into a deep truth. If he lost, it was the universe sending him a distinct message: you cannot find romance if you are not honest.

He did his best, but on the final turn, he knew he'd failed. An open frame on the tenth? That had to be nerves! His spin had been all wrong. And now he just had to deal with the consequences. Carter was carefully selecting a ball, and glanced his way. The blue eyes were keen.

Declan changed from the bowling shoes and snuck off to the restroom as his opponent prepared for victory. In the mirror, he looked past the makeup to the haunted eyes.

"You have to do this. You know you do."

What would Carter's reaction be? Of course he would be angry. Who wouldn't be? But would he carry that anger over into the school year and turn it into revenge? Declan checked his phone. Nothing from his fairy godmother. She'd known, when she cajoled him into this date, that there was the risk Carter would discover the truth. With that possibility looming, she hadn't batted an eye, so there must at least be some chance that she knew something he didn't about Carter's personality and how he might react.

He shied away from calling her. Whatever she said to do, he'd do, but not because she was right. He would do it because he was afraid, and making it her responsibility would be easier than owning the decision himself.

He fixed his makeup and took a deep breath. He'd stall and wait to tell Carter until they stood at the door to his house. Then he'd slip inside while the poor boy dealt with his emotions, and that would be that until school started. It was a cowardly move, but it was the safest way to break such news. If Carter wanted to talk about it later, he'd know how to find him. And that bridge could be crossed when it came to him.

Declan opened the bathroom door, his stride filled with purpose, and walked squarely into Prince Charming.

"Carter!"

"Layla! You missed my last turn."

Declan's blood ran cold, and a leaden horror was sinking into his guts. "Figured the conclusion was foregone."

He shrugged. "Too bad I choked."

"What?"

"Dropped a spare. You won by one pin." He snatched Declan's hand and led him to the exit. The alley was shutting down for the night, all but one lane dimmed. "That was way too much pressure to put on a guy on the first date."

Declan managed a sound in the appropriate place. Carter didn't press conversation on him. Simply held his hand and guided his unsteady feet back toward the car. Halfway home, Carter cleared his throat.

"My mom says that trust is never on your terms. Like, it's the one thing I guess you have to completely give up in order to have. Guess that's why the phrase is 'to put your trust *in* someone.'"

Declan glanced his way; the eyes were locked on the road as if peeling it back in layers.

"Makes me wonder if I've ever really trusted anyone, and whether or not I can expect anyone to trust me, knowing how I can be about things."

Declan swallowed and felt the warmth return slowly to his fingers and toes. But now it was stained by a black poison. Carter was truly an amazing boy, who would one day be an amazing man, and Declan was deceiving him in a way that was so despicable, it made *him* angry.

Carter parked and turned off the engine.

Declan shook his head. "You threw the game, didn't you?"

"You looked miserable."

Declan squeezed his eyes shut and fought back tears. He was not going to cry. He was not going to make Carter worry that he'd done something wrong, when it wasn't his fault at all. The passenger door opened and Carter ran his knuckles down Declan's upper arm. The gauntlet wasn't over yet. There was still the good-night kiss.

Declan busied himself with his keys, wondering if there was a way to squirm out of it. But how could he form a convincing argument against something he'd never experienced? After how gentlemanly Carter had been, it seemed like a cheap shot to fake a headache, and to be honest, he didn't want to. He wanted to kiss Carter more than he'd ever wanted to do anything, even breathe, but not in a perfunctory way, with this anxiety hovering in the background. He wanted to kiss Carter when it meant something.

But they were at the door, and there was no way out.

"Layla?"

Declan turned. Carter was leaning against the porch rail, that pensive look on his face.

"I had a nice time. If it's okay, I'd like to call you tomorrow. Maybe we could do something."

Blinking, Declan took in the distance between them, the tilt of Carter's head, and the arms crossed over his chest. It was clear then that the young man wasn't going for the kiss. Face burning, he grappled with mixed emotions, both relieved and disappointed in equal measure.

Carter shrugged in his casually enticing way. "I'd rather you have fun and enjoy being with me, instead of wondering every five seconds if I'm going to fall on you like a ton of bricks."

Declan's mouth opened, but Carter had already turned around. Unsure if it was the influence of the chemicals in his blood, or some greater compulsion, Declan dropped his belongings. His limbs were being controlled by his hindbrain, and suddenly, inhibitions seemed the stupidest of vestigial reactions. Compared to the dejected look on Carter's face and the idea of letting him wear it home, nothing mattered.

"Carter?"

The prince turned, and Declan threw his weight off the steps. Wrapping his arms around Carter's neck, he dragged the mouth to his.

The world swayed a little. Sounds were muffled, the tang of Carter's aftershave was delicious, and when the tongue slid against his, it was the greatest pleasure he had ever known. He raked his fingers through Carter's hair, rested in the arms as they wrapped around his waist and lifted him off his feet. Distantly aware that they were moving, he kicked off the ridiculous shoes. The door was cool against his back, but offered no support as his knees finally gave out. Instead, he was held in place by another body, and it terrified and satisfied all at once. Warm hands were wrapped gently around his chin, a thumb stroking his cheek and tracing his bottom lip. Every breath shared, all the senses mingled, they stood.

For what seemed like the first time, Declan was truly happy.

Carter pulled away, but only with kiss after kiss of farewell, leaving Declan propped against the door, accessories littering the ground. Carter took a few teetering steps backward, and swiped his hands over his face.

"Yeah, next time, I'm gonna lead with that."

The laugh tickled Declan's chest, amplifying the shiver as it tumbled forth. "You can't *lead* with the *goodbye* kiss."

"Can if you're this cool."

"*I* kissed *you*!"

Carter took the stairs backward, grinning like a fool. "See, that's how charming I am! So tomorrow, when I pick you up at noon, I'm gonna open with *you* kissing *me*, okay?"

He didn't wait for a reply, but Declan was trembling so hard he wouldn't have gotten one.

Chapter 7
The Architect

Delia answered the door. She was wearing sweats and a baggy T-shirt. Her hair was twisted up haphazardly.

"Layla's almost ready. Want a sandwich?"

He chuckled and followed her into the kitchen. "Hi. How's it going? I'm well, and you?"

She stuffed a piece of avocado in her mouth as he sat down at the breakfast bar. "Is that a no?"

"Has she eaten?"

Dee shook her head. "She doesn't eat much."

"She ate last night."

"You cook it?"

He nodded and stole one of her tomato slices.

"That's why."

"I hope that's a testament to my skill and not to her sympathy for me."

Dee smashed her sandwich together and shook her head. "To be honest, this is the first time we've really spent a long time together. But I really like her. We mesh. She's like a sister."

He leaned forward expectantly. "Yes?"

"She's like you, in a lot of ways. She thinks about everything, from all the angles. I think, to her, even if your food had sucked, she wouldn't have wasted it, just so your feelings wouldn't get hurt."

"I worked hard on that dinner!"

"It was probably great! I'm saying she was more interested *that* you cooked, not that it was tasty. If you want to keep her attention, you'd better show her more. Like the real you. The one that hides in the back and keeps to himself."

"That guy. I remember him."

"Tell him to look up from his drafting table once in a while."

He picked at her cheese crumbs and didn't look at her. She was, in many ways, the most perceptive person he'd ever met, except for Layla. It was what had made dating her possible, because she had never pushed, always backed down whenever he had seemed withdrawn. He still couldn't believe she'd stayed with him as long as she had, but it had made so many situations easier to handle, and he was grateful for that.

"You're not going to tell me anything about her, are you?"

She gave him a sardonic look for his trouble, and took a bite of her sandwich. Carter knew that was Delia for *Go to hell*. She could put away a hamburger like she was taking a deep breath and loved food. In lieu of communicating, he could always cook something and count on her to shove it into her face as a form of affection they could both handle.

"Where's your bro? I could use a good first-person shooter about now. He used to be logged on Xbox like all night long. Haven't seen him in a while."

She choked down a bite. "Camp."

An absurd image came to mind, of a skinny, unkempt Declan, shoving his glasses up his nose while attempting to start a fire by rubbing sticks together.

"Last person I would have expected."

"It's some kind of nerd camp."

"*Zombie survival* camp," Layla corrected from the top of the stairs. "Like *Walking Dead* crossed with an episode of *Man vs. Wild*."

Shockingly pretty as usual, she wore a pair of capri pants and a plaid button-up shirt. She was smiling brightly, but looked a little tired. That meant she'd possibly been dreaming about him, which was good, because he hadn't slept a wink. He wondered if she remembered his parting joke, until she climbed up onto a stool next to him and kissed the corner of his mouth tenderly.

"Told you," he whispered as she pulled away.

"You were right! I couldn't resist your animal magnetism."

Delia gagged. "If you need me," she slurred, "I'll be in the other room trying to swallow my food."

Carter tapped his phone and sent her an emoji of a kissy mouth. "Let's go."

"Where are we off to? I hear there's this amazing water tower where drunk kids pile beer bottles. Or there's the mall."

"Thought I'd keep you all to myself today."

Layla hopped down and followed him out to the Charger. "How entertaining will that be?"

He made a face. "I am the most entertaining man alive! So very. Do you know how to use a table saw?"

Layla's eyes were already huge, but when she blinked in astonishment, it was more adorable than a video of puppies and kittens playing together. He let her stew, saying nothing until they reached the first stop.

She got out of the car, bemusedly looking around as if he'd driven her to the fairy kingdom. A forklift trundled by them, blocking the entrance for a few seconds. She had the opportunity to ask, but let him have his fun. He stole her hand and drew her past the piles of reclaimed lumber.

A large man in a green polo shirt emerged from behind a stack. "Hey, Carter. Garret just went out back."

"It's cool. I wanted to look at the lot before I sign."

He nodded and gave Layla the once-over. "Careful of the sandals, miss."

She thanked him, and didn't appear to notice his perusal of her ass as she walked over to a large cross-segment of a tree trunk.

While she occupied herself with reasoning through why he'd brought her here, he went into the warehouse and looked through the cuts his grandfather had given him. They were minimally warped. A pile of really solid chunks of pine, nicely planed, an entire pallet of wooden shingles, stacks of discarded panels and slats. It was exactly what he needed.

Garret appeared with his clipboard. "Nice, right?"

"How much?"

"Not bad at all. You want me to bring it by on my next go?"

"When will that be?"

"Couple hours. There's a remodel over on Cyprus that's ripping out pine to put down cork."

It would time out perfectly. He signed the paperwork and smacked the bill of Garret's ball cap. "Leave it in the driveway."

"When do you start back up?"

He shrugged. "Busy year. Not really sure."

"Got time for a girlfriend, though?" he said with a ruddy grin. A nudge of his chin was directed at the pretty young thing who'd meandered into the shade. "Better than polishing your own timber, eh?"

"Ah, Garret, I never tire of your lumber jokes."

"You're the only one who smiles anymore."

"Just keep carving away at them."

"Ha! I'm using that."

They left the yard and stopped by the Sonic for lunch. By the time they got to his place, his mother had gone back to work, and they had the house to themselves.

Delia's insight had only served to flesh out the silhouette he'd crafted of the girl holding his hand. He had made the decision to invite her upstairs at about 1 a.m., when he had yearned to text her so acutely his stomach hurt. He'd sent her some z's. She'd replied with a chubby kitten tipped on its side in slumber. The exchange had gone on in pictures for some time, words not seeming enough, until he knew for sure.

His sanctuary was off-limits, even to his mother, and that was a well-respected law in their home. Delia had seen it once, and had shown an appropriate amount of interest, but something told him Layla would be different.

She sucked down a slushy and followed behind him, patient but taking in everything.

"So, last night we both got too caught up in my sex appeal to recall that I lost the bet."

"You cheated."

"It's not cheating if you lose at a disadvantage. That's called sucking at strategy."

"I thought it was noble."

He glanced at her face. Her eyes were veiled. "Noble or not, I still lost. So I'm about to introduce you to my one and only secret, as far as I'm aware. And it's not even that secretive, because my mom and Delia know about it. Actually, technically, a lot of people know about it, they just don't realize it."

He drew her attention to the door at the end of the hall. It had a lock on it, but was only barricaded during parties. For the effect, he'd secured it earlier in the morning so that he could put the key in and turn it in front of her.

"Welcome to my inner sanctum."

She slid past him, her gaze captured first by the balsa wood shape hanging from the ceiling. She stepped around the many cylinders of drawings, small models, and woodworking tools, and toward the professional drafting table in the center of the room. His latest sketch was lying there in plain view, but she was taking her time. She flipped through a few sheets scattered over the worktable, to his delight, wiping her fingers on her pants to be sure they were clean before she handled the expensive vellum.

She really was a rare creature that guys dreamt of. A mermaid, or a unicorn, or a comic book girl.

"Is this . . .?" Layla glanced at the large window that faced the backyard and pointed to the fire pit.

"I built the fire pit last summer. Got bored."

Distractedly, she cast around for a safe place to set her slushy. He took it from her and enjoyed the tripping in his heart as she fingered through the many sketches and schematics. There were buildings, improvements to existing structures, reproductions of classic cathedrals, really anything he could get his hands on to study or work over. Her eyes were picking out every detail, comparing duplicates for changes. Eventually she discovered the unfinished plans on his table and leaned over them cautiously, her hands tucked to her stomach.

"Carter, this is amazing!" she breathed. As his abdomen lurched, she traced the line of the organic element in the drawing with a fingertip. "Wait . . . this is the tree out by the trampoline!"

"Yup."

She stood up and clapped her hands. "Are you going to build this?"

He grinned. "Well, that's the plan. I work at my grandfather's lumberyard, as you saw. We specialize in reclaimed stock from torn-down houses and factories and stuff. A lot of times there's cast-off material that can't be used for any major application. He collects them for me after I've made the plans, and I turn them into things. I've built two treehouses this summer for kids to practice for this one."

"Can I help?" She bit her lip, and a shadow passed over her visage, as if she remembered how little time she had. "Please? I don't know how to use any power tools, but I can learn! I love treehouses!"

The back of his neck was burning, and he felt intensely awkward with pride. "Really? You sure? It'll be hard work."

"I don't mind! How long will it take to finish?"

He stood up and pointed out the window to the posts sticking out of the ground around the tree. "If I hadn't done those a couple weeks ago, it'd take a month, but with the posts up, the concrete cured, and two of us, it should be pretty quick."

"I thought those were like tree supports! I can't believe you built the fire pit! I love that place! It's the best part of the backyard!"

He shrugged, but her praise warmed him in a way not even his mother's had. "I built the deck too, but that was with my dad, before he left."

She cocked her head and gave him a glorious smile. "Why do you keep this all a secret?"

He sat down at the drafting table and slid the straight edge up to darken a line. "I won't always. It's what I'm going to study in college. I just . . . don't want anyone messing with it yet. It's mine, and right now, I can make whatever I want, or at least—"

"Imagine it." Her voice had softened. His ear pricked and his chest clamped down on each breath. "While it's in your head, it's flawless, every line and angle. No snags or patches, nothing that has to be overcome, only the creation. That moment *is* the thing, until the thing is built. The moment, though, is always perfect."

Carter swallowed and blinked furiously, but it didn't help. He hooked her waist and towed her down into his lap, surprised she didn't stiffen in his arms like she had before. He found her mouth with his thumb first and coaxed her lips open with the tip of his tongue.

The kiss was flavored blue, but still as amazing as the night before. Every time he thought he could pull away, she would tease him back, and when she slid her arms up around his shoulders and neck, he felt as if he could crush concrete with his bare hands. Or maybe curl up in a warm little ball at her feet when she asked.

"I knew you'd get it."

He sniffled and refused to look at her, but she managed to slither in his lap until she could find his eyes and stare into them like some kind of healing miracle worker. "I'm honored. I have serious misgivings about the saw, but you still have all your fingers, so I'm sure I'll be in good hands."

With a strangled laugh, he set her back on her feet. "The lumber will be here soon. Come out to the workshop and I'll show you what we'll be doing."

She smiled as he rolled up the plans and handed them to her, but there it was again, that curtain of sorrow behind her gaze. Maybe a few hours of hard work would banish it. If not, maybe he could kiss it away. Maybe this time, she would let him.

Chapter 8
The Mystery Girl

It was so hot, Declan felt like he'd been tarred and feathered, inside out.

He stretched along the bench and let out a tremendous yawn, muscles already protesting. From his vantage, he could watch Carter finish bolting in the last crossbeam, hugging the ladder with his bare legs. His shirt was off and tucked into his belt loop like a tail, and his skin glowed in the pink sunlight. No wonder the young man was so beautiful without the accompanying conceitedness: he didn't spend hours a day isolating muscle groups in a gym while looking in a mirror. His body was tailored to the thing he loved. That was something truly attractive.

When Carter's arms went above his head, Declan could see the lovely groove that led from hip to groin, and could feel his own stomach tighten in reply as he considered running his fingers over it.

Whimpering and squirming in misery, Declan chewed on his painted lip. The more time they spent in stolen glances and careful brushes of skin, the more Declan became sure that he was going to hell, if such a place existed.

He covered his smudged face and wished he could take off his own shirt. The air was humid and stifling, and he'd begun to feel dizzy with the effort of moving the lumber from place to place. Being a woman was hard work. For Declan, just as complicated as trying to be a man, but with the additional inconvenience of uncomfortable body modification. Beneath his clothes, he had the silicone breasts and contouring shorts. He'd had to go to the bathroom at regular intervals to mop the sweat off his chest so the stupid things would stick.

This lie was getting too difficult. He had a feeling it was all going to end badly.

A shadow fell over him, and cold droplets of condensation landed on his exposed stomach, burning like coals. Declan gasped and convulsed upward to find a glass of tea before his eyes. Carter took advantage of the opportunity, slid behind him, and went back to being the best pillow ever. Sucking the beverage down gratefully, Declan leaned back into his self-loathing. The young man was slick with his exertion, but Declan didn't care. He was cooler than the open air, smelled amazing, and the feeling of bare skin canceled any trace of disgust. If they were in Carter's bedroom, twisted up beneath the covers, it'd be just as slippery.

Declan shivered at the image, cursing the sweeping tension in his abdomen.

"You look tired," Carter said quietly. His voice was so enchanting, not quite a rumble, but a purr strong enough to send a pleasant tingle over the back of Declan's neck.

"It was worth it. I can't believe how great it's turning out. So are you going to put the floor in tomorrow?"

"Think so. Probably not until the evening though. It doesn't take long, and it's better to do it when it's cool."

"That's a good idea. Can I come help?"

His fingers found Declan's upper arms and stroked them gently. "Nothing would make me happier. Besides the fact that I intended to kidnap you all along, you're a lot stronger than you look, you skinny thing."

Declan smiled, but in this weary state, it was so much harder to fight off the feeling of dread and suspended grief.

Carter was his ideal mate. And in his female form, they harmonized. But the more he pranced around as Layla, the more he missed the comfort of being . . . whatever it was that he was, without a costume or a predestined chromosomal path. He knew now, after hours of continual, agonizing deception, that Layla had always been a construct, a projection of who he wished he could be. She was the blueprint. She wasn't him, any more than the spectacled Declan was. The real Dex was somewhere in between and at home with neither.

How could he expect anyone to love him if he didn't know his own pronouns?

He sighed. The sway of the swing, powered by Carter's legs, began to make him seasick. His head was throbbing.

"I've been thinking."

"Does it hurt?" Declan whispered.

Carter chuckled. "Honestly, a little."

"You should probably knock it off, then."

"I have a list."

"Of what?"

"Things that don't bother me."

Declan frowned and held the cold glass to his throat.

Carter purchased a sip from Declan's straw with a kiss to the top of his head. "I want to run them by you."

"Okay . . . not exactly sure—"

"It wouldn't bother me if you were a runaway."

Declan's throat seemed to swell shut.

"I wouldn't care if you were a criminal, or used drugs, or had a mental illness, or if you were a cat hoarder who had a shopping addiction."

He would have laughed, if he hadn't known where this was going.

"It wouldn't bother me if you had a child. I love kids. Or if you had to quit school to work a shitty job to pay for your mom's medical bills. I wouldn't care if you changed your name, or your address, or if you're defensive because someone hurt you. If someone tried to hurt you, I'd . . . well. I wouldn't leave if you were sick and had only weeks to live."

There was a lengthy pause, as if Carter was waiting for the breakthrough, but he would be disappointed, and that added a whole new batch of needles to the metaphysical voodoo doll standing in for Declan's soul. He spent the time berating himself in an onslaught of cruel names, his wretched innards twisting and his thoughts evaporating in the heat.

"I wouldn't care if you killed someone, unless you did it for the hell of it. I might care about that, but it would depend on the circumstances."

"I'm glad that murder was the *last* thing you thought of."

Carter shrugged beneath him and pulled him closer. "Have I gotten close?"

"No." His voice was shaky. The heat seemed to vanish then, and he felt the cold creep of adrenaline.

The sun finally slipped from view behind the tree line. Fireflies began to wink in and out around them, and the cicadas began to slow their incessant buzzing. But the air remained still and close.

"Will you ever tell me?"

Tears stung Declan's eyes and threatened to erode the carefully applied cosmetics. "Does it matter? Do you really care who I am when I'm not with you?"

"Yes."

"Why?"

"Because I'm a greedy son of a bitch, and this perfectly lovely girl isn't enough."

A tiny sob escaped in the guise of a laugh. "Please Carter, just . . . just let me have this."

This new silence stretched like the shadows, falling over the whole yard with a haze. The roughened fingers stroked his wrists and hands, tracing lines as if memorizing them. Declan's heart began to skip erratically, and breathing became a labor.

"Tell me what you need," Carter whispered finally. The smooth veneer was gone, the notes sounding brittle as they tumbled out of his mouth.

"I . . . I need to forget. I need a place to hide."

"From what?"

"Myself."

"Do you hate who you really are that much?"

Declan thought that yes, he was starting to.

"What if I could help her, this person you are when you're not here? I feel like I could. I feel like I could make you really happy."

"I wouldn't want you to have to deal with that. There's nothing wrong with you Carter, but sometimes we have to do things for ourselves. If you really want to help me, leave it alone."

"I can't."

Declan pulled free and stood up. It was a sudden impulse, but he felt that if he didn't obey it, he would suffocate. His vision swam.

He touched his face and felt the heat radiate off his skin. Moving in a swift series of trips over the deck, he grabbed his purse from the table and fished out his phone. The house was cooler than the outside, but he still felt sick.

Delia answer his call instantly.

"How soon can you come get me?"

She muted the television. "I can be there in five minutes."

"Please."

"Are you okay?" He heard her voice change as she jumped up, and the clatter of her keys.

Suddenly, the phone was out of his hand. He spun and the room danced with him.

"Layla is fine. I will handle it." High-pitched insect noises came from the phone as Carter stood staring sternly at him. "She's fine. I will take her home when we are finished having this conversation."

Declan's heart was hammering against his rib cage. Carter wanted an answer, and he wasn't going to stop until he got one. Declan felt weak, ill-equipped to handle the situation. And as he tried to hang on to thoughts, they flitted out of his grasp.

"I will, Dee! Will you stop mothering, please?" Carter hung up, keeping the phone hostage in his fist. Then he crossed his arms and took a deep breath, but the searching look in his eye didn't dim. Maybe Declan had finally gone far enough.

"Help me understand this, Layla."

Declan shook his head. Best to let him think Layla was a crazy bitch with more baggage than he cared to lift.

"You like being with me right? I'm not imagining that."

Swallowing hard, Declan wanted to lie, but somehow he knew that Layla, being what she was, wouldn't. "Yes."

"But you don't want my help?"

"No."

Carter ran a hand through his hair and looked around. The stare broken, Declan felt his limbs turn to jelly. When the young man came toward him suddenly and pulled him close, his strongest shove barely glanced off the bare chest. The kiss was insistent, furious even. Declan fought for oxygen, but couldn't find any, and then his vision darkened.

When it cleared, he was shaking. The world resolved itself over a series of dizzying waves. The cold was breathtaking, and when he lifted his arm to escape it, he found himself wrapped around another still form, up to his neck in water. His head was resting against Carter's throat, his arms slung limply around his shoulders.

"Stay still." The pulse drummed steadily beneath his lips. "Can you talk?"

"What . . . Why are we in the pool?"

"You passed out. I'm pretty sure it's heat exhaustion. This was the quickest way to cool you down."

Declan lifted his head and looked up at Carter's face filled with worry. It was the only time he'd ever seen that expression there, but it was one time too many. He tried to pull free, but Carter wouldn't budge.

"You feel okay, but you're not. I need to get you a glass of water. Are you awake enough for me to leave you for a sec?"

Declan nodded. Carter set him on the stairs and jumped out of the pool, shedding a flood as he ran into the house. Declan closed his eyes on a splitting headache. Then, as if the thought had had trouble cutting through the disorientation, it hacked its way to the front of his mind.

He was in the pool, in his Layla gear. He looked down and padded himself in a shaking frenzy. Little rivulets snaked up between skin and silicone augmentation. Everything was still in its place, but that was no guarantee it would stay put for long.

That would be an "easy" way to resolve the situation before it could go any further.

Carter returned and dropped back into the pool, handing Declan a large glass of ice water. He gulped it down as his favorite pillow took hold of him insistently. He must look a sight, but Carter didn't seem to notice, and when Declan pondered the reasons, he realized Carter's fingers were wrapped lightly around his wrist, taking his pulse with focused care.

"Just breathe, okay?"

Carter wasn't blind; he simply didn't care, which made the situation that much worse. How could Declan do this to someone so completely kind and gentle?

His head began to clear and the migraine dissipated. The sky was glowing a pale purple and pink. He listened to the slow rhythm of Carter's breathing and tried to match his own to it.

"I've always claimed I could knock a girl out with a kiss, but I thought I was kidding."

"Don't know your own strength, huh?"

"I'm really sorry. This is my fault. I shouldn't have acted that way. You were about ten seconds away from me stripping you naked."

Declan blinked. "I'm flattered."

"That's standard first aid. This is my fault. I should have made sure you had more water. Why didn't you tell me you were feeling sick?"

Declan braved another shudder as it ripped through him. His body had gotten so used to the heat, it had no idea what was happening. "I thought I was okay."

"And you didn't want me to worry."

"That too."

"Number one on my list of things that don't bother me is 'taking care of Layla,' so you know."

"I've memorized the whole thing, so that when I begin my insanity-fueled criminal rampage, I'll know who my friends are."

"This isn't a joke for me." A series of kisses swept from the nape of his neck to the collar of his blouse. It was a delicate reprimand. "I've thought about what you said last night about caring for someone the way they need you to. I was up all night thinking about it. I agree with you. And if you need a place to hide, I can do that, but I wouldn't really be helping you if I didn't try to help you *every* way I can."

"You can't fix this, Carter! I—"

"I'll drop it."

"Thank you."

"For now."

Declan's heart sank, and he knew for certain, that no matter how he proceeded, they would both end up heartbroken.

Chapter 9
The Liar

Carter stood in the dining room and scowled at the phone still in his hand. "Why should I bother going to him? Why can't he come to me?"

"Did he say why?" Carter's mom asked him. The pot of soup was bubbling away, and she was adding a pinch here and a pinch there. "Your dad hasn't called you in a while, has he?"

"Not since that counseling session where I told him to go to hell."

"Carter, he's your father."

"And he's a son of a bitch."

She shot a glance at him. "I know you would really love to believe that your parents are perfect, but it's not true. We're people. We make mistakes."

He picked apart his dinner roll. When he was younger, his dad had been his hero. He'd even thought about becoming a civil attorney when he grew up, but now he was lucky if he could stand being in the same room with the man without clenching his fists. Their whole relationship had been based on who the man had *appeared* to be, and rather than correct the misunderstanding, his father had allowed the illusion. He'd let Carter worship him, and when it all came crashing down, hadn't tried to lessen the shock. He'd just packed up his boxes and gone.

"Why do you defend him? He cheated on you!"

It was a question Carter had wanted to ask her for a long time. He'd found the photo albums sitting out, the piles of Kleenexes. The strong warrior-goddess she had seemed had proven to be yet another mistake he'd made. She was more delicate than he'd ever imagined.

"He did what he had to do," she said quietly.

"Why do you say things like that? How can you accept it?"

"Because I understand exactly what happened and why. I was there."

Not for the first time, the secret life of his parents became tangible. They had been children together, built their own world and language before he ever existed. He was their child, but more and more, he felt like he had never known them, nor had any right to ask questions.

"Why did it happen?"

She brought him a bowl of soup and ran her fingers through his hair. "Sometimes people mistake affection for love. They're not the same thing. I loved him, so I let him go be happy. He was fond of me, so he left."

Carter shook his head, stabbing at his food with a spoon. For some reason, he thought of Layla, and her faraway eyes. He pictured her passed out in his arms. She needed someone to look after her, of that he was certain, but it might not be him. She could be happier without him. Maybe all her secrets would resolve themselves without his interference.

"I can't think that way," he whispered aloud.

His mother smiled. "That's because you always want to save everyone. You're not responsible for us, Carter. We made this mess. We have to clean it up."

He glanced at her. She had such a soft face, such large, warm eyes. Once, she'd seemed to know everything. Now she seemed lost. He wondered if she always had been.

"Dad doesn't see it that way."

"He doesn't have to. I'm the one who didn't stop him, who let him lie. I did what I did for him, of my own accord. I don't expect him to return my feelings."

"Here he is, off building his second family, ignoring us completely. Here you are grieving. He doesn't give a shit!"

She stared down at the table. "That's unfair."

"How can you still love someone like that?" He realized too late that he was shouting. It wasn't her fault. She didn't deserve to be punished any more. He wasn't angry with her. He was angry with himself for repeating the mistakes he'd watched them make.

Layla was going to vanish, with all of her mysteries intact, and he was going to let her, because there was no other way to stay by her side *now*. But the knight in shining armor that dwelled in the back of his mind refused to accept that. There were no "no-win" scenarios. There had to be something he could do, some way to save what he could see forming between them. He needed a plan, a blueprint.

His mother drank her whole glass of wine before she answered, her face flushed. "I've asked myself that a thousand times, babe. Obviously I didn't see him clearly when we were kids. I wonder if I loved him, or if I loved the person I thought he was. First, I was angry with him, like he kept it hidden from me, but then I was angry with myself, for making that his only option. What if I'd been different? If he could have come to me with his feelings, we could have tried . . ."

"Mom, you're great! You don't need to be anything more than you!" he insisted. "If he wanted you to be different, then he's still an asshole!"

Her smile was so sorrowful, he almost hugged her compulsively. "And I'm learning that, Carter, I really am. But the issue is still there. Right now, I am trying to figure out if it matters."

"What?"

"We all have different aspects of ourselves we show to different people. You wouldn't want your friends at school to know how many nights you and I sat on the couch making fun of bad movies. And you wouldn't want me to know all the times you snuck out and did crazy shit with your friends. Those are two separate people."

"But . . ." He shook his head. "I wouldn't be crushed if either of you found those things out. Are you saying that if he'd told you about his girlfriend, you would have been okay with it?"

She took a deep breath and considered him. "No. After I found out, I waited to see how long he'd keep lying. Eventually I realized it would go on forever, because he was afraid. I realized he'd broken a promise to me. I wanted to keep you insulated, but then the bickering started, and we said hurtful things we couldn't take back. And then it all collapsed."

He thought of the Layla he knew and the one who had a complicated life back in Chicago. Which was the real girl? He wondered if she had made promises to anyone there that she was trying hard not to break.

"How are we supposed to deal with him, when we have no idea who he is?"

She poured another glass of wine and looked at it forlornly. "Now you're caught up to me."

Carter slammed his hands down on the table. "So why aren't you asking him? Why don't you knock on his door and refuse to leave till he talks to you?"

"You can't solve every problem with force, Carter. I know you know that."

He stared at his food and felt not the least bit hungry. He was letting his feelings about Layla drag up every other similar emotion he'd ever had. Was he falling for a girl who didn't really exist? Layla had asked for a place to hide away from her *real* life, and he'd promised her that, but now he wasn't sure if he could deliver. Now he wasn't sure it was fair for her to ask. If she loved him, would she?

Maybe her secrecy was proof that he was a fling to pass the time.

He refused that thought with a shake of his head, stood up suddenly, and snatched his phone from the table.

She glanced up at him. "Carter—"

"He wants me to go over there? Fine! I'll go, but he's going to answer me."

She protested, but he stopped listening. She was too kind to do it for herself, to make his dad squirm beneath her consideration, but Carter was not. He got into his car and drove the thirty miles, his memory flicking over the arguments that had halted because he'd come home from a game, or the shouting that had been stalled because they hadn't wanted to upset him. Well, he was upset now, and he'd have an answer. If he was the reason they'd never talked through it while it was happening, he'd be the thing that solved the problem for once and for all.

When he pulled up to the house, he had to remind himself that he was here to have a conversation, not to blow a gasket. He sat in the car for a long time, counting, breathing, divorcing himself from his feelings, planning what to say. The porch light came on, and a familiar black shape appeared. It walked down to the curb and got in beside Carter.

"Don't want to upset your girlfriend, huh?" he spat, before he meant to.

His dad sighed and took a piece of paper out of his wallet. "This is the money for your track stuff. There's also some in here for your college applications and tests and whatnot."

Carter set his phone on the dash. "You see that?"

The check in his father's hand drooped.

"That's your name in my contacts list. You're going to talk to me right now. You're going to answer my questions honestly, without bullshit, or I'm going to block you. You understand me?"

"I don't have time—"

"You'd better make time, or you'll have wasted a huge chunk of your life, you fucking coward."

His voice echoed in the silence.

"I guess I deserve that."

Carter's ire cooled. There was real defeat in that voice. "Did you ever really love Mom? I want to think that you did, but if you did, then you couldn't lie to her, and yet you did, for years."

"I lied to protect her." But the words lacked conviction.

"You lied to protect yourself."

The accusation hung in the air for a long while. Finally his father leaned back into the seat and covered his face. "You're right. Both are right."

"Did you love her?"

"I don't know. I know that I didn't want to hurt her. I know I didn't want her to see me being such an asshole. I know that I wanted her to be happy. In the end though, it all somehow managed to come out exactly the wrong way."

"Because you lied!"

"You're right! Is that what you want to hear?" The car door opened and he got out, tipping forward to talk through the opening. "I wasn't the person your mom wanted. I wasn't the man she deserved. The more I knew that about myself, the harder it got to deal with her expectations, the easier it was to lie. It's easy to be an asshole when you believe you already are one. So I guess I just lied for the wrong reasons. Figure that shit out and you're a better man than I am."

"How could you let her love you?"

"How could I have stopped her?"

"You could have warned her. You could have left."

"I tried, Carter. A thousand times. She wouldn't let go." The lines of his face had softened, and he suddenly seemed old. "Everyone is responsible for what they feel. We see who we want to see."

"So you're telling me that it's all a bunch of bullshit. I wonder if your girlfriend knows that's how you feel."

His dad slammed the door. The check blew into Carter's lap. He folded it up and shoved it into the center console. When he looked at his father's picture in the contact list, he debated deleting him. Instead, he drove home, feeling like shit.

His mother knew him well enough to read the look on his face and leave him alone. He went out to the backyard, turned on all the lights, and started laying the floor of the treehouse.

As he measured and cut, fitted and nailed, the more fluid parts of his mind took over the dilemma. He was falling for Layla, through no fault of hers, and when she shied away, tried to fend him off, warn him, he barreled straight ahead and ignored her protests. She'd run out of his party, for crying out loud, and he'd chased her down and kissed her without her consent. How could he be angry with her for keeping things from him, begging for privacy, protecting herself from a persistently nosy teenager?

She hadn't lied yet, as far as he knew, but if he kept pressing her, would she? Would it be for the wrong reasons? What were the wrong reasons?

He stretched out on the platform he'd created, high off the ground amidst the branches, and looked up at the stars.

He'd never really thought about things like "love at first sight" or "soul mates" or anything like that before. But when he'd seen Layla walk through that door, something had hit him. It was the *potential*, like his mom had said. The potential for a lifetime. It would exist for another six days, and then . . .

"There has to be a way."

Chapter 10
The Promise

Layla stretched out across the boards on her stomach, her sandaled feet kicking in the air. In the span of an hour, she'd assembled the entire railing along one side, without a single question. He glanced at her occasionally, comparing her to the other girls he'd met.

He'd dated a few before and after Delia, but none of them had clicked. What he'd liked best about Dee was the way she handled things. She would observe, and when the situation finally called for her to comment, she was careful and precise. When it was time to cut loose, Dee could easily match him in enthusiasm. She was a calm person that people went to when they were hurting, and a happy person that people gravitated toward like bees to a flower.

Delia made him feel comfortable, but Layla . . . There was something unique about her, something that fitted her into his world better than any girl . . . hell, any *person* ever had.

It all came together flawlessly, like he'd known her forever.

The banter was hilarious, and she got all of his jokes. She didn't misinterpret his swagger even a little. She didn't overreact or ask endless questions. When she looked at him, his blood ran hot, and he could feel himself being picked apart with a wary touch.

And on top of all of that, she was . . . incredibly beautiful in a way he couldn't quite describe. Delightfully awkward, gracefully guarded—Layla was a form he couldn't draw, because it was the movement that was the poetry.

He glanced back at her. She was lying on her side, looking at him with a playful grin.

"What?" he prompted.

One of her shoulders hitched. "Enjoying the view."

"I'm trying to work, ma'am. Let's keep this professional."

Her laugh slithered over his nerves. "Then put your shirt back on."

"Are you suggesting that my physical prowess in any way affects you, Princess?"

"If I took my top off . . ."

"I'd probably nail my hand to the tree. Stop sexually harassing me."

"If you don't want to get harassed, you shouldn't dress like that."

He gasped, but she was back to her measurements, and mischievously ignoring him. He dropped his nail gun and crawled over to her. They'd already kissed three times today, and it still didn't feel like enough. He grabbed an ankle and dragged her closer. In a single movement, he had flipped her over and caged her in his arms.

He felt it, that moment when her whole body stiffened as if he had thrown a bucket of cold water over her head. That was the line, and he wasn't to cross it. She twisted beneath him, until she was resting on her side. He rolled and lay staring at her upper back, bared by the swag of her top.

Nervous in spite of all the times he'd framed this moment in his mind, he began with a deep breath. "I want to ask you a question, not to pick a fight, but . . . because I need to know the answer." She nodded. Carter ran his fingertips down her shoulder, his heart slamming into his ribs when she shivered. "The girl from Chicago, with the complicated life . . ."

"Mmm?"

"Or the girl up in my treehouse. Which one do you like being most?"

She turned and replied by wrapping her arms around his neck. Her nails raked over his scalp as she tugged him close. Her lips were sweet, some kind of gloss that smelled like cherries, and the feel of them was bliss. Every stroke of her tongue pulled a current down his spine that spread out over his midsection and paralyzed him. He wanted to take hold of her and squeeze her, but there was the line, like an invisible wall.

She murmured in his ear; it was lovely but unintelligible. He was catching his breath slowly, returning to the world a few heartbeats at a time.

"Chicago isn't that far away," he begged hoarsely. "And people have long-distance—"

"No."

He raised his head. Her eyes were fixed sternly on the branches overhead. This was a command, a directive, and it was more definite than he'd ever heard the word said before.

"You're killing me, here!"

Her voice broke through a melancholy smile. "It'll be over soon enough."

He stared, the horror of having less than a week left finally dawning on him. "But why? Why can't we—"

She rolled away and went for her bag. "You're right. I need to leave. I'm making everything—"

"No!" He imprisoned her again and hauled her backward. To his tremendous relief, she relented.

"This is only going to get worse."

"I know." He snaked his hands beneath her knees and lifted her up into his lap. Her head turned and nuzzled him. They were a tangled knot for a long moment, trading tiny kisses as if marking time. "I'd rather have every second I can, even knowing you're going to leave."

"That's masochistic."

"No. We all know death is coming, but we don't all jump off bridges."

"Fair point."

"When you go home, back to your complicated life, are you going to forget about me?"

She pressed closer to him. "No."

"Then why would you want that instead of this?"

"Because this is the dream, and that's the reality. I don't want it, but it's the way it is."

He didn't bother to insist that it didn't have to be that way. She would take it as yet another sign that he didn't understand the boundaries of their brief relationship. There were other things that he needed to know, more important things.

"Answer me this."

"Okay."

"Have you ever lied to me? Of the little you've said . . . was any of it a lie?"

He felt her body react to the sting in his words, but she didn't balk. "Yes."

Carter took a steadying breath. Suddenly, he knew what the right reasons for lying actually were. Last night, he thought that he'd want her to always tell the truth, or only lie if she was doing him a favor. If she wanted to protect him, then that meant she liked him. But no. He knew that if there was a chance he could love her, he could never let her be dishonest on *his* behalf.

"I know you didn't ask me to get attached to you. You ran away and I chased, every single time. It was all me, so don't say you lied for my benefit. Please."

"I didn't."

He nodded, somehow grateful. "Don't, okay? Promise me you won't lie to keep me happy. Only ever lie if it protects you, okay? Even if it protects you from me."

She reached up and rested a hand across her face. After a few moments, she sniffled. He didn't want her to cry, but it wasn't his place to stop her. "I promise."

The warm wind picked up, shaking the branches in a gentle sway. They sat quietly for a long while as the sun moved in a slow drift across the sky. Carter heard the back door open and his mother emerged. She came to the foot of the tree and knocked on the ladder.

"You up there, babe?"

"Yeah. Just taking a break."

Layla's eyes were shut, but she was visibly listening.

"How do you feel about fried chicken for dinner?"

"Sounds great, Mom. Can Layla stay?" She shifted in his arms. He pressed his mouth to her ear and shushed her.

"Oh, I didn't realize you had company."

"She's asleep."

"Well, there should be enough for three. I'll go get started. If you wanna come help at any point, it'll go faster."

"Sure."

She walked back into the house. Layla unfolded from his arms and stretched like a panther released from lifelong captivity. "I should really go home."

"Are you saying that because you *want* to go home, or because you're worried she's going to ask you about yourself?" He raised a knowing brow and tugged his shirt back over his head.

She gathered her things. "You asked me not to lie."

"I'll take care of it."

Carter climbed down the ladder and held it for her, then followed his mother into the house. From the kitchen, he watched as Layla lifted her phone to her ear and curled up on a deck chair. The more he wondered about it, the more worried he became. He'd given her quite a comprehensive list of fucked-up lives, and she'd denied all of them. But if that denial had been *the* lie, then perhaps the "running from a mafia death squad" and "escaping an arranged marriage into a cult" possibilities didn't need to be raised.

"Come cut up the vegetables for the salad," his mom said.

He got out a knife and cutting board, his eyes still glued to Layla as she wrapped her hand over her face. The conversation on the phone was certainly with Dee, but Layla seemed anxious and upset. Perhaps she was just as sad to leave him, more so if her life was really bad.

"This the girl from the date?"

"Yes."

"She okay?"

He turned to his mother suddenly and set down the knife. She was midway through dredging a piece of raw chicken in flour, and she stared at him blankly.

"Can you promise me you won't ask her any questions about herself, please? She's here to take a break. She doesn't want to talk about it, and I told her I wouldn't ask."

She blinked in surprise. "Don't you want to know about her?"

"Of course I do."

"Then why would you promise that?"

"Because I don't want her to lie to me."

Their eyes met and held, and understanding passed between them like an electric current. Her hands moist with egg, she leaned the side of her head against his shoulder.

"She must be pretty special."

He swallowed till he could find his voice. "Yeah. Remember that pit-of-the-stomach thing?"

"You going to be okay when she goes home?"

"Not even a little."

He looked out the window at Layla. The phone conversation appeared to be winding down, but the worry on the pretty face remained. His mom was right about his hero complex; all he wanted to do was gather her up, tuck her into his bed, and protect her. Until someone called the police and forced him to give her back.

"She's attractive."

"Yeah . . . But that's not the least bit important."

"No? Hmm. Someone must have raised you right." She elbowed him.

"She's one of the smartest people I've ever met. At least when it comes to me."

"Smarter than Dee?"

He nodded. "With the added bonus that we have chemistry."

His mom made a noncommittal noise. In her opinion, no girl matched Dee, and if her future grandchildren did not have the trademark dark hair and hazel eyes, she wasn't interested. When they'd broken up, he found out afterward that Delia had driven out to the lumberyard to break up with his mom first. They'd gone to lunch and spent about two hours hashing out his weak points. She still sent Dee a birthday card, and still asked about her at regular intervals.

"What could be so bad that she doesn't want to talk about it?"

"I keep hoping it's nothing, and that she just doesn't want to involve me in it."

"Or she just doesn't want that much from you."

He could barely manage a shrug beneath the weight of what she was saying. "Maybe."

Layla finally got up and came inside, smiling shyly. "Delia says for me to bring her a leg."

His mother smiled, but she was giving poor Layla the once-over. "I'll wrap one up for her."

"Is there anything I can do to help?"

"You could set the table."

Layla went about the task mutely, taking direction in nudges from his chin. His mother watched her with a keen stare.

Then Carter got a bright idea.

"I thought about adding a second level down below. What do you think about that, Layla?"

She glanced up. "You mean around the pylons on the ground? Like a deck?"

"Yeah. Thought it might be cool to have tiers, connected by a couple swinging plank bridges."

Layla's anxiety broke for a winning grin. "That would certainly make it a much more awesome Nerf war zone."

"Is that what you've been envisioning all along?"

"No, I was picturing a shaded loft, where I could sit with a drink and read . . . and shoot from above while you try to gain the ladder."

He rolled his eyes. "Girls can't shoot."

She stowed her tongue in her cheek and gave him a dirty look. "Keep telling yourself that, Carter. I once tattooed a guy's ear neon green from half a football field away."

"You paintball?"

"Like a boss."

He laughed and shook his head. It didn't seem uncharacteristic. In fact, it enhanced his image of her. He could picture her in fully coordinated gear with a high-powered rifle at her side. He spared a look for his mom. She was pressing her lips over a smile.

This required investigation. Carter couldn't help a grin. "You ever play Xbox with Declan?"

Layla bent over to retrieve a fork she'd dropped. "Uh, sure, all the time."

"I'll worry if you can hold your own against him. That kid's got magic trigger fingers, or something."

When she emerged from behind the bar, her face was screwed up in an unimpressed expression. "Well, if you weren't caught up in *Minecraft* on creative mode, you pansy."

"That's the one with the blocks, right?" his mother wondered as her frying pan began to spit.

"Yup, I can just see Carter sitting around for hours at a time building pagodas and castles and stuff."

She nodded. "He even plays it on his phone while he's in the bathroom."

"Mom!"

The women shared a glance and then exploded into laughter, and Carter knew the evening would pass in an easy camaraderie. He kissed his mom's cheek and thanked her with a whisper.

Chapter 11
The Game

Carter appeared the next morning, breathtakingly handsome in tight black jeans, a leather jacket, and combat boots. Declan had hardly enough time to prep his appearance and throw on a robe before the boy waged an assault on their door. His hurried insistence that Declan "dress to get messy," inspired slight hesitation, but Delia hauled her butt out of her creative chaos and pieced him together from her treasure trove of clothing.

"He's wearing the boots. Better put you in my motorcycle outfit," she muttered, digging through a pile of laundry.

"You have a motorcycle outfit?"

A pair of leather pants flew out at him. "Found it at Thrift Club. Couldn't pass it up."

Declan looked out her window at the Charger. Carter was organizing the trunk. He caught sight of a pair of kneepads and a breastplate.

"What do the boots tell us?"

"He calls them the 'Mighty Boots of Stomping,' and he wears them whenever he goes out on some macho quest."

"Such as?"

Delia groaned and handed him a black T-shirt that read *Self-Saving Princess*, and her knee-high lace-up boots. "Last time it was laser tag, before that he wanted to rent a dirt bike and go out to the motocross track to take lessons from a twelve-year-old. Before that, it was his seventeenth birthday, and he insisted on hang gliding." She shoved a matching motorcycle jacket on top of the pile. "Go with Glob, my son."

Declan retreated into his room and donned the disguise in a frenzy. All of those adventures sounded fucking amazing, but letting Delia know he was the least bit excited was a poor way to thank her. She'd probably dreaded the Mighty Boots of Stomping, but Layla couldn't wait.

He knotted a scarf around his head and searched through his chest of paintball gear. As an afterthought, he strapped on elbow and kneepads, fingerless gloves, and the utility belt. Hooked over his arm were a studded purse and some serious goggles, just in case.

At the door, Carter's blue eyes lit up. "Are you psychic?"

"Well . . ." He stood up on tiptoe and kissed him greedily. When they parted, Carter had a hold on his waist and was grinning like a fool. "I was warned of the Mighty Boots, and I do recall that we discussed my predilection for sniping with an actual gun, not the way other people do it."

"This Declan's gear?" He laughed.

"Yup. Fits okay. Should I grab his rifle?"

Carter's brows shot up. "Never touch a man's rifle. He might spaz out and reorganize something."

"Are you slandering his exceptionally orderly space?"

Carter shrugged and followed him inside. "He's like the most meticulous sixteen-year-old I've ever met. Probably dusts his action figures with a Q-tip and distilled water."

Declan made a face. "What's wrong with that? That's what all the care manuals say will retain their resale potential." Carter snorted, and Declan realized he'd let the line blur. It was much too close a call. He was supposed to be pretending to be a girl, and though he'd learned about action figures from Yuki, boys didn't think girls knew about that sort of stuff. He shrugged and took the stairs two at a time. "At least, that's what he says."

Carter waited for him as he grabbed his gun and ammo. At the bottom of the stairs, he gazed longingly at the compressed gas tank and scope.

"That's some piece of hardware."

"It's certified by the Army."

"And you know how to handle it?"

Declan cleared his throat. Almost another misstep. "We all got matching."

"Who's 'we'?"

"Dex, Dee, and me."

They got in the car. Declan fiddled with the radio; the nearest range was quite a ways away, and they'd need tunes. But soon Carter was pulling up in front of another house and honking.

"I hope you don't mind. Today is team day at the range, so I called a few friends to join us."

Declan's heart sank. Instead of a relaxing day of being himself, he'd have to be "on." Not only that, but there was no guarantee that the other boys would be as easily fooled as Carter in the broad light of day, minus the assistance of alcohol.

He smiled, but his misgivings were obvious.

Carter leaned over and kissed his cheek. "I promise they'll behave. If they don't, I'll beat the shit out of them."

One by one, they acquired three more senior-aged boys. As each one crammed himself into the Charger in various states of preparedness, Declan waited behind his dark sunglasses for someone to say *Who's the fag?* But no one did. He was introduced as Carter's girlfriend, which made his chest cramp, and soon the boys were busy ignoring him or talking around him as the "female" in the car.

Aside from the fact that they were all athletes, all exuding machismo like a car full of *lucha libre* dressed for combat, they were perfectly normal human boys. Most of the small talk centered around the upcoming sports seasons and whether or not the cheerleaders would date them. Declan loaded his mouth full of chewing gum and tried to stay out of it.

"I asked Sophia out last year." A guy they called "the Goat" swallowed down half a breakfast burrito in one bite. He was wearing a camo jacket and smelled like cigarettes and deodorant. "Told her I'd let her drive Sadie."

The other boys were impressed.

Carter looked in the rearview in surprise. "She's like Fort Knox. What did she say?"

"That I was a nice guy, but she'd rather stay friends. That and that she didn't have a license."

"Translation: you're too childish," Declan muttered.

The boys snickered. The Goat leaned around the seat and frowned at him.

"Is that what that means?"

Declan's mouth hung open. It would be obvious to anyone looking. From the stupid chin fuzz to the self-congratulatory belch, the Goat was a giant child on a hormonally accelerated growth spurt.

"Yes, that's what that means."

"So, like," Andre Parker interrupted, "what does it mean when a girl says that it's not you, it's her?"

Declan rolled his eyes heavenward. "Most of the time it means that you're like a puppy she doesn't want to kick."

"What if I like being kicked?"

"Then you're an even sadder puppy."

The car filled with abrupt laughter. Declan gritted his teeth. A hundred years ago, all these children would have had jobs and wives, instead of slowly bringing down the average of the human race. How could someone like Carter have friends like these? They seemed light years apart in terms of maturity.

As the conversation carried on, he barely listened. These were exactly the type of boys who worried Declan the most. They drove muscle cars, hid in locker rooms, listened to violent music, and never read books that contained words bigger than three syllables. If they found out he was cross-dressing, he could end up dead.

"Layla." Andre leaned between the front seats. Delia had been friends with Andre since junior high, and Declan had seen him a few times. He was a loud-mouthed comedian type. Always making rude jokes at other people's expense. "What kind of girl goes paintballing?"

Carter glanced his way with a smirk.

"Any girl who enjoys marksmanship, I would think."

"Can't imagine there are many of those."

"Actually, some of the world's finest sharpshooters are women."

"Yeah, but paintball is a man's sport. One shot to the chest and you'll probably be like 'Oh my god, my lady parts!'"

His faux female voice dragged across Declan's mental chalkboard.

Carter squeezed his hand. "Knock it off, Andre."

"I can take care of myself, Carter Aadenson," Declan warned. "My gun is a US Army Project Salvo Elite Sniper Rifle with a twenty-inch tactical barrel and a cyclone feed. It fires at the maximum range-safe velocity of three hundred feet per second, the approximate speed of a musket ball. If you shot me in the tit with the hand-pump bullshit you're about to rent, I'd hurt just long enough to get pissed. If I shot you in the balls, Andre, you'd need a fucking surgeon. Do we understand each other?"

The car went completely silent. Declan stared straight ahead, his right boot wedged onto the dash, and blew a gum bubble.

"Shit!" Andre finally whispered. "Glad you're on my team."

Declan was not amused, in fact, he was fairly certain he'd once again ruined the rest of his life, but when he caught Carter's eye, the boy was grinning proudly.

"I told you guys to be nice to Layla. If you thought I was saying it because I was worried about her getting her feelings hurt, then you misunderstood."

In that moment, through some bizarrely ironic transformative magic, he became "one of the boys." Before long, they were demanding he translate all things "girl." From giggling in the halls and hair flipping, to slamming doors in their faces or refusing to call them, he was the source of knowledge. It was intensely amusing, but uncomfortable. If he didn't believe that the girls of his high school were better off with his intervention, Declan would have shrugged off the questions.

Was he appropriating female culture, or was it his culture too? Did he have the right to claim it? Delia would say yes, but she wasn't the one living in both worlds uncertain where to tread to offend the fewest people.

Declan wasn't sure how else to get through this situation, and the boys needed serious enlightenment, deep psychological reprogramming. Most of the girls he knew had their own troubles; they couldn't waste their time trying to fix these guys. They shouldn't have to.

"Every time I talk to a girl," Andre revealed, "I think, 'Man, I'm gonna make some stupid joke, and then I'll end up pissing her off.' And then I get nervous, and I do that, and then I get slapped."

Declan turned and looked at him. He was sheepishly playing with the zipper on his coat. He would have said Andre was immune to defeat, but in reality, the boy seemed painfully shy.

He realized, in that instant, he'd misjudged this motley crew. They were all really nice boys who spent too much time trying to read the cues that society was giving them. Except all those cues were wrong. If society knew what it was talking about, there'd be a place for Declan, and there wasn't.

Sighing, he turned off the radio and sat up straight. "Okay, I'm going to give you guys the best advice you will ever get in dealing with a girl."

Carter's face was stretched in a superhuman grin. "Can't wait to hear this."

"You ready?"

Andre pulled out his cell phone. "I'm gonna take notes."

"Girls are not a separate species. They're *no different* from you when you get down to the core. They're not the enemy. They're not secretly planning the many ways they can humiliate you."

"You sure?" Hunter muttered.

He made a face. If that was really how they thought about it, no wonder. "Yes, I'm sure. And the fact is, if you had to live the way women do, you'd understand. Suddenly *everything* they do and don't say will make sense to you."

"Are you going to tell us what they want?"

"They want the same things you do. They want to be your peers. They want to know that their opinions and thoughts are important to you, not just important, but *necessary*. If you find yourself worrying more about your fantasy football picks than what's coming out of her mouth, then you should not be with her."

The Goat frowned. "Yeah, but they don't want to be *equal* equal, because they all go nuts for a guy who can pick them up and carry 'em around and shit."

"You could pick up any girl in school, Goat."

"Well . . . yeah. I bench two sixty."

"Uh-huh. So why don't you have a date?"

He shrugged. "Because I'm emotionally immature?"

"You're definitely *playful*, but that can be appealing to some girls. The problem is, most boys at this age are just looking for fun or sex for fun's sake. Girls don't have that luxury. Society has it out for them, doesn't fund their sports, or pay them the same money for their time, and pounds it home that if they have sex, they're forever tainted. Imagine, for a second, how you'd feel if you faced that kind of life."

The Goat nodded thoughtfully. "Yeah, I guess that makes sense. Guys do have it way easier, especially when it comes to sex. If I get laid, it's like, hooray. But then everyone talks shit about the girl."

"If every day you had to convince everyone that they should take you seriously, trust your opinion, not reject you because of your gender, and all you ever got back was that your appearance was the only thing that mattered about you, in spite of your intellect or feelings, you might make sure your hair was perfect, your makeup on. In fact, you might get downright crazy about it. You might be terrified that if you don't look the way magazines look, you aren't worth it and no one will love you."

"Shit. That's gotta be why you guys don't like your hair touched," the Goat whispered.

Declan glanced at him. "With a life like that, you'd think that if you aren't careful as hell in every way, you'll end up alone, and that is horrifying. You would try to find people you could trust and you'd do it as soon as you had any freedom. Does it make sense now?"

"I barely brush my hair," said Andre, "my grades suck, and I wear whatever my mom tells me to."

Declan nodded encouragingly. "Exactly. It's hard work. Girls don't have time to waste. Many will eventually have children, which is a huge commitment for them. They want to be sure they find a guy who will defend not just their rights, but that child's too, not because he's *a* man, but because he's *the* man who must deal with a masculine society. He represents her to the world that won't let her speak for herself. She wants a guy who will shoulder the responsibility, not leave it all to her. Essentially, girls want a *partner*. Even girls like Bambi are mean out of fear."

"That explains a lot," Hunter finally let out.

Andre frowned. "So, when a girl is, like, talking to you a lot, about random stuff. What does that mean?"

Declan sighed. "She's throwing anything she can at you to get a read on you. She can tell if you don't feel strongly enough about her to be that partner she's looking for. If not, she is forced to keep looking till she finds one, because for her, the world is a dangerous place. It's full of ways she can fail, people who will judge her, societal trends designed to keep her from realizing her potential. A girl wants a boy who can mesh with who she *wants* to be and help her *become* that person."

That was something he understood very well. He'd spent a long time thinking about what gender meant in this world, and knew the theatricality of it had nothing to do with what it felt like. Much of his identity was considered feminine, while some of it was designated masculine. That made it almost impossible to see either as a comfortable fit. But for most people looking at him, he was a boy. As long as he avoided discussing half of his identity, he could slip under the radar. But it was just as bad when he allowed himself to explore femininity, because then he was hemmed in by what everyone thought *that* meant. He could imagine how it felt for women—trying to find who they were while constantly fighting with that idea of what they were supposed to be.

He'd learned so much from the girls he knew. Without the women in his life, he would have been stuck in his depression, hating himself and thinking that there was no way anyone could understand what he was dealing with. Without Yuki and Delia . . . he could be dead.

He owed them. He needed to make sure that while he was here, playing dress-up to figure out who he was, feeling so guilty, out of place, and afraid that his palms sweated, that he gave something back to them.

Maybe because he was a little in both worlds, he could at least help one see the other a little more clearly?

There was a long silence as the boys hopefully pondered his words. Carter was staring at the road as if to use its blank surface like a sketch pad. Declan wondered what he was thinking—if he was wondering about Layla.

Hunter made a sound. "That's heavy. What if you just want to take a girl out and have some fun?"

Declan lifted his sunglasses and stared at him. "Then tell her that's what you want. Let her know you respect her as an equal and just want to hang out. It shows you understand what she's worried about and why. If you can get around that mental reflex, you might have a date. And she'll have some fun too, instead of feeling self-conscious, or afraid, or second-guessing herself for taking the time to play."

The Goat frowned. "So if I went up to Sophia and was like, 'Hey, girl, it's cool that you don't wanna be my girlfriend. I wanna hang out with someone awesome, and I think you'd have fun,' she might say yes?"

Declan pinched the bridge of his nose. "Do you guys have good relationships with your mothers?"

There were some sounds that equated to adolescent agreement, because saying they loved their moms was seemingly forbidden by ridiculous boy culture.

"Would you ever call your mom 'girl,' or be cool with someone else treating her like a second-class citizen by not using her name?"

The Goat grumbled something about his love of killing.

"So why would you do that to that beautiful girl who might one day be someone's mother, or a CEO, or a president, or a military commander? Think about what she *could* be, what she wants to be, not just what she is."

Carter steered the Charger down a dirt lane. Declan had probably secured his safety for the rest of the day. He spent the remainder of the trip breathing easily and letting his nerves relax.

They stopped in the dusty parking lot in front of the range and piled from the car. He pulled his gear out of the trunk and strapped it into place.

"Hey, Layla," Andre murmured. "I get why Carter likes you."

"Because he's a shit shot and really needs the suppressing cover?"

The boy shook his head, grinning. "You know, guys are looking for all that stuff too. It's just . . . I guess that there's not as much pressure on us. If I was a girl, I'd probably go apeshit and have, like, an eating disorder or something."

"Instead you mask your low self-esteem with humor. How's that working out for you?"

"Pretty shitty."

"That's because girls don't think you're serious. If you feel vulnerable, a girl isn't going to hate you for it. If you let her know that that's how you feel, she'll completely understand, because that's what she's probably feeling too. You have to be strong when she needs help and let her be strong for you when you need help. Girls have guts. They will scratch out eyeballs to protect their partners' hearts."

Carter dropped an arm across his shoulders. "Let them be warned, huh?"

Andre raised a finger. "So the next time a girl wants to talk about her feelings—"

Declan walked past him to the entrance. "You damn well better see it as the honor that it is."

At the rental building, Declan bought some more ammo and wandered just inside the gate to prep his rifle. He'd configured it to be fully automatic a few weeks previous, which ate up pellets like a bastard. He poured some into the feeder and hooked the bipod onto his chest.

The boys joined him at the gate as he donned his safety goggles and tied his scarf back around his head. The other team was sitting on a bench nearby, eyeing them. They had nice guns, extremely accurate at about fifty feet. Nothing compared to his rifle, which had a laser sight accurate at one hundred.

"So, gentlemen, who should we nominate as team captain?"

A look was shared. Hunter glanced over his safety glasses at Declan, decked out in his impressive getup, rifle braced on his padded hip.

"How often do you do this?"

"Yeah." Carter nudged the air with his cleft chin. "I'm beginning to wonder about that."

Declan popped his gum. "A girl's gotta relax."

Andre held up a hand. "I nominate Layla!"

Chapter 12
The Night

Carter pulled himself out of bed sometime in the early afternoon. Paintball had been about as fun as constructing a barn. He ached all over, and the three center-mass shots he'd taken had raised welts that were still a bright shade of purple. It didn't matter though; they'd walked in half-assed with rented gear and walked out with five flags and ranking in the stats. All thanks to Layla.

Who knew such a general could be hiding behind a pair of green cat eyes and a luscious smirk?

He had two thumbs and a cocky grin.

Carter's mind ran over the details of her face, the husky tone of her voice, her complete confidence when confronted with four seventeen-year-old idiots. She'd put them through the paces, tossing hand signals from her vantage point over the obstacle course, and when the battle was done, as a reward for loyal service, had taken her knights out to the river bed to shoot cans with the sniper rifle. They'd made stupid jokes, foul smells, said ridiculous things, and she'd accepted it all in stride.

He couldn't quite figure it out. Most girls he knew, even Delia to some degree, were awkward around boys. Probably because they were worried about how they were being perceived, and how the boys would treat them. It had to be difficult, to be mocked for liking things that were supposedly "boy things"—like treehouses and paintball. It had to be uncomfortable to feel judged and measured the way boys measured a girl. It had to be a little frightening for some girls to be surrounded by a group of boys, who could be a threat. At first, Layla had seemed stiff and awkward, but after that conversation in the car, it was as if her shield was put aside.

Truth was, the boys had gotten much more out of the encounter than she had. If Andre stayed single this year, Carter would be surprised. That kid was like kryptonite to the fairer sex, but with Layla's tutelage, he might come through with some seriously necessary skills in observation and sensitivity. Her only payment had been another notch in her utility belt, and yet that had seemed enough.

"Princess Paintball."

Carter chuckled. He pictured Layla stretched out on the roost above their flag, gun set up on the bipod, one eye to the scope and one to the direction of the wind in the trees. Every time she took a shot, she would lean sideways and pop her gum. It was adorable and did something to his stomach that felt eerily like falling off a roof.

The best possible thing was that she hadn't corrected him when he'd introduced her as his girlfriend.

As he showered and got ready, he thought back on her advice about women. Maybe, at first, Layla thought he would be good for some fun. But perhaps she was slowly beginning to realize he was the other type of guy, the one she could count on for defense against the world. Maybe he had a shot at not losing her when their time together ended.

He picked her up and took her to lunch. She completely overlooked the salad portion of the menu and ordered a giant cheeseburger. Eating like her cousin, she loaded her fries with ketchup and her burger with pickles. He wondered if that meant anything. According to her, if a girl was relaxed, she'd stop worrying about being "the perfect female" and just be the awesome woman she already was. Carter celebrated this little victory by ordering them milkshakes, which she happily tucked into her shapely bottomless pit.

They went back to the treehouse and worked until the sun began to set, flirting stupidly and making eyes at each other through the branches. Occasionally, he'd get a kiss, or make her laugh with a monkey impression. But mostly, Layla was focused on the construction. To have her actually there beside him, working, satisfied Carter in a way that was indescribable. It was the first time *anyone* had helped him on one of his projects; the act of creation had always felt entirely too private to share with someone else, but as was the case in all other ways, she was different.

While Layla bobbed her head and sang along with the music from his iPhone, he snuck back into the house and gathered up a pile of blankets, sleeping bags, and pillows.

He was going to make this evening special. If girls wanted boys who could protect them from a hostile environment, then he was going to offer her that. From the way she blushed when he smiled, the way her head tipped away when he held her, and the way she froze whenever he pulled her close, he knew that was exactly what she needed.

Carter Aadenson was not the kind of guy to back down from responsibility.

Besides, the feeling was so strong he had to tell her. If he didn't and she went back to her complicated life without knowing, he'd be crushed. There were only three days left, after all. There was no time to be a coward.

Layla had turned the platform for which she was constructing a bridge into a stage, and was dancing, drill in hand. He watched her admiringly from the kitchen window as he collected a tray of snacks. She leaped out, dropping about ten feet to grab more slats, and clambered back up as if her crocheted tank top and manicure meant nothing.

When the highest level was fully stocked with all his supplies, he climbed up and stole the drill from her hand.

"Let's call it a day."

To his immense happiness, she seemed disappointed. "But there's still a whole section to—"

He swept her up in an adamant kiss before she could make a reference to recorded time, and how it was steadily marching on. She felt so light, like he could throw her over his shoulder and carry her there, but that would hardly be polite. He wasn't trying to club her over the head like a caveman.

"Come up to the crow's nest."

A little disheveled, she sank back to her feet and cleared her throat. "Okay. Gimme a sec."

He pulled out his phone on his way to the perch and texted Delia his plans for the evening.

Her reply was a frowny face.

It's not like you can tell on her. She's staying with me.

Bad idea. You're gonna scare her.

He hesitated and surveyed his little love nest. Would it frighten her? If it did, he wondered why . . . until he didn't wonder anymore and had to calm himself down before she saw the frustration on his face and assumed it was directed at her. Should he treat the encounter differently? How could he handle that? He hadn't broached any subject like that aside from the general "Has anyone hurt you?" which could be interpreted any number of ways. But if Layla had been . . . assaulted, would Delia have gone apeshit?

Why?

Keep your hands to yourself.

Scowling, he typed a furious reply, demanding to know when he'd ever made *her* feel uncomfortable.

That wasn't our problem and you know it. It *is* a problem for her.

Layla shouted to him, her head popping up from the ladder before he could get any more information. She looked around at the fluffy bed and candles, her expression shifting right before his eyes.

"What's all this?" she said, but there was a catch in her voice.

Kicking himself, he altered course in midflight. "Well, we've worked pretty hard. This project was supposed to take a while, but we're making so much headway, I thought we could take a break. I don't want your last few days to be—"

"A shared work of art?" She crossed her arms indignantly. "Am I being politely kicked off the project?"

Carter ran his hands back up through his hair and tried to find his old bravado. If he could hold form, it might go okay. "No, not at all. I was going to try seducing you, but I figured it might be too much for you. You might faint again or something."

Her chin dipped and brow rose as she made a long appraisal of him. "So you arranged a perfect little love nest and thought, what . . . that I'd seduce you instead?"

"Seemed like a good strategy." He approached her cautiously and hooked her up in an embrace he knew would not make her cringe.

It afforded him access to the back of her neck, which was one of his favorite places to adore, because it got such an obvious reaction from her. "Is it working?"

She squirmed out of his arms and, still tethered by a hand, tugged him into the pile of bedding. He was exiled beneath a mound of pillows and told he could work his way out with little acts of kindness. Content, he fed her grapes and massaged her feet, and told her about all the ways she impressed him. With every contact of their skin, a little jolt moved through him, messing with all the carefully calibrated machinery in his chest. It was excruciatingly slow, but for that, completely wonderful.

Again he found himself wondering about why she felt so different, and also so right. Maybe she pulled different things out of him. But how? He couldn't quite put his finger on it, and wasn't sure if he wanted to.

The sky darkened and little lights began to blink on. His mom came home and went through her nightly routine without disturbing them. As the air cooled off, they cuddled closer. He lit the candles and opened some Coronas he'd lifted from the fridge. Eventually, she rolled onto her stomach, and when he ran his fingers down her exposed skin, she didn't shy away. Instead she laid her head on her arms and watched him in the dim light, something lovely and melancholy about her face.

There were few words. What could he say to a walking cipher who dismissed time-wasting small talk? He couldn't yammer on about his friends, his college aspirations, his hopes for how the year would play out to such a graceful creature. It would just cost him her favor, and then where would he be? So he stared into her eyes and was fulfilled by watching her shiver occasionally at his touch.

"I should go home," she whispered, as it neared the wee hours.

"No, you shouldn't."

"I can't stay here."

"Sure, you can."

She smiled. "Your mom won't like that."

"My mom already knows."

That seemed to surprise her. "If *my* mom knew, I'd end up in a coma."

"Good thing she's in Chicago."

Her expression wilted, as if he'd reminded her of something painful. For the hundredth time, he wondered what could possibly be so horrible about her home that she'd run away. And for the hundredth time, he felt ashamed to be glad that she had.

"I guess . . . I could stay," she granted, and hid her soul away behind a pair of painted lids. He watched her doze in and out, worked out what he was going to say as if drawing up plans for a cathedral. Finally, he had it right, and all that was left was the courage to say the prayer.

She opened an emerald eye and smiled. "Aren't you tired?"

"It'd take me a long time, I think," he murmured, "to get used to sleeping next to you."

"Why is that?"

"Be too busy watching you."

She blushed a deep shade of pink and turned away. Carter knew he'd finally found the right moment, or rather, the moment had found him, as if a vacuum had formed in the space between them. Slowly, painfully if need be, it would pull the words out of him.

"I love you, Layla."

She went absolutely still, and the curve of her shoulder halted in the regular drop of her respiration. He traced the line of it gently, stopping at her elbow. Then he couldn't contain himself anymore and dove headlong. Putting his arm around her waist, he cradled her close, running his hands over her hands, her thigh, anything he could touch that wasn't out-of-bounds.

"I don't know why you don't want me to say it, but I had to, just once. I know I can't say it again. Remember that I did, okay?"

When he nuzzled her neck, her jaw unclenched and she finally took a shaky breath. "Carter—"

"I told you to lie to protect yourself. I know you will, too. Which is why I want you to listen, okay?"

Her assent was almost inaudible, but her pulse was hammering beneath his lips.

"I think you know I'm *that* guy, the one who is always thinking about who you could be, who you want to be, not just who you are. I don't understand why you won't tell me anything about yourself, but I think you want to."

She said nothing, and eventually he wondered if she ever would. Her eyes were squeezed shut, her face stony. His kisses landed on a brick wall of self-control, until he was sure he'd failed utterly. She didn't want to hear his stupid, boyish confessions. So he lay there in misery, petting her spine in supplication, hoping it was at least pleasurable. He could feel the weight of her thoughts piling on top of him like a punishment for heresy, pressing the air from his lungs. If he didn't claw a way out now, nothing he had said would matter.

"Layla, I know you love me too."

She made to sit up. He caught her and pulled her back down.

"Don't! Don't run away, because I'm freaking out right now. I didn't want this! You think I threw that party so I could go through the complication of falling in love with an amazing girl who just happens to be out of reach, but right under my damn nose like some kind of . . . fucking . . . fishing lure! I wasn't looking for this!"

Her voice was quiet, far away, and breached the silence like an echo as she apologized. She was already leaving. He could feel it, and rejected it. How could she possibly understand how serious he was? He wasn't a dumb kid making a stupid vow he'd never keep. He was the sort who didn't fuck around.

He squeezed her harder.

"You didn't want this. So let me go."

He swallowed. "I didn't want it, but now I don't think I can get by without it! Please say something. Say anything! I'll take anything."

Suddenly, her body relaxed, until she was simply resting there calmly in his arms. Perhaps, finally, he'd made the point, and her lack of confidence in him had been the only hurdle to overcome. Maybe she'd finally surrendered. His stomach in knots, he waited.

"Say it again," she whispered.

He sighed and slid his hand around her hip to caress her smooth stomach. "I love you."

"Now the other thing."

"I think you love me too?"

She nodded and his heart lurched.

Chapter 13
The Dawn

"I think you're right."

It was the end. In one small exhalation, Declan knew. This connection they shared was a cascade of emotions, urges, subtleties that consumed their minds whole. He understood now why his mother had always warned of the pitfalls of being a teenager, of how emotions could completely overwhelm all reason. If it went any further, he'd lose all will to stop it, like being sucked into quicksand.

It was so easy, and in any other case, it would end in simple regrets. But if Declan wasn't careful, it could terminate in something unspeakably awful. He had to put a stop to this. Carter's desires were a force to be reckoned with, and he didn't have the strength. But maybe Layla did.

Rolling in the downy tangle, warm to the point of sleepiness, Declan found Carter's throat and slid his tongue over every curve in slow progression. Carter murmured and his Adam's apple rose and fell. His arms tried to force Declan into submission, but *she* had other ideas.

Moving quickly, Declan caught a wrist, and drove his knee between Carter's. With one seductive tilt of his hip, he had the young man on his back, looking up at him hungrily. He tipped forward and seized the proud mouth before it could use bombast as an escape. When starving hands rose to again overpower him, he pressed them to the floor. Once Carter was taking every breath as if racing to keep up, Declan straddled him and looked down appraisingly.

"You like to touch my back."

Carter nodded, his eyes wide and shimmering in the moonlight.

"Because you like to make me tremble. Because you think that means you have some kind of power. You think you can take control of what I'm feeling and measure it. Trim it down. Make it fit."

He was speaking poetry, and Carter's mind was clearly fighting to make sense of it. Declan, however, had pored over these cravings and images for months, years. He knew exactly what to say.

"This thing is not made of numbers," he breathed in Carter's ear. "You don't get to tell it what to do. And every time you touch me, all you're doing is giving in a little more. We both know you're not in charge here."

He made a decision then, watching the dawn play out in his mind's eye like it had been predestined. He would cast his little spell on the poor unsuspecting prince, and when the slumber came, he'd erase every trace of himself, and steal away into the sunrise.

Layla would be gone for good.

Declan took a deep breath and felt as if with each movement of his hand, he was tracing his own shape, creating himself like a sculptor. The mask made him brave, but in the most ironic twist, it also gave him a place to cower.

He trailed his hands down Carter's bronzed chest, following the hollows of his collarbones, the planes of his pectoral muscles. When fingertips failed to adequately inform, he leaned forward and retraced his steps with the tip of his tongue. He found a nipple, a wound from combat, an old scar, and paid each one of them the proper amount of attention. Carter lay as if transfixed, his ribs flexing with the labor of breathing. As Declan found them too with his lips and teeth, Carter's arms reacted, constricting around him snugly, but he would not be dissuaded.

Shoving the embrace aside, he pinned Carter with a stern look. "No."

"Layla, please—"

"Shut up and look pretty for me."

Carter's breath caught, and for the first time since they'd met, Declan saw all the intricately fashioned walls fall to pieces. It was finished, a foregone conclusion. All that was left was one moment of calculated recklessness.

He dropped his head back to the furrows and tripped over them with his mouth, allowing his lips to find that wonderful little ridge he'd fantasized about for so long. It fit his thumbs perfectly. He molded the muscles there with a sweep, his fingers curving over the hip bone possessively.

Carter was already writhing in anticipation. This was going to be too easy, and in a way, that terrified him, because it was by far the most egregious offense he would commit. As he found the elastic waistband, Carter's abdomen tensed, reminding Declan just how much authority he had. It was the strongest he had ever been, in or out of his borrowed skin.

"Layla—"

The sound of the lie jangled his thoughts; he banished them with a vengeful stroke of his tongue. The rest of Carter's clever words crumbled into incoherent whispers, and Declan had his permission.

He lost himself in it then, eyes lifted to watch his triumph over Carter's every nerve. From far away, he wondered that such an assertive personality could be laid low by so simple a dance. Finally, Carter could no longer take it. Calloused hands broke their bonds and tangled in Declan's hair. He allowed it, but only because he knew the sun had nearly risen.

Carter's whole body convulsed, and he let out a wonderful cry that rang in Declan's ear. He swallowed and rested his head on the flat of Carter's stomach, waiting.

"You're incredible," Carter hissed.

"In the truest sense of the word," he replied, but Carter was already slipping into dreamland, and when the breathing fell into a slow rhythm, Declan carefully slithered free.

Carter's phone was sitting on the bannister. He took it and laid it against Carter's thumb. It unlocked on a picture of Layla looking indomitable in her paintball gear, her rifle braced on her shoulder. Declan blinked back tears and chose the Settings icon. In a few commands, he'd robbed Carter of a year's worth of records, deeds, and the girl who would love him best.

Gathering his things, he climbed quietly down the ladder and along the side yard to the driveway. He didn't put on the hard platform shoes until he'd reached the corner. Calling Dee, he waited for the slumber to clear from her voice before he permitted his emotions to overtake him.

"I'm walking toward the house, but I don't know how long he'll sleep. He could already be awake."

"I'm on my way. When you get to Atlas, take a right and walk up one block. If he's looking for you, he'll drive the opposite way. I'll hook around and pick you up."

"Thanks, DeeDee."

"It's okay, kid. Be careful. Remember that you look like a girl. Shit's dangerous."

He did as she instructed and found that the house on the corner had a lovely little tree stump just inside the fence. He sat down on it and looked up at the sky. It was turning a pale violet and the eastern edge was ringed in gold.

He had a moment then, to run his tongue over his lips, to taste, to regret, and then fall to pieces. When she found him, he was sobbing uncontrollably, and she had to practically carry him to the car. They didn't go home, but drove to the national park and sat on a hillside turnout. Once the birds began to sing, Delia's phone commenced ringing.

She glanced down and silenced it. "That's four."

He was numb. He looked out the window and watched a squirrel climb down the nearest tree.

"If I don't say something, he'll flip out. He needs to know you're okay and haven't been eaten by wolves."

"Do what you want."

It was like he'd been drained of all feelings except pain, and that was slowly expanding to fill the empty space like a fungus. When she began speaking in her hushed mother-voice, he cringed. Carter's fury was easily audible.

"She's fine," Delia said. Carter became irate, but her voice stayed even. "I'm not going to talk to you if you keep shouting at me, Carter. I understand that she left . . ."

Declan opened the car door and got out. The turnout was small, and didn't afford much space to wander, but he made do. Squatting down near the base of a tree, he balled up and went back to weeping like the world was ending. In a way, it was. Layla was dead. He'd have to resume life as plain old Dex. Go back to the novocaine of video games and the concealment of ugliness.

She tapped the horn. When he could pull himself together, he met her by the trunk. She had a paper bag in her hand. Her eyes were puffy, and she was clutching her phone.

"These are boy clothes. Change out. We're going to need to get you squared away before he comes looking."

"What did you tell him?"

"That I had to go pick you up from camp, and that Layla called me from her cab to tell me she was leaving, but didn't say why."

Her voice was taut. He took the bag and bowed his head in shame.

"I'm so sorry, Dee. I didn't mean to make you lie. I know he's your friend. Please don't be angry with me—"

She grappled him into a fierce hug and refused to let him go for some time. "Shut up! I'm the one who made *you* lie. If I hadn't been so stupid, we could have had a nice summer, and none of this would have happened. I realize you've been in a terrible situation, compromising your boundaries, and I let it happen. Some big sister I am."

"No. It's okay. I knew what I was doing."

She combed his hair with her fingernails and squeezed the tears out. After a long time, they both gathered enough strength to step apart. Declan walked just into the woods behind a bush and stripped off one identity to swap out his latest. It took a handful of cotton balls and a quarter bottle of makeup remover to clear all the smudged femininity. He traded the green contacts for the nerd-goggles, and slid his feet back into his Vans.

"I'm taking you to get a haircut, and then we're going to the mall. Mom left us her card so we could get stuff for school. I'll be damned if I let you go from my classy closet to a bargain bin at Walmart."

Declan appreciated her humor, but couldn't participate. His mind kept tracing the damp skin, kept hearing the shallow, ragged breathing. If he closed his eyes, he could almost pretend he was back there, warmed by Carter's body heat.

The stylist hacked off the shaggy bob and replaced it with a tousled boy cut, straight from the cover of *GQ*, tinting the whole dapper mess with henna, so that Carter wouldn't be tempted to see Layla. At the mall, Dee loaded him down with armfuls of garments to try on, and he did so without struggle. She practically replaced his entire wardrobe with something she called "geek-chic," even purchasing him new glasses and a pretzel while they waited for them.

He hid inside the restroom for about twenty minutes, after a group of teenage girls swept by talking about boys at school they were most looking forward to seeing again. Carter's name was prominent. While he was fighting back tears, in this locked stall that was somehow less safe because of the sign on the door, he changed into a new outfit and threw the old one in the trash can.

"Time to shed skin."

He washed his face and stared down his emotions. He was being a child. This was the thing that *had* to be done. No one would get anything they needed from the other way. Sure, he'd have wonderful conversations, companionship, but never the closeness he wanted, the way he wanted it. How could he have a romance without being able to have physicality? He would have to wait until college, until he could get out of this town and into the wider world.

There were kids living in war zones, wondering if they were going to survive. There were people dealing with starvation or terrible diseases. In the scheme of things, his stupid drama was a drop in the ocean. He had absolutely no business feeling sorry for himself. If anything, he should be feeling sorry for sweet, handsome Carter.

And he did. Overwhelmingly. So much so that when he stepped outside and caught sight of the argument taking place, he nearly dropped to his knees.

Carter's face was rigid, he was so upset. He had Delia backed up to the drinking fountain, and was whispering furiously at her. She fought back valiantly, until he drooped against the wall and covered his exhausted face with his hand.

"This isn't fair, Dee! Why are you doing this?"

"I'm not doing anything! I'm telling you, she said she's gone. I haven't been back to the house since I left to get Dex."

Just then, Carter glanced up and found him. Declan would have been startled by the anguish he saw there if not for the fact that he was feeling the same thing. It was clear he believed Delia had been lying to him, and Declan's presence was bitter proof she had not. Carter gulped down some air and got back a modicum of composure.

"Hey, shrimp."

Delia shot a look at Declan, but he raised a hand. "Hey. Everything okay?"

Carter's face was a mask. "No. The whole world is a fucking shit-pile. How was zombie camp?"

"Not nearly as cathartic as I thought it would be."

"Yeah, I could really use an apocalypse right now."

Delia cleared her throat. "We have to finish our shopping, Carter."

He gave her a fearsome look, but she didn't budge. "Give it to me, Dee."

"I said no, and I fucking meant it."

"This is bullshit! Why the fuck would she vanish like this without letting me say goodbye?"

"I don't know, okay, but that's her business."

He kicked away from the wall and held up his finger. "I'm going to find her."

"Good luck with that."

"You're the one who told me to ask her out! What the hell is your problem?"

"You're my problem! Get out of my face before I break your nose!"

Declan stepped in, wedging himself between them and shoving Carter back. The brief physical contact impacted his own senses like a tank, and seemed to have a withering effect on Carter.

"Hey! Back up."

Carter did, because his emotions were raw, and his blood was still tuned to Declan's voice, even if he didn't know it.

"I'm sorry, Dex. You're right. I . . ." And he was gone, rushing into the bathroom before Declan could blink.

He grabbed Delia's arm and the shopping bags, and steered her toward the parking lot. Once safe inside the car, Dee breathed a sigh of relief.

"What the shit did you do to that boy?"

He shook his head. "Lied to, betrayed, and manipulated him."

"He's never shouted at me before. I . . . really misread this. He's not going to drop this."

"Bet you never guessed your beauty makeup skills would be so formidable. You should, like, become a pro."

She shook her head solemnly. "There's some things even makeup can't do, Dex. I'm telling you. Did you ever think that one of the reasons you actually *pass* to him is because he doesn't care? I think you are better off explaining the situation to him."

"That's how school shootings happen, Dee."

"Carter isn't like that. Trust me! I've been inside his head a long time. He makes everything his fault, his problem. If you don't tell him, 'Layla' is going to end up tattooed on his body somewhere, and he will always think that he did something terrible."

He thought of all the tiny kisses he'd used to stitch that skin over a coursing heart, and closed his eyes.

"I can't do that to him."

"I'm telling you it's the only way. He will definitely surprise you."

"Dee, no prince is *that* charming."

Chapter 14
The Welcoming

The front of the school had been transformed into a fairground and was teeming with people. Already sure he was going to have an anxiety attack, Declan took his measure in the visor mirror and sighed. There were the new horn-rims, the tousled hair, the silver bow tie Delia had insisted he needed to wear. "Why am I dressed like this?"

"Because it's perfect."

"A TARDIS sweater vest is perfect?"

She grinned. "You got way too used to wearing uniforms, okay? The school colors are blue and silver! Just trust your stylist."

"You realize this nerd gear screams, 'I'm a loser, please clock me in the fork,' right?"

There was a long-suffering sigh. "Remember how you felt when you dressed like Layla?"

He looked back into the mirror and endured the flood of cold shame sweeping through his blood. "Yes."

"Pretend like you're still dressed that way. Be her in *this* skin. I'm telling you, this *will* work. You'll feel great . . . or . . . well, better than you did at St. Cat's."

"That isn't saying much."

She huffed. "Look, I don't know how to help you other than to tell you to be you and find a way to make that mesh with what people see! You need to cooperate with me till we find a presentation that works."

He licked his lips and blinked at her emotional outburst. "Okay, Dee. I'll try."

"Good. Thank you!"

They got out of the Bug. Declan shaded his eyes and surveyed the sloping lawn at the front of the campus. It was covered in tables with painted signs, upperclassmen wearing sports uniforms and regular clothes in their colors. A cheerleader was doing flips on a grassy stretch, and a section of the band was playing pop music. As people meandered up the central walkway, they were assailed from all sides by the many activities they could do to add to "the school spirit." He was pleased to see Yuki sitting off to one side in a pair of cat ears, her action figure collection staging a reenactment of a gunfight from a classic dust-punk anime. It would be a gauntlet just to get to her cozy little safe haven.

"Any advice?"

Delia was holding his arm as if they were at home watching a scary movie. She smiled at him and squeezed. "This is the first time we've been at the same school in like . . . ever, Mr. Accelerated Curriculum."

"True. But let's be honest, St. Cat's was an obstacle course I avoided by hiding in the library. I had nothing to do to distract myself *but* study, while you had a social life."

Her hands slid to his shoulders, her cheeks flushed with pride. "You helped me with my homework before you even took the classes. You're a genius with school stuff, but I'm a genius too . . . with people. This is the first time I've been in a position to do anything for you. So let me."

"What are you planning on doing?"

"You'll see. Be *one hundred percent* yourself, okay, and everything will be fine." She tousled his hair. "Have fun. There's no such thing as a permanent record. Do your best, but this is your last chance to be a kid, so feel free to be one."

"We both know I've never been a *kid*."

She laughed and waved at a group of boys who broke ranks to greet her with a pack of goofy, lovesick smiles. "True, much to my chagrin."

"'Chagrin,' huh?"

"Trust me, Dex. Please, be the geeky, nerdy diva that I know you are. Be confident, be feminine if you want. That's the secret to liking who you are . . . just doing it and learning how to say 'fuck you' if necessary."

"I can do that. If I get into trouble, I'm telling Mom you told me to say it."

Delia halted in her tracks and swept her bag up over her shoulder. For a moment they were face-to-face, and she took advantage of it to peck him on the forehead. Declan glanced around, blushing furiously. In normal circumstances, getting a good-luck kiss from a big sister on the front lawn of a school was strictly forbidden, but for some reason, it didn't count against him. As she danced away to a swell of music and was swallowed by a wall of people who all seemed to know her, he was left standing there in his nerdy clothes, in peace. No one mocked him or shot him anything but speculative looks. Apparently, knowing Delia was a good thing.

A Goat in a football jersey brushed by him, stuffing his face as usual. "Are you Dee's little bro?"

He nodded, trying to hold on to her advice as he watched the athlete size him up with something like skepticism.

"What grade are you?"

"Junior."

"Not what I expected. You're like . . . a tiny person."

Looking around at the crowd, Declan searched for a polite response. "Um . . . thanks?"

"Nah . . . I mean like . . . what's the word?"

Declan shrugged helplessly.

"Never mind. You know Layla?"

"Yeah."

"She told me she taught you how to shoot, and Carter says your stats on *Call of Duty* are like, out of this world."

"I don't like to brag, but don't come at me or I'll waste you."

"Right. So I expected . . . I dunno . . . like, a scary dude . . . Never mind."

"Right."

"I hope you realize that means you're filling in for her as team captain when we match up against the Squid Army in a few weeks."

Blinking, Declan froze. "Me?"

"We ranked. It means we have to play another team, and the Squids are run by Spencer Barrett from Singer Valley. He's their quarterback and a serious dick. I wanna see him without his smug face on." He held up a fist, and for the first time in his life, Declan felt like he might have a leg up.

He bumped the fist after a slightly awkward moment. "Well, I'll be happy to ping it for you, but you jerks need to invest in proper gear. Layla told me about your bullshit, and frankly, I wouldn't be caught dead on a range with you."

The Goat's face slid into a dorky scowl. "Yeah. Fuck me, man, I never thought we'd do any damage. Get my number from Dee and send me a few gun specs, yeah?"

"Sure!" he called, as the Goat and his herd smashed through the crowd like a crash of rhinos.

He took some time to look over the many tables. Bambi Weatherton sat primly at one piled with heart-shaped cookies. The sign indicated the organization was "faith-based." Didn't appear to matter what "faith" you had, just that you had it. He looked at her stretched smile and prissy demeanor and knew he had more faith in dingoes. At least you always *knew* they were about to steal a baby and eat it.

He caught sight of Carter, taking up all the oxygen at the student council table, looking like the loss of Layla really wasn't so bad, until Carter caught sight of him with a razor-sharp glare. The breath knocked out of him, Declan turned away and bumped squarely into a thin figure wearing a baseball tee, skinny jeans, and Keds. As the person spun around to apologize, he realized he had no idea if they were male or female. For a moment, his heart soared.

"Oh my god! It's so crowded, right?" The voice was girlish, but her fifties-style boy cut and suspenders cast serious doubt.

He nodded. "Hard to figure out which clubs are worth it. I'm not really a social person."

"Here! Read this."

She handed him a flyer. In huge letters it advertised a safe environment for all those in the LGBTQ+ community, their supporters, and family. Delia hadn't said anything about this club, and as he had in freshman year when Yuki told him she was starting the St. Cat's anime club, he felt like he might have found kindred spirits. But it would mean sacrifice. He scanned the smaller print, his mind racing over the map of his life.

Delia had told him to *be* Layla, and he dearly wanted to, but if he joined this club, he'd be declaring his approval of the "lifestyle." If he reached for acceptance, he'd find it in only a few, and be ostracized from all the rest.

But how was that any different from Catholic school?

"How many members are there?"

The girl smiled shyly. "Well, it's a new idea. If I can sign up ten people and get a faculty advisor, it's a club. If not, it's basically a wash."

Declan looked around. Tables were swamped, sports teams were signing up new recruits right and left, and the cheerleaders were giving scathing assessments to the line of hopefuls who dared sign their names on the line. Here was this androgynous angel, standing alone, fighting for people they couldn't even see. People like him. Who was he, if he could lecture Carter Aadenson on being a coward, and then acted like one himself?

"I'll join," he declared.

The face lit up, and he felt instantly like he'd won the lottery. Shuffling her items, she handed him a clipboard and waited impatiently as he signed his name, snatching it back from him before he could read the other two names on the list.

"Declan Elliott? Are you Delia's brother?"

"Yeah. You should ask her too. She'll sign up, for sure."

"You think so?" Items were again shifted and a hand came out. "My name's Chloe. Thanks for being an advocate for the LGBTQ+ community! This is the next leg of the civil rights movement!"

With a grin, he shook her hand, the disconnect between high school and real life finally corrected, if only by a bit. She gave him a rainbow-colored sticker he could easily discard, but Layla would never be such an asshole, so neither could he. He squatted down and stuck it to his binder right in front of her, so she would know that he was proud of himself, and proud of her for being his champion.

"Cool bow tie, Declan!" she said by way of thanks.

"Call me Dex. I was eyeing your suspenders."

"I have a huge collection. Anyway, I'll send you an email if we manage to get everything set."

"I'll try to direct more people your way."

"Awesome! Have a good Welcoming!" And she moved on, glowing with encouragement.

Well, that was a great way to start the mad dash to adulthood, if ever there was one. Kind of like falling off a cliff with a perilously tiny parachute. When he found Yuki, she made huge eyes at him.

"*Hisashiburi, Dekusu-kun*!" She fixed a pair of cat ears on his head and hugged him tightly. Yuki was his closest friend, his mentor, and he loved her like a sister. Knowing he would have the safety of her confidence had been the final push he'd needed to escape the toxicity of St. Cat's. She knew all his secrets, everything except Layla, but in a way, Layla couldn't have existed without her. He swore in that moment, he was going to wear those goddamned cat ears all day long, out of fealty.

"I love your ensemble," he said with a wave. "*Obā-chan* ran you out, huh? Or did you run her out? Will Harajuku rue the day?"

Yuki giggled. "You should have seen her. She was mincing around in her kimono like she was on crack, her face all *Attack on Titan*. I thought she was gonna pummel this kid in eight-inch platforms when he tried to help her up a step."

"Kids these days, huh?"

"I'm surprised you didn't show up in your pajamas in protest!"

He shrugged. "That's not really a protest, is it? I mean, if they beat you into giving up, then you're not really apathetic at all, are you?"

Her brows shot up into her turquoise wig. "You've gotten philosophical in your old age, my son."

He wrapped his arms around her waist and buried his face in her strawberry-scented cloud of Otaku-goodness. "Man, *aitakatta*. I'm so glad I followed in your colorful mad dash to freedom, Yuki-san."

"They still talking about my uniform strike?"

"Well, when you show up in a floor-length dress made entirely of fringe . . . it tends to make an impression."

"I looked like a bright-orange tornado when the nuns hurled me out the door."

She took out an eyebrow pencil and gave him cat whiskers, and they sat at the table for the first two periods, signing up new members and debating fandoms with all the older kids who had come up without the collective unity of a club. When Carter turned up toward the end, he blanched, but the attractive young man kept it stiffly civil and signed up, opening the door to a whole new wave of kids who'd been ignoring the flamboyant table. By the end of the Welcoming, they'd swelled the ranks by nearly twenty people, and the first meeting promised to be an amazing one. But it was hard to go wrong when your entire gig was watching cartoons and eating Pocky.

Declan wandered happily through his morning, getting a host of reactions to his cat ears and bow tie, but giving not a shit. This was the proving ground, and teenagers feared standing out. Being different meant subjecting yourself to ridicule. Well, he wasn't afraid. He had his people, and the ridicule of a pack of idiots meant jack. He diffused sarcasm with authenticity and accepted compliments with Chloe's charm. By the assembly, he had acquired all of Yuki's girlfriends and a new clique of freshmen who flocked to their beacon of truth like moths. They packed their rows in the auditorium trading jokes, many of them decked out in elements of cosplay. It was a colorful group, and he was at home.

Chloe came by with her clipboard and complimented their ears. Yuki gave her a pair and didn't bat an eye when she mentioned Declan had signed up for the newest club. She wrote her name down, in a silent display of loyalty, and put her sticker on her chest. When the young lady had moved on down the aisle, her aura sparkling, Yuki leaned against his shoulder.

"Took you long enough, *Bishōnen-chan*."

"*Ah*," he agreed.

"*Yūki ga aru na*."

"*Arigatō*. I'm learning to be."

"So"—she poked his ribs—"you still crushing on—"

Carter stepped out on stage to give his opening remarks. They were informal, but it was clear he'd won his election by a landslide. Who could argue with that handsome face when it cracked that ridiculously self-assured grin? Better men than Declan.

The pun made him cringe even as he thought it.

Yuki muttered under her breath in Japanese that Carter was too gorgeous to be real. Declan sighed and clutched her for dear life, vowing to tell her about Layla as soon as possible. But as Carter stepped back from the mic, Declan saw the tension in his shoulders, the speed with which his face fell back into stoicism, and the distance in his stare. He looked tired, and though he was hiding it well, he was upset.

Declan felt the lump forming in his throat, but steadied himself. This was how he knew it would be, loving someone from far away and wishing the world were a more forgiving place.

Principal Taggert welcomed them with a weirdly passive-aggressive speech, directing them to the gymnasium to collect their schedules and ensure their name appeared on the roll for the day. As he went on about lunch being the end of the day, Declan became certain that he couldn't stand the guy. He reminded him of a used-car salesman and was all too happy to announce that as of seven thirty the next morning, it was all business and all tardies would be counted as absences.

As they filed out, he spotted Carter standing next to Delia. She was punctuating her sentences with her hand, which meant she was annoyed. Carter didn't seem to care. She finally shoved him out a door with a sigh and made some kind of agreement. While Declan stood in line for his schedule, she came up and leaned on him as if fighting for serenity.

"He's so fucking obnoxious when he fixates! How did I not see that about him when we were dating?"

"He tell you he loved you?"

"Nope."

"Probably why."

"Well, I'll count myself lucky." People were looking his way. Delia was popular, and when she stole his cat ears and settled them atop her own head, they became an instant fashion classic, and he became her sidekick. "I signed up for Chloe's club."

"Nice!"

"Carter did too."

Declan bit his lip. "Does he edit? Or does he just sign up for everything?"

"Chloe is like his best friend besides me. She ran his campaign."

"No shit. What the fuck! How am I supposed to be myself if I can't get a moment's peace from that boy?"

"Tell me about it. He asked me out to lunch tomorrow. Scratch that, demanded I go out to lunch. I said yes," she said in his ear as he gave his name to the teacher handing out schedules.

He looked up, aghast. "What? You know you can say no to him. He doesn't have the right to boss everyone—"

"Well, it's kind of a tradition that we go to lunch every Tuesday, even though I know he's just going to bring up *her*."

"Promise me you won't say anything!" He slid away from the line and towed her with him. "Promise!"

"It's *her* business. I plan on yelling that at his stubborn face, if necessary. Trust me," she said, when his look turned to concern on her behalf, "this isn't him being a boy treating a girl like shit. This is him being him with his best friend."

Yuki pranced back up to Declan and stole him from Dee. He was pushed into the cafeteria with barely enough time to recover.

Their table, when he found it after getting his lunch, was crowded with characters within minutes, some old, some new, some he knew he'd love, and some who would drift away as soon as they found their true places. A new pair of cat ears appeared from Yuki's bottomless swag bag and made a home on his head. These matched his vest in a brilliant shade of blue.

"You need a matching tail."

"Yes. Yes, I do."

And there Carter was, like the good witch Glenda, settling in front of their table in an impervious bubble of arrogance.

"Yuki-chan! You were at my party in a sick Goth-Loli dress. *Oboeteiru no*?"

Yuki gasped and clapped her hands. "Of course I do! We had PE together last year!"

"You were the queen of the girls' soccer team!"

Shooting Declan a meaningful look, Yuki dug through her bag and retrieved a pair of black ears for Carter, which he set on his head with a winning smile.

Declan crossed his arms, certain this was about to get ugly, and not entirely sure why. It was something about the blue of Carter's eye, the flex of his jaw, the way he focused on Declan's face and refused to look away.

Carter hovered expectantly. "Have you decided on what anime to show at the first meeting?"

He straddled a chair that seemed to magically appear, in a spot that cleared as if he'd waved a wand. The others at the table were suddenly in rapt attention. Who could blame them, when the president of the senior class and most popular kid in school deigned to sit down at their table and recognize their strangeness in front of everyone? But Declan could see it in the brittleness of Carter's features. This was The Politician, and he was about to do something sleazy.

Carter waited for a passably polite gap in the conversation, and turned on Declan with a row of flashing white teeth.

"So, Cat-boy, about your cousin . . ."

Declan scowled at his food. So it was like that, then? Carter got a week under his belt and then went back to being a coward. *How easily people forget.*

Yuki glanced at him. She was reading his glare and the set of his shoulders. She nudged him as the silence stretched. He looked straight at Carter's mask.

"What about her, Carter?"

"I was hoping you could give me her phone number."

"Go fuck yourself."

He stuffed a tater tot into his mouth. Barely tasting it, he watched the table ripple with his bold dismissal, until the discomfort spread to the surrounding tables.

Carter blinked in the silence. When he finally chuckled, it rang hollow. "Come on, dude. I'm sure she'll be okay with it."

He stood up and planted his hands on the tabletop, his heart struggling to get free of his ribs and end its suffering in some ketchupy self-annihilation.

"Will she? Because I'm pretty sure she has a 'no fake assholes' policy, which pretty much rules you out, you smug prick! Go plow your bullshit somewhere else."

There were audible gasps. Carter got slowly to his feet, pure shock written all over his face. "Dex—"

"Don't pretend like you don't know what I'm talking about! This conversation has already been had, and the outcome is not going to change because you come over here and put on a pair of cat ears. You don't get to *buy* what you want by *gracing* us with your presence. Layla gave you her answer when she ditched you, and I won't break her trust to gain the acceptance of a pack of teenagers!" He grabbed his stuff and pushed away from the table. "I'm out, Yuki. I'll call you tonight."

And he left, walking calmly in the hush to the trash can, where he bussed his tray with shaking hands. Delia met him at the Bug a short time later, her mom-face unchanged by her fluffy ears.

"That went well."

He looked away petulantly. "He's obnoxious."

"Mmm. That'll make lunch tomorrow such a blast."

"Sorry, but he pissed me off."

"Because he loves you?"

"Because he lusts after *her*. He has no idea what love is. If he did, he'd leave her alone like she asked."

"You mean you, right?"

"Shut up!"

Chapter 15
The Fairy Godmother

L ying awake all night, Carter ran over the day in his mind a thousand times, and wondered when he'd lost it. For once, his ingenious plans had gone completely awry, and he wasn't sure how or why. Sure, he'd done something slimy, totally motivated by how easily his fellow classmates were manipulated, but he could scarcely believe Declan had called him on it. He saw the junior's fierce expression, heard his disgust, saw him storm away, and every time he examined the memory, it hit even harder. He had completely misjudged that kid, and the vicious but accurate declaration that he was "fake" haunted Carter.

Is that what Layla had seen? With her piercing bedroom eyes, she *must* have known how quickly he'd fall back on old habits when it served his needs. She had been right not to trust him, because he wasn't even close to being the person she needed.

And then there was their last night together. Had she gone that far . . . just to escape? Had he pushed so hard he'd forced her to compromise her body just to find a way out?

The thought made him physically ill. He needed to find a way to apologize, to atone, but without a way of finding her . . . and if he did find her, what could he do? If she didn't want to hear his apology, then he wasn't allowed to speak it. Those were the rules of apologies.

His mind ran in ever lower circles, until his stomach ached with every thought.

At four in the morning, he got out of bed and went down to the kitchen, all future machinations scrapped. It was as Layla had said: he could not trim his feelings down to size and press them into the shape of his stupid teenaged existence. They were wild and raging, and he barely had the strength to hold them in check; things like that had no place in the high school drama of gossip, competition, and games. But what could he do when he was ready for a real relationship and the rest of the world wasn't?

He dug through the cupboards and pantry and threw together a pot of soup. He struggled with soup. It all went into a haphazard jumble, and yet somehow, was supposed to come out right. It was nothing like a building, a piece of furniture, a swing. But it gave him room to think, removing his mathematical mind from the equation with the tiny monotony of chopping and tasting. Packaging it up into a picnic basket, he added a loaf of bread and a couple bottles of sparkling water.

Then he went back out to the treehouse and buried his face in Layla's pillow till the sun came up.

As he drifted through his day, the sensation grew that she was somewhere far away, as if she'd ceased to be as soon as she parted from him. It had all been in his head, maybe. Reality began to alternately blend or grate on his nerves, and the lunch bell couldn't come fast enough. Dee was leaning against his Charger, casually beautiful as always, nibbling her sunglasses while she waited.

Catching sight of his colorless, slack visage, her guarded body language melted. She reached for him, but he couldn't do this here, in front of everyone. He got into the car without a word and drove out to the old park. When they'd been children, the gazebo had been painted white and the willow trees had created little hollows of shade. Many an Easter egg hunt and birthday party had been held here. Though everything felt smaller somehow, shabby, he instantly felt safe as he unfolded a blanket on the concrete.

Dee watched him lay out their meal. "When was the last time you had a good night's sleep, Carter? You're shaking."

Her voice was so soft. He remembered that about her, how calming she was, how comfortable. It was easy to like Delia. She was warm the way Layla was fearsome, and cool the way Layla burned like ice. She was exactly what he needed, and also, the only person he knew would not judge him.

"I don't know."

"Talk to me."

"You're going to tell me what you've already told me, and you're right to do that. I just . . . don't have anyone else to talk to about this."

She sighed and pulled him close, until his head was across her knees. Stroking his forehead, she shushed him as he eventually lost his grip.

"I don't know what I did. I keep thinking about it, over and over. She never gave me any sign! There wasn't an argument, nothing! It was the opposite, in fact! At least, I thought it was . . ."

Her breathing was slow and deep, but he could see the miserable look on her face as she leaned over him. "I know, Carter. I know."

He sat up and smeared the tears across his face. "She erased my whole phone! Every picture of her! I'm not even allowed to remember her! It's not fair!"

Delia's eyes fell as she appeared to work through her own emotions. He didn't want her to misunderstand him, to react as Declan had to being caught in the middle. He was grasping for the tiniest scrap of information, and she was the only person who could bridge that divide.

"Did I do something—"

"No, I'm positive you didn't, honey. Layla just . . . nothing I say is going to make sense!"

"I told her I loved her. She acted like I'd stabbed her. I've been thinking about this all night, and I finally get what my dad was saying, what she was saying in the car."

"I'm not sure what you mean." Her fingers raked through his hair and soothed him a bit.

"She doesn't love me—"

Delia was shaking her head. "I don't think that's true at all! I think she does love you, very much."

"Then she wouldn't have snuck off while I was asleep. I made her promise not to lie to me. Maybe she left because I backed her into a corner, and when I told her how I felt, it was like I dropped this huge burden right on top of her. I know it was selfish, and I broke the rules.

She said that loving someone the way they need to be loved was hard." He laughed crazily, his nose running. "She really wasn't kidding."

Delia shoved the forgotten food aside and moved so that she could sit knees to knees. Each of his hands ended up in one of hers, and she massaged his palms with her thumbs. "I know you're confused."

"Did I come off as fake? I keep hearing myself make jokes, and she laughed at them, but now I wonder if she wasn't really laughing. Maybe all the time, I was scaring her away—"

"Carter, no!" She palmed his face and stroked aside the tears beneath his eyes.

"It felt so good with her, Dee. Like there was this buzzing in my head all the time that went silent when she was around. I can't go back to it! It's too painful!"

"Listen to me. Layla *is* the truth, and the life she went back to . . . for her, *that's* the lie. She loved being with you. That's why she ran away, because when you told her you loved her, she knew it would hurt a thousand times worse when she had to stop living her honest self, and leave you for a lie."

"But why does she have to go back to that? Whatever she is dealing with, I can help! I gave her a list of things—"

"You and your damn lists, Carter!" She huffed in exasperation. "It's so much more complicated than you could possibly figure out, and the longer this goes on, the more upset you get. I love her but I'm gonna kill her for this."

He sniffled. Watching the determined look on her face, he hoped that at last she was going to put his heart at ease. He'd take anything, but Delia continued to sit there, her eyes flicking back and forth as if lining up words in orderly rows.

"When we were together," she whispered, "you never felt it, did you?"

"What?"

"You know."

Carter shifted uncomfortably. "Dee—"

"Let's talk this through! We never did before, and now we need to, so bear with me." Sitting cross-legged, she braided her fingers in her lap, her face composed and sober. "You didn't *want* me, did you?"

"I'm sorry I let it go so long."

She shook her head dismissively. "Any of your other girlfriends, before or since. You feel it with them?"

He swallowed and looked at his hands. "No."

"But Layla . . ."

"Yes."

"Why?"

"Because she's . . . I don't know! She's just . . . she's perfect!"

"How?"

With a giant shrug, he waved his hands. "I don't know! In every way. From the sound of her voice to the way she thinks. I can't figure it out! It's like some kind of magic, or something."

Delia's smile was indulgent. She reached up and traced the crease in his brow. "You are so cute when you're in love."

With a grimace, he leaned away. "She didn't think so."

"Yes, she did. I doubt there's a straight girl on this planet who wouldn't."

"What Declan said in the cafeteria . . . that's not who I am. Yes, I fucked up and I was being slick, but when I was with her, I wasn't. Please tell me she knew that! She called me a coward once, but I was brave from that moment on, I swear! I was completely honest with her."

"That's part of the problem! The worst thing you've ever gone through is your parents' divorce! Your life makes it easy for you to be honest. You've never once had to face someone else's irrational hatred. You've never had to face a gang of mean, stupid kids and defend yourself! Layla has!"

Dee pulled down her hair and hiked it back up into her messy topknot, her face creased with worry. But she was right. People didn't make vows for the good times. They made them for the times when a promise would matter, when the world was banging down the door, when nothing seemed to be going right. A pledge of honesty was much the same. He never really had had to stand up for anyone or anything. He had never had his resolve tested. He'd never had to lie to live.

If Layla had . . . then he really was no match for her.

Silenced, he leaned back against the railings and looked out over the grassy hills. God, what had she thought of him? As he'd gone on and on about his own goals and his many "achievements," she must have been rolling her eyes. He'd never once done anything for the principle of the thing, when it was doomed to fail. If he hit a wall, he backed out. Being the king of bullshit was easy, but having integrity, being selfless, those things were difficult, and those were the only things that mattered.

He thought of everyday people who leaped into dangerous situations and rescued perfect strangers, or spectators who talked down people jumping off bridges. He wasn't noble. He was a bag of hot air, a smug prick, like Declan had said.

"How did I fuck this up so badly?"

Delia roused herself from her thoughts to smile at him forlornly. "The person who would fit you best, Carter, isn't going to allow you to just sit there being the same old you, never progressing. They're going to push you, hard if necessary, to meet them in the middle, and then walk beside them, no matter what happens. You have incredible potential, and you need someone who is going to inspire you to realize it."

He thought of his mother and took Dee's hand. It was cold, as always, but sat in his comfortably. "Who taught you all that?"

She shrugged. "I've thought about it a lot lately, is all."

"Okay, because it wasn't me."

Her laugh had a sardonic brittleness to it. "No. We kind of fell in together and couldn't be bothered to roll our asses out."

"It's because I'm a good cook, and you like to eat."

"And I'm a good mother, and you obviously needed one while she was busy divorcing your dad."

He cringed, but she was right. "That stings a little."

"Look, let me say something, okay?" She glanced at her phone and then tucked it away. "I think Layla is *the one* too. She's going to energize you. You're going to give her confidence. I think you fit amazingly well together, and I know she feels that way too."

Bracing himself, he closed his eyes. "Okay."

"You know me. You know that if I thought two people were being pigheaded, I'd bring them together, by force, if necessary."

He chuckled, thinking back on fifth grade when she'd dragged three older boys by their ears into the basketball court so that she could be taken seriously for her free-throw skills.

"Yeah, I know you would."

"But I'm not, in this case, am I?"

"No."

"Because I understand her worries, but her decision is where we disagree. I know you and I know that when you finally do make sense of this riddle, you won't do what she expects."

Carter shoved his container of soup back into the basket untouched and shook his head. "How should I know what she expects? I already told her I didn't care if she had a kid, or was married, or killed someone. It's hard to know what else there is to give two shits about."

Delia snatched the food away from him and set it down with a definite air. When he looked at her, her gaze was eerie in its focus. "I need you to hear this and record it to hard disc, okay?"

"Okay!"

"I know how smart you are, Carter Aadenson. I know you understand all these technological things, all the *numbers* and *pixels* whizzing through the *clouds*. I know you're going to *recover* her phone number, but what I want you to hear me say, is that I *know* you will sort through this calmly, in as *organized* a way as you always have with every other puzzle you've faced. I *know* you're going to put yourself in Layla's shoes, because you are *compassionate*. And I just *know* you're going to understand *exactly* why she lied, why she ran, why you don't *need* to chase her. Okay?"

Carter blinked back at her confusedly. Every word had seemed like a period at the end of a sentence, but he couldn't make sense of them.

"Skip the rest of the day. Drink a bottle of NyQuil and get a good night's sleep. You'll be ready to tackle this fresh in the morning. And when you finally do, you'll have the right head on your shoulders to deal with it. Yes?"

"Yes, Mom."

"I mean it."

"I know." He lifted her hand to his lips and gave it a quick kiss. "I'll drop you at school and take your advice."

"And when you get back," she warned, "apologize to my brother. Mark my words. After how he shut you down, he's going to be popular with the subculture kids. He's in the right place at the right time, with the exact right personality. If you don't make friends with him, your last year will be shittier than you think."

He saluted and followed her back to the Charger. She was starving, he knew, but she walked with a skip in her step. When she got out at the school, she beamed at him and leaned in through the window.

"I love you, Carter. Please be the guy I think you are."

"What if I'm not?"

Her expression hardened. "Then I guess you'll get to see my rage-face."

As she trotted back inside, he shook his head. If Declan was any clue, he wasn't sure he wanted to see that side of Delia.

Chapter 16
The Apology

Declan looked around at the maze of bookshelves and felt safe. Libraries had always been the best place to wait out a bully or regain some composure. Just the smell of the bindings and paper was enough to relax him and put a smile on his face.

"That's quite a schedule." Ms. Folger signed the class assignment sheet and shook her head. "No wonder they screwed it up. How has your first week been, so far?"

"Good, but confusing. I'm used to nuns and mandatory chapel hour. I'm glad this slot was open and that I didn't have to sit around for a whole week while they figured out where to put me."

"No one ever wants library duty."

He glanced at the mess of books around them. "Am I your first TA?"

She smiled, but it didn't detract from the eternally miserable look on her youthful face. "Let's face it, the district should just switch to ebooks and get it over with. If they're not going to fund the library so that we can keep it up, then why do we bother having it? Kids all have their devices, their backpacks would stop giving them scoliosis, and the technology is already adaptive to disabilities, but for some inexplicable reason, they feel it necessary to maintain what amounts to a pile of outdated recycling."

Declan blinked. "That bored, huh?"

Her expression changed suddenly, as if she'd remembered that he was a kid. "Don't get me wrong! This is a great place to find reference material, and because libraries actually have a part in higher education, it's good that kids encounter them—"

"You don't have to sugarcoat it for me." He looked at the three carts full of books that needed to be tagged, scanned into the system, and put onto shelves. Most of them were older than ten years, donated by community members. "I don't think I've ever once had an accurate science text book, and I came from a rich prep school. No one prioritizes books. At least if the books were digital, they could be altered instantly. And . . . they'd be cheaper."

"Yes! Thank you."

She demonstrated once again how he was to enter a book into the system, all the while carrying on about funding disparities that were due to the board's outdated way of thinking.

"And that's not even half of it! Anyway, I shouldn't be talking about this with a student. I could get fired."

"Only if I told someone who gave a shit," he said sweetly, a huge grin on his face.

She blinked at him. The horn-rim glasses and bow tie must cancel out the impression that he might be deliberately disrespectful. Her perusal ended with a chuckle. "I think I'm going to like you."

"Same here."

"Once we get this pile of . . . *knowledge* entered into the catalog and on the shelves, it really becomes mostly a study period for you, which I think you're going to need with your class list. The only time you have to do anything is when someone checks out a book, or when we have a big enough stack of returns that I need your help sorting them."

"What are you doing while I'm studying?"

"Good question."

"You're reading your iPad in your office, aren't you?"

She made a face and pointed to the sign on the wall that commanded all devices be turned off unless they had been cleared by the district for educational use. He put his finger up to his lips and grinned.

It wasn't a difficult task, if a trifle repetitive. All he had to do was log the title and ISBN of the book in the computer. It spit out a Dewey Decimal number and printed a label. He attached that to the book, and then put it in the pile of books to be placed in the appropriate slot on the shelf. If he could keep his mind from wandering to his personal life, he'd be done inside of two days.

Declan clicked the mouse through the series of windows that popped up for the book in his hand. The door opened behind him. He glanced back. "I'll be right with—"

Carter was standing at the end of the counter with his arms crossed. The look on his face clearly said that he was not here to check out a book. In fact, he looked like he couldn't decide if he wanted to continue their fight or pretend like it hadn't happened.

"Cushy gig. Usually transfer students don't get perks until they've been here a while," he said, casually, though his eyes were gleaming.

Declan had not seen him for three days, as if Carter had been avoiding him with the aid of the CCTV cameras. All of a sudden here he was, in the flesh. Declan had the span of only a few breaths to become the person Carter was expecting, not the lovesick bundle of confusion who remembered an erotic night beneath the stars.

"Yeah, well . . . I'm special."

Carter seemed to suddenly tire of their standoff and draped himself over the counter like a wilting plant. "Yeah. I caught a peek at your transcripts. All honors? That's pretty tough. I should know. You're on track to be valedictorian. Maybe you should run for president too. But I'm told that's what assholes do."

Declan ran his eyes down the muscled forearms and calloused fingers that were leafing through the books stacked behind the counter. "Don't you ever stand up straight? Why are you always flopping over everything like you're too bored to be bothered?"

Carter shrugged lazily. "Too bored to be bothered. So why are you in here instead of some other stupid elective?"

"Like what? Art?"

"Art's not stupid."

"Are you in it?"

"Yes. We're doing animal hybrid sculptures. I'm making a lizard-pit bull."

Declan winced. Of course Carter would be in Art with the level of skill in his drawing. He probably aced every single assignment. Well, at least if Declan insulted Carter, he might learn to stay away.

"Don't you have a class right now?"

Carter swiveled his head to face Declan, sleepy body language belied by an intense blue stare. "This is Student Government period. We have our first meeting tomorrow, so I have nothing to do for now."

"So what, you're just wandering the halls?"

"I came here specifically to see you."

Declan's heart did a flip-flop. The book he was holding slipped from his grasp and crash-landed into a pile, sending them all over the place. Cussing, he dropped down and hurriedly righted them, glancing up occasionally as Carter's amused face dawned over the edge of the desktop.

"How'd you know where I was?"

"Saw your schedule too."

Declan busied himself with the mountain of texts. "So why are you stalking me, or should I guess?"

"I wanted to apologize to you."

"Apologize? Funny! I have work to—"

"Do what you're doing." Carter slid along the wraparound counter till his head was resting on his arms near the computer, and though Declan tried to ignore it, he could still see the focused gaze in his periphery. "You just have to listen."

"This is a library."

"With no one in it."

"Carter, has anyone ever told you that you are as stubborn as a mule?"

"How many mules have you met in your sixteen years?"

Declan grumbled, but Carter's grin said he would not be turned away. He stood up finally, and braced his hands on the edge of the counter as if thinking about leaping over it. He was tipping forward and backward in a thoughtful exercise that slowly pressed at Declan's last nerve.

"Will you spit it out, please?"

"I wanna have this convo, man to man."

"Better go find some then," Declan muttered, peeling the backing from a sticky label.

"Dude to dude. Person to person. Shit."

Declan shrugged and continued to sift through the piles, but his ears were tuned to the soft sound of Carter's voice and the nervous tremor in it.

"I'm sorry."

"That you're a fake person, or that I noticed?"

Carter's constant motion came to an abrupt halt. "I'm not sorry you noticed. You're like your sister in that way. That's why she's my best friend, instead of just my ex. But she's a girl, and this conversation doesn't go the same way with a girl."

"Why should her gender have anything to do with your authenticity?"

"Stop using big words to confuse me." Declan looked over. Carter was smiling, but the expression was not his usual million-lumen beam. "It matters because she doesn't know how a guy *feels* about things in the world the way it's all arranged, I mean. Like, a guy's perspective on it. You're a guy. So you'll get what I want to say."

"If it's a legitimate thing from the heart, then *any* person will understand it, Carter."

"Okay. Fine. Be logical, but I was going to—"

"I'm not giving you Layla's phone number."

"Hear me out!"

Declan dropped the current volume onto the counter and scowled at the gorgeously petulant face before him. "You act like a dick, then apologize for acting like a dick by again acting like a dick. Is that simple enough for you to grasp?"

"Just listen to me. Please?"

"Trying to convince me of why you should also be allowed to be a giant douche is not going to go well for you."

Carter retreated, his expression unreadable, until he could sit on a nearby table. He covered his face with his hands as if trying to give himself a moment of peace and privacy to think. Declan obliged him and turned back to his work, though secretly he longed to watch the thoughts pass over those handsome features.

That one three-word phrase, once uttered, was like a perfect chord in a sea of disharmony. Declan felt annoyed by all the noise between them. He wanted that one flawless note, and if not that, then at least a whisper of it.

The sound of it sang through him, leaving sorrow in its wake.

"You knew her for a week," Declan said quietly. "No one loves someone after only a week."

"I disagree." He came out of hiding, his face resolute and determined. "Until you've felt it, you don't understand. I'm telling you. I love her."

Looking at the book in his hand, he felt the answering call fighting inside him to get out. He *did* know what Carter meant. He *did* understand, but better than Carter did, because the person he loved was real.

When he wasn't busy being political.

Carter's face brightened suddenly. "You're a geek."

Declan managed a swallow. "Is that an insult or a compliment?"

"It's a compliment. You play with Legos."

"O-kay."

Carter renewed his assault, attacking the counter with a full-on lounge over its curved surface, his hands outstretched. "It's like you're building this thing, right? And you're looking for a red two-by-four block. You look and look, but the stupid bucket has no red two-by-four blocks. You find all kinds of two-by-four blocks that fit the space, you could use two two-by-two blocks, two one-by-fours—"

"The combinations are many. Does this have a point?"

Carter's spirits were clearly undaunted by Declan's attempts to distance himself. He began stacking a book fort and peeking through the gaps at him playfully. "So, okay. You have all these possibilities that can fit in that slot, but the red two-by-four block is *the* one. You would know it if you saw it, even if you've never seen a red two-by-four block before, because the slot is—"

"Eight pegs and in a red zone. I get it."

A blue eye found him from between two spines, smiling. "Delia is a two-by-four block, for sure. Structurally sound, but not the right shade. I could manage, but I wouldn't be happy."

Declan pictured Carter measuring and measuring before he finally cut and bolted a piece of wood in place. He was a perfectionist, and that was why his structures looked so professional. He thought in geometry. Then Declan's mind stumbled across the image of him with his shirt off, carrying a beam on his shoulder like a sweaty Adonis, and he rattled it loose with a shake.

"My previous girlfriends were all like two one-by-fours. Some were red, but not ideal to the structure."

"But how do you know that Layla is a red two-by-four and not two two-by-twos stuck together or something? Appearances are deceiving. Especially when your dick is involved."

Carter laughed. "Not true! That's all a part of it."

"You can tell if she's a red two-by-four if you use your dick? Dude, you're ruining a classic toy for me."

Carter finally threw his hands in the air with a laugh. "Point is, I'm satisfied with the way she fits. So satisfied that I built all this stuff on top of her—"

"Phrasing, please!"

"Dude! I'm trying to explain how I feel here!"

"Like, your *real* feelings?"

"Yeah, those things."

Declan surrendered. Carter was besotted. He was euphoric and wanted to share it. He was alone and desperate to find his girl. There was no way to stop him. It didn't matter how Declan felt, having to stand there and be his masculine confidant. Declan loved this boy, and no matter how badly it hurt, he needed to offer his support.

"So..."

"So . . ." Carter again slumped over the counter and stared up at him forlornly. "Layla is the one. She gets me the best, helps me feel confident. When we were together, I was my real self for the first time. I didn't know who that guy was before I met her."

Declan kept his eyes averted, feeling the sting as they began to fill with tears. His voice came out husky even as he tried to clear all emotion from it. "How do you know she was her real self with you?"

"I don't know, but I think she got pretty close. That's the point. I am who I need to be because of her. I'll let her be whoever she wants to be. That's all that matters to me. That's what I want to tell her."

"It's sometimes not that simple—"

"She doesn't trust me yet. Maybe she thinks I won't like who she really is, maybe I never got a chance to show her I'm more than talk, but I'm going to fix all that. Delia said she'd keep Layla in the loop, and I hope you will too."

"In the loop?"

"Yeah. I'm hoping she'll see that I'm being real, that I can help her deal with this problem she's got, not just perv on her. She said she loved me—"

Declan looked up sharply. "Did she, now?"

Carter shrugged. "Okay, not in so many words, but that's because she didn't want to make it worse when we had to be apart. She has her own definition of love, but she loves me. I know she does."

Swinging his face heavenward, Declan prayed for the bell to ring. If he didn't get free of that stare soon, he was going to fall over. "You do realize that saying that makes you sound even more arrogant, right?"

"Sure I do. I just don't care. It's the truth."

"Carter, I'm saying this to you as a friend—"

"We're friends again, huh?"

"Find another two-by-four or a really sexy pair of red one-by-fours. Okay?"

"No. You don't get to tell me to settle. No one does! I've already fitted her in, Dex. I'm not undoing everything after her to swap out pieces."

That was it. Declan couldn't take it anymore. He slammed a book down on the counter. "Carter! I am not giving you her phone number!"

"I know! I get it. That's not what I came here to say!" His jaw was set and his eyes were ablaze. "I'm apologizing still, remember? This explanation is part of that."

Declan's mouth fell open uselessly, and his mind went blank.

"I was stuck . . . waiting for the time when I could get back to building who I wanted to be." He swung his hands around for words. "Now I can keep building, and the character, the *man* I want to build is not the asshole who came up to you in front of your friends and put you on the spot. I'm sorry I did that. It wasn't cool. You were right to call me out. You were right about everything you said. I *was* trying to swap popularity for something I wanted, instead of getting to know you or your friends. I love her and I was pushing ahead without thinking about what I was doing. I. Am. Sorry."

After a few long moments of staring, Declan remembered that his mouth was still dangling in open air. He shut it with a smack. "Okay."

"Thank you."

"That's all you wanted to say?"

"Yup." Carter stood up and stretched. "So, are we square?"

Declan moved a pile of finished books to the rolling cart. "Just because you dated my sister—"

"Who practically worships the ground you walk on and demanded I apologize. I also dated your cousin, who taught you everything you know about paintball apparently. And I know you have to be a pretty stand-up guy. I mean, most would have given me the phone number to avoid the drama. But you stood up to the most popular guy in school in front of everyone . . . while wearing cat ears."

Carter was grinning again. He'd made some kind of headway in his own mind, at least.

"What can I say? I'm not a giant coward."

Carter blinked at him, suddenly stoic. "See? Just the kind of guy I need to know."

The bell rang. Declan looked at the mess of books. Ms. Folger would be reconsidering him. He'd done less than twenty. He scribbled a hasty note of apology and stuck it to the monitor. Carter waited for him to grab his bag and followed him out.

"I'll see you on Xbox, Dex."

He shouldered his coat and tucked his blushing face into it. "Yeah, thanks for tainting my love of stackables."

Declan felt the fingers as they slid up through his hair from his nape and tousled it. The jolt sent him upright on a stiff spine, and then sideways into a locker. Carter didn't appear to notice, and sauntered away.

Chapter 17
The Meeting

Slumped against the table, smile fixed, Carter secretly wished he could pull out his cell and play *Minecraft*. The junior class representative was putting them to sleep with a long diatribe on the yearbook photobomb competition. Looking askance at his vice president, Brianna, he winked. She wrote *This statement is false* on a note and slid it to him.

He barely stifled a laugh. The rep had only been elected because he'd run unopposed, because how could anyone oppose a robot? It was fact that only paradoxes could shut them up, and Carter knew that most of his peers thought *paradox* meant *a couple of doctors*. So there he was, the long-winded protocol droid, droning on in a nasal tone. Maybe if he used Brianna's line aloud, Carter could short-circuit the kid's brain and cause it to grind into silence.

"If I can interrupt, since we're so close to the end of the period—" Carter held up a hand. "What I hear you saying . . . since your presentation was so . . . detailed . . . is that you want people to join clubs because they're motivated; *however*, last year, the third-semester club enrollments were up by almost a quarter. Some of the larger clubs managed to have more fundraisers for activities, because even though people joined for the club photo, they got to like the group. Why don't we solve the problem this way: let's ask the clubs and yearbook to hold off on their photos until closer to the end of the year. Maybe by then, the people who joined to participate in the contest will get bored and drop."

This seemed to make everyone happy. Carter sealed the mood with a grin. "Besides, I'm a shoo-in to win the award. Wouldn't want to help anyone else out."

Carter asked for any more business. Heads shook in desperation. All in all, it had been a successful first meeting of his student council. Priah Sangupta stretched out backward over the table as the class reps filed out and released a tremendous yawn that sounded more like a howl.

"I didn't sign up to be treasurer so that I could listen to children bicker about nonsense!"

Carter chuckled at her upside-down head and her crisp accent. "What? You didn't find the concerns over the painting of the cafeteria with low V-O-C paint to be stimulating?"

She stared. "No, Carter, I did not."

"Better than watching it dry."

Brianna tipped over him as if she were melting. "I hate you for talking me into being your running mate. Is this all we're supposed to do, all year? I swear, I thought they were kidding when they told us it was boring."

He remembered the look on the face of the previous council president, who announced their victory and then immediately mocked them for being so naively ambitious.

"Count yourself lucky. You get a free period, and all you have to do is look busy." As he said it, he could picture Layla shaking her head at him in dismay. "If you're bored, we could brainstorm a way to stay busy. Pick a charity, or a cause or something and use our spare time to do something for it."

Priah rolled over and propped her face up on her fists. "That might be fun. We could put it on our applications. Like a food drive or something."

The door opened. Chloe appeared, but her head was bowed and her face pale. She moved slowly through the desks as if running on the fumes of some adrenaline rush. She looked as if she'd seen a ghost, clutching a manilla envelope as if for dear life.

Carter stood up. "Chloe? Are you okay?"

She blinked at him and held out the envelope. "He banned it."

"What?"

"The Rainbow Corps. He . . . Taggert banned it."

Brianna shot out of her chair and came around the table. As Chloe collapsed, Brianna caught her and slid her into a seat. Besties since kindergarten, Brianna shushed her as Chloe quickly came unglued. Priah managed to get the envelope out of her grasp. It was the paperwork for the LGBTQ+ club. Leafing through the papers, Priah frowned at him.

"She has everything she needed," she said.

Carter knelt down in front of Chloe and took her hands. She'd begun to sob, her whole body shuddering with each gasp. Instantly, he felt the familiar twisting of his stomach and the awful burning behind his eyes. He hated watching people cry. It triggered horrible memories of his mom slumped over a pillow on the couch, still in her pajamas at three in the afternoon, her hair a mess, a wine bottle tipped over on the coffee table.

"Calm down, Chloe. Take some deep breaths. Tell us what happened."

"He called me . . ." Her words came and went on a tide of sorrow and self-doubt. She had been so excited about the club. Surrounded by understanding friends, Chloe had finally made her statement to the world, and now the world was apparently fighting back. "I came to the office . . . He said that the . . . Rainbow Corps was . . . unacceptable material."

Priah's face screwed up on an expletive. "'Unacceptable'? On what planet? Every public uni in North America has an LGBTQ+ club!"

"Yeah, but . . . we're still kids." Brianna shook her head. "Did he say why?"

Chloe accepted a wad of tissues and mopped her face. "He said he was disappointed in me . . . for what? Why? I don't understand."

Carter's body ran cold as reality washed over him. So much for an easy A and a free period. So much for a bullshit-free year. He could turn away and throw his hands in the air, but how could he explain that to Layla, or indeed, to a sharp-eyed Cat-boy? How could he look in the mirror? If he didn't do something, he really was fake.

He turned to the council secretary, who was putting away his things. "Does anyone know club bylaws?"

Martin looked like a deer in headlights as all faces swiveled to him. "What do you want to know?"

"Can they do this?" Priah blurted out. "Can we stop them?"

He dodged her anger by running for the bookshelf. He leafed through the book frantically and finally emerged with a blink. "We'd have to petition the school board to rule on the club. They'd have to reverse Taggert's decision."

Getting to his feet, Carter picked up the packet of materials. "Stop freaking out, everyone. I'm going to figure this out. Just hang on."

He shot from the room, limbs strengthened by righteous fury. He pictured the man's insipid demeanor and his weasely little face and wondered if Taggert spent hours practicing his delivery in the shower so that he could get the most condescending tone possible. Opening the office door, he failed to acknowledge the secretary as he usually did, with witty banter and a roguish smile.

"You okay, Carter?"

"I'm sorry, Mrs. Nelson, but can I please talk to Principal Taggert right away? It's important."

She nodded and tapped an intercom key. The principal emerged from his office with a forced smile. "Mr. Aadenson! How did the first meeting go? I look forward to reading the minutes. Have some business to bring to my attention?"

He was ushered into the office and directed to an uncomfortable chair. He ignored it. Instead, he put the envelope on Taggert's desk and crossed his arms. This would be a touchy conversation. He had managed, in the past, to behave in a friendly way with Taggert, but that was only politics, something he was discovering he liked less and less.

"Chloe Shannon turned up in the council room bawling her eyes out. She wasn't making much sense. Did you really *ban* the LGBTQ+ club?"

"Yes, I did." Taggert sat down behind his desk and donned a supercilious expression.

"Can you explain the decision?"

"I don't have to."

So it was like that, then? Carter changed tack. "Then how am I supposed to keep her from going to the school board?"

Taggert relaxed in his throne, poking the envelope as if disgusted by it. "You're her friend, aren't you?"

"Yes."

He nodded. "Explain to her that the district has specific policies regarding sexual education. A club that focuses on sexual orientation circumvents our curriculum on the subject."

"The purpose of the club is to provide gay teens with a support network so that they don't drop into depression. All of the club's planned events are geared toward raising awareness for equal treatment. It saves lives and teaches tolerance. It has nothing to do with sex."

"Yes, I'm sure that's what she told you when you signed up." Taggert had a narrow eye pointed at Carter's feet. His tone implied enough to make Carter clench his fists—namely that Chloe, his friend, was somehow a disgusting person and an influence on others.

"I'm the one who suggested she try to start the club," he seethed.

"Well, then I can see I need to instruct you too. The fact is, it is entirely dependent upon the concept of sex. She put forth the idea of inviting a local author to give a talk on the history of sexuality in American media."

Carter tried but could not halt the grimace as it bent his features to its will. "That author is a professor, and that book is about *all* sexuality, not just queer."

"Precisely."

"You don't think that'd be beneficial for a bunch of horny teenagers?"

"That is immaterial. Do you need to take a moment to calm down?"

Rocking back on his heels, Carter's voice was knocked out. Chloe's packet was sterling; she'd planned to organize trips, talks, and fundraisers dealing with everything from date rape to transgender psychology. This was the exact opposite reception Carter would have anticipated and, in some way, perhaps he was to blame for her disappointment. He'd made light of the club, shoving off her concerns with a winning smile and some bullshit about how no one would make fun of Chloe for being gay because she was his buddy.

He took a steadying breath. "If this falls outside the curriculum, then maybe the curriculum needs updating."

"That's an issue for the board to handle," the principal said nonchalantly, as he picked up a cup of coffee and emptied a sugar packet into it. "You know, I'm surprised to see you in here about this. You've always struck me as a laid-back boy."

"I'm not sure I know what you mean by that, sir."

Taggert shrugged, but still would not make eye contact. "You're popular, you do well in school. You're not the type to cause problems."

Carter's mouth dropped open. The unfairness of the entire situation was suddenly becoming clear. Adults made all the rules, so they got to tell teens what to think and feel, and if the teens objected, they were making trouble.

"I wasn't aware I was causing problems. You made a decision. I wanted an explanation. It's in my job description to be a liaison to the student body. People are going to wonder where the club went."

"Well, then I leave it to you to explain it to them. I'm sure you'll make the point completely clear. You're late for your next class. Have Mrs. Nelson write you a pass."

Carter felt the dismissal keenly. He turned his back on that beady-eyed little stare, but couldn't bring himself to leave. "What do you plan to do to help queer students at this school if you won't let them form a club?"

Taggert balked. "We have school counselors for a reason, Mr. Aadenson. They have the 'safe space' stickers. If LGBTQ students have an issue, they're welcome to seek help."

"That's pretty weak. Most queer students don't seek help because they're terrified of being outed. The club helps them feel like they have friends, peers, straight people who will understand."

"Then we put ourselves in the dangerous position of allowing other students to be responsible for mental health issues."

"But Principal—"

"Mr. Aadenson, I was happy when you won the election."

Carter turned and caught the dangerous look in the man's eye. He repressed the desire to shout, barely. "Really, sir?"

"I thought, 'Now here's a boy who will keep his head down and get things done quietly.'"

Standing there, feeling the scorn like the glow off a fire, Carter burned with indignation. "What does that mean?"

"Politics, Mr. Aadenson. I knew you understood politics."

Muscles turned into coiled springs. His blood was hammering in his ears. He fought the urge to jump across the desk and tell the man what a small-minded asshole he was with his fist.

"Yes, I do, Mr. Taggert. But you know what else I understand? Bigotry."

He slammed the door behind himself and took the pass. Instead of going to class, he went out to the track and ran in circles for the next half hour. Stretched out on the turf, he stared up at the clouds and generally felt like shit until a face wearing a pair of horn-rimmed glasses eclipsed the sun.

"Are you dead?"

Carter sat up and waited for the dizziness to subside. "Not yet. But I'm starting to wish I was."

Declan plopped down beside him wearing a PE jersey. "It can't be that bad. The year just started. Even I'm having an okay time. I'm practically a cast member on *Revenge of the Nerds*, and I have a posse."

"That was a great movie."

"You look like you've been running for hours."

"I run when I'm angry and don't have my chainsaw."

Leaning back, Declan covered his face with an arm. "That's funny. I get angry when I have to run, *unless* there's a chainsaw involved."

Carter looked back at the class Declan was supposed to be attending. They were practicing volleyball technique on the far end of the field. Couldn't be too easy to play ball games when a person wore glasses like Declan's. He was more of a marksman anyway.

Carter couldn't have wished for better company at this moment. "What would you do if someone called you a loser?"

Declan made a sound like a chirp. "Is this someone I hate, or someone I like?"

"Someone of authority."

"Hmm. Well, I guess it depends."

"On what?"

"Authority isn't the same thing as respect. If you respect the person, then you accept their guidance, but if the person is a—"

"Gummy-faced contemptible cock with a halitosis problem?"

"Okay . . . that." He uncovered his face and shrugged. "Then disobeying him is exactly the same thing as telling a bully to sit on it and spin. You have to be willing to accept the consequences."

"That's my point, though. There shouldn't *be* any consequences! People like that shouldn't have that kind of power."

Declan let out a long-suffering sigh as if he couldn't believe he had to explain such a rudimentary concept to someone older than him. He shook his head. "Carter, a bully's fist isn't going to hurt less because you think the world is unfair. Pick a course of action and stick to it. When the consequences come, choose how you will handle those too. The point is, integrity means strength, fortitude, like a wall with no weaknesses, a building with a solid foundation. If you're going to have it, you have to have it in rain or shine, easy or hard, under pressure or in relaxation. If you don't plan on doing anything about the situation, then you don't get to complain. Choose."

Carter sat there looking at him for a long moment. He'd never noticed before that Declan had a small brown birthmark above his lip. It was exactly the sort women faked with makeup or had tattooed. It drew the eye straight to his mouth, which was wearing a slightly bemused smile on a pair of full, feminine lips.

Forcing himself to look away, Carter shook his head. "How is it that simple for you?"

"What?"

"To know who you are and what you should do?"

"*Simple*? Are you on drugs?" Declan let out an explosive laugh. "It isn't! Think of it this way: what would you want someone else to do if they were in your position?"

He already knew the answer to that. He would want the student council president to take the fight to the school board and slam the point home in an awesome display of public speaking that included dropping the fucking mic. But that other person didn't exist. It was just him, and he was the one to whom everybody would look.

"Whatever it is you want *them* to do, that's what you have to do," Declan said softly.

"Why? Why does it have to be me?"

"Why not? Aren't you the coolest guy that ever was?"

Carter looked askance at the skinny kid. He had raised his arm to the sky and was pinching the fluffy white clouds into shapes. Carter had never noticed how long his fingers were, or how delicate his wrists appeared against the blues and grays.

If Declan were president, faced with the decision to antagonize the entire adult leadership of the district, he would do it. Hell, he spent all day shooting the RPG characters of fully grown adults in the face and listening to the fully grown operators scream in dismay; it probably desensitized him to the feeling of getting into trouble. But the question was: would Carter want him to handle this? The answer was yes, because he knew Declan *could* handle it. But he wouldn't want him to have to do it alone.

"I'm not sure I'm good enough. I can try, but—"

Declan sat up and picked some grass. "Do or do not. There is no try."

"Did you just quote Yoda?"

"The point is, Carter, you fail *until* you succeed, by *definition*. I know you're used to getting everything perfect on the first attempt—"

"Wait . . . there's another way of doing stuff?"

Declan stood up and looked down at him with a knowing smile. "There he is. Now hit the showers."

Chapter 18
The Question

Declan leaned over the check-out desk and searched for Carter. As had become his custom of the last few days, Carter was tucked into a corner behind a reference shelf, with a pile of books that he continuously leafed through as if annoyed. Declan never found out what they were, because Carter would always replace them before the bell rang. Despite his reservations about getting too close, he found himself looking for excuses to bother Carter instead of studying. His heart still ached, and every glimpse of Carter filled him with an intense longing.

Picking up a stack of returns, he snuck through the shelves until he could get a better look at why Carter was wearing such a scowl. When he smelled pencil shavings and caught sight of the sketchbook, however, he lost interest in deception.

"You're drawing?"

Carter didn't react. Which meant he'd either seen Declan coming, or he didn't care. He was staring at a textbook of some kind, and slid the art pad toward Declan without a word. It was the treehouse, only it wasn't. There were several more tiers, and more than a few extra means of ascending. Biting his lip in anticipation, Declan turned pages, seeing exactly how every little alteration could be made even without Carter's helpful notations about materials or measurements. On the final page, he stopped and let out a gasp.

"You like that, huh, Cat-boy?"

Declan frowned, but it was a nicer nickname than *shrimp*, which was what Carter usually called him. He was on the point of asking if the young man planned to erect a second high tier around the back of the tree to accomplish the drawing, but realized there was no way he could know anything about it. *Layla* was the one who had built this little palace with the boy of his dreams.

"Is this a real treehouse?"

"Mostly. I'm still building it. That's an addition. I've sunk posts for the little platform. The larger one is already in place." He turned away from his books and pointed to a part of the sketch. "I'm going to put a rope swing here, and then here—"

"A hammock!" Declan grinned uncontrollably. He'd seen pictures of stuff like this on the internet, suspended over stairwells, lofted above bedrooms, like giant spiderwebs where people could lounge in a less conventional way.

"Hey, you wanna come help me this weekend? Layla kept me moving on the project, but now I actually *need* an extra set of hands if I'm going to get this roofed portion up, or set the hammock in place."

Declan swallowed down his immediate, enthusiastic yes. Being in close quarters with Carter on a regular basis outside the strictures of school could be dangerous. Especially if he made a mistake and let something slip like he'd been about to.

"What do I get out of it?"

Carter was indignant. "Besides my company?"

Declan stared him down.

"I'll help you with your classwork."

"I don't need help."

"No, you probably don't." Carter went back to his books. "I guess all I've got is my company."

Declan's heart performed an inconvenient twitch. "A little lonely, huh?"

"Always. Just didn't notice before."

The candor caught him off guard, and for a long moment, he stared at the sketch vacantly. It wasn't possible; he couldn't let Carter be so miserable when he was right there with the ability to at least mitigate some of it.

"Well, in that case, I guess I *could* help."

Carter smiled, but he was clearly pondering something weighty. He shifted a new book into place and absentmindedly flipped pages.

Declan caught a few words in a bold font that nudged his eyebrow upward.

"You've been in here every day this week. What are you up to?"

"Research."

He closed the cover on the nearest volume. It was a psychology textbook. "Are you in psych?"

"No. This is for my rumble with the authority figure I mentioned the other day."

"What was it? The gummy-faced cock?"

"Yeah." Carter let out an exasperated sigh. "Did you hear about what happened with the LGBTQ+ club?"

Taking a seat on the long table, Declan shook his head. A sense of foreboding was dawning. He'd seen Chloe a few times in the halls, and she'd looked as if she were sick. When he didn't hear from her, he assumed that she hadn't gotten enough members for the club and was upset about it. He hadn't been brave enough to ask.

Kicking himself for not following through on his plans for his life at this new school, Declan braced himself for bad news. "Chloe said she was going to contact us when the club was approved."

"You signed up too?"

This was what it meant to stand for something. It wasn't always pleasant. In fact, it could sometimes be downright terrifying.

He swallowed. "Of course. It's a civil rights issue."

Carter looked away. "Yeah, well, apparently the district doesn't see it that way. It's been summarily banned."

The bottom fell out of Declan's stomach. Visions of camaraderie dissolved into the certainty that there was no place for him in this rigid world. It was as bad as the day Father Ryan had given the sermon on why the gay agenda was rotting their souls. Suddenly the familiar look of crushing dejectedness on Chloe's face was clear. How had he not recognized it for what it was? It was easy; he'd been too caught up in his own head to care.

"But . . . how? Why? What happened?"

Carter set his chair on its back legs, heedless of how it teetered on the brink as he stretched like a puma. "Chloe was called into the office and basically told that the club was a disgusting breach of school rules. I've never seen her cry like that before. I've never much liked Taggert, but fuck if I don't want to rip his face off now. I almost did when I asked him about it, and he essentially patted me on the head and called me a good boy. I'm starting to get tired of people underestimating me."

His eyes were little shards of blue glass. It was clear his words were not bluster. Feeling as if he'd broken through another of Carter's defensive walls, Declan took a deep breath and prodded the opening.

"How close are you two?"

"I was the first person she came out to."

Declan's mouth fell open, but it made perfect sense. The safest ally to have was someone in whom you had no interest, and who could protect you if you needed it. Carter gave off the dashing-prince vibe at a thousand paces, like a shiny, floral skunk.

"We used to hang out all the time, back in the day. I went to her house once, and she dropped it like a weight she couldn't carry anymore. 'I am a lesbian,' she said. And I just stood there like an idiot."

Declan drew his knees up under his chin. "Had to rethink the person you knew, huh?"

Carter shot a look at him. "Nothing about *her* changed just because I found out."

"Except that she had someone she could trust."

"Yeah." Carter shrugged. "I guess that's true. A person is different when they feel safe."

Declan closed another text. It was a book on human sexuality. "You see more of them."

"Exactly! I had this epiphany, you know, that by telling me her secret, she was basically forcing me to reveal how I would react. Like we were both telling secrets."

That was a charming idea, but few people thought of that type of confession so fondly. "And how did you handle it?"

"It surprised me that she treated it so casually, like, 'Here's this thing I've never told anyone, and it's, like, crucial to my identity. Here you go!' So I stood there, wondering, like angry even, that she'd be so nonchalant about it. Then I realized . . ."

"What?" Declan whispered, tightening his grip on his legs.

"That it *is* something she *should* treat casually! Who the fuck cares? I mean, holy shit! Nobody asks me if I like girls like the answer could end life as we know it. Why should she have to be so careful?

It killed me, thinking of how long she had been afraid of the best part of herself, the part of her that could love. Broke my fucking heart."

Declan unfolded with an acute self-awareness; he had been barricading himself around the same deep dark secret, making certain that the person he loved above all others would never find out. But here was Carter himself, saying that the secret was not a good enough excuse to keep him out. But would Carter still say that if he knew how precious he was to Declan?

He envied Chloe then, that she had grown up alongside this boy, and had seen a part of him Declan had not. But then again, who was to say Carter's kinship with her hadn't been the thing to sculpt him into a tolerant individual? She had laid a foundation in his mind and heart, and being a builder, Carter had built.

With a nebulous prayer, Declan propped himself up on his elbows and put his feet on the chair beside Carter's. "I'm proud of you for that."

The young man glanced at him, somewhat shyly. "Thanks. Means a lot."

"Chloe must be too."

"She worked hard to stand up for who she is," Carter said quietly. "And here they are, shoving her back in her closet and telling her that she is inappropriate. They have no right."

"I agree completely. So what are you going to do about it, Mr. President? I mean, she did run your campaign for you, right? But she probably only did it so that you could hide out in here."

Carter took a steadying breath, glaring fiercely at the book in front of him. "Yes, thank you for being so encouraging."

"No problem. It's just, you know, a man who can't be bothered to stand up straight probably doesn't stand for much."

"Wow . . . that's how it is?" There was a smoldering look in his eye. "I'm way ahead of you. I've been reading and rereading bylaws and trying to get a handle of the biology of it all."

Of course he had. He was too rational to think of feelings and urges as shifting patterns of light and color. To him, they were grounded in blood and DNA.

"You think being gay is biological?"

"To some degree sure. Everything is. I mean, you eat Pocky, right, Cat-boy?"

"Only Nazis don't eat Pocky."

"Right, well, the reason you like it is because it's sweet. That's your body rewarding you for giving it glucose sugar, the fuel that your brain uses to do all of your deep thinking. Even the urge to prefer Pocky to something else that is sweet is biological."

Declan stared at him, uncertain if he was more surprised that Carter had actually retained knowledge from his classes, or that he had applied it to any serious issue. But that was an entirely erroneous impression that Carter undermined time and again, with his structures, his grades, his alacrity in dealing with the people around him. It wasn't Carter who changed by unveiling his intelligence or focus, it was Declan who changed for the hearing.

"I think the LGBTQ+ community shies away from that for a reason."

"Right! We can't talk about XXY or XYY chromosomes, low testosterone or estrogen production, and genetic inheritance, because that might make a person think that being gay is 'predictable,' and therefore 'curable,' when in fact it's probably as curable as having brown eyes. And really, that's only *part* of sexuality."

Intrigued, Declan stole the *Human Sexuality* book and looked up *homosexuality* in the index. "What's the other part?"

"Well—" Carter huffed indignantly "—I mean come on! If you tried Indian food for the first time, your opinion would be pretty jumbled. Maybe you like the spices, but hate the chilies, you know? And maybe later, you change your mind. It's the same thing with sex. People don't come out of the womb 'pure,' and stick to missionary position their whole lives."

With a laugh, Declan shook his head. "Principal Taggert probably has."

"Oh, great! Thanks for *that* image."

"You're welcome! I suggest pulling that one up anytime you're supposed to be taking him seriously. Everyone looks stupid while having sex. It's a fact."

Carter had a flirtatious lilt to his voice. "I don't know. I imagine to your lover you don't look stupid."

Declan felt his blush rising as the memory came back for the millionth time, as if it loved to appear when he was trying to get away from taking Carter seriously. "That's very true."

Carter looked at the clock and began closing his volumes. "Anyway, I guess what I'm saying is that sexuality is pretty complicated. Some of it, for some people, could be biological, part of it could be learned behavior, fetishes, things like that. Some could be interplay between the two, or a response to trauma, or any number of completely unpredictable factors. It could be a phase, or forever. Hell, maybe you just like it when you come across it, like a new flavor of ice cream."

Looking back on his own reality, Declan pondered. For him it had been a fact, from as young as he could remember, that he preferred boys. What was less cut and dry was his gender. Sometimes he was okay with jeans, and others he desperately wanted to wear a dress; he wanted to be both and do both simultaneously, and the only way to accomplish that was to have an alter ego. But he wasn't sure that either side fit, and leaping back and forth was disorienting. He still had no idea if he'd created Layla to do what he could not, or if she was an integral part of the experience. Could he be with another boy *as* a boy, or did he need her like a kind of bridge? And if he did, why did it matter to anyone else?

That was the question at the heart of it all.

"Why should anyone else care?" Declan muttered.

Carter leaned over his stack and nodded. "That's why I looked at the psychology books. I realized that I couldn't do anything until I understood how the school board rationalized this decision and could find a way to explain to them why they're stupid."

"Sex is threatening, obviously."

"But why?" Carter closed his sketch pad, much to Declan's sadness, and tucked it into his bag. "Why do straight people get so freaked out by gay people? That's one of the reasons Goat and I are friends and he's one of my best friends."

Blinking, Declan tried not to read into that statement. "Huh?"

"Goat, he's the giant football player with the goatee."

"We've met. I meant . . . is Goat gay?"

"No. But back in sixth grade, his uncle came out. When people at school found out, there was a shitload of drama. A bunch of boys refused to let him into the bathroom. His parents had to get involved."

"No one picks on him now."

"Well, that's because he's over six feet tall and weighs as much as a small lion."

Declan pictured him, crammed into the back seat of Carter's car, chowing down on his breakfast burrito. So, to keep himself safe, all Declan had to do was grow until he became imposing. He looked at his skinny legs in his straight-leg jeans and shook his head. Yeah, that would never happen.

"It got bad for a while, and I was the only person who would talk to him. Eventually people got bored with it, but it always made an impression on me, that sexuality was something people can't deal with. And if a person is open about it, the rest of society turns away."

"There's this idea that it's somehow contagious."

"Well, so what? *Knowledge* is contagious. We learn new things all the time that change us as people. Why should we be afraid of it?"

Declan raised a brow.

It was an excellent point, but secretly, he wondered what Carter would do if confronted with an adoring cat-boy all coy smiles and compliments. Declan wandered back to the desk under the pretense of fetching his stuff, but in reality, he was looking for a way to hide the blush that refused to leave his face.

"So are you saying that if you met the right guy, Carter, you'd suddenly turn bisexual, or just full-on gay?"

To his shock, Carter shrugged. "I'm at least open to the possibility that there exists such an amazing person in this world who could make me see past all that stuff, and if a boy came to me and told me he liked me, I wouldn't flip out and hit him. I'd say the same thing I say to all the girls who like me."

"Oh, *all* those girls, huh?"

There it was, that crooked, cocksure grin. "There's a lot of 'em."

"Well, of course there are! You're the most interesting man in the world!"

"I'm working on it, but honestly, it's difficult to find anything else that needs tweaking."

Laughing in spite of himself, Declan dropped behind the counter and shoved his things into the pockets of his backpack. "So what would you say to him?"

"That I'm flattered but not interested, unless I am. In which case, I'd do the same thing I'd do with a girl, and take him out on a date."

Declan couldn't resist the urge to tease him. "What would you look for in a guy, Carter?"

"You making fun of me or seriously wondering, Cat-boy?"

The bell rang, and to Declan it couldn't have come at a more auspicious moment. He'd backed himself into a conversational corner. It was either lie about himself and undo all the honesty they had shared, or reveal himself to the one person who really shouldn't see him as a sexual creature. If he took the bullshit route, Carter would dismiss him utterly, but if Declan was brave, the consequences could be just as painful.

"As much as you've talked about being nonjudgmental and open to the possibility, I doubt you've ever really done any serious thinking on the subject."

Carter followed him into the hall, a frown already in place. "That's not fair. Sure, I have."

"So answer the question."

"The same things I look for in a girl! Good qualities are universal. Intelligence, humor, compassion, motivation: all of these things are the same no matter what body they're in."

"That's not what I'm talking about, Carter, and you know it."

"Ah . . . you're talking about *sex*!"

Declan paused by the drinking fountain and waited for some eavesdropping students to pass before he responded. Carter was staring at him impassively, arms crossed.

"That is what we're talking about, yes."

With one casual shrug, he brushed Declan's momentous point to the ground to be stamped over by loitering kids. "I like what I like, when I like it."

"That must be nice."

"It's a highly advantageous position."

Declan rolled his eyes. "You're good at finding those, huh?"

"I read this book about sexual positions that bring health—"

"Oh my god, Carter! Edit!"

"Take notes, Cat-boy, this is what 'not being fake' looks like."

"Some of us already have that one down."

There was a sly glimmer in his eye as Carter reached out as if to give Declan's hair its familiar parting fluff. He didn't anticipate that the young man would grab hold, chain him to the spot, and peer into his face from an inch away.

"Oh yeah? You sure about that?"

Declan swatted at him. "Yes, I am."

"So what do *you* look for in a boy?"

Paralyzed by Carter's knowing look, by the sidelong glances of his classmates, by the tremendous cacophony of mental voices all shouting contradictory things, there was no way out. He had promised himself when he signed that membership form, when he'd put on the ears, when he'd stood up to the young man in the cafeteria, that he would be brave.

"That's between me and him."

Carter let go, freeing him to breathe again. With a smile, he stepped back and held out his arms. "My point exactly!"

Chapter 19
The Castle

Declan appeared beneath the tree at about ten in the morning, looking chipper in blue jeans and a black T-shirt, skateboard tucked beneath his arm. Carter blinked down at him, feeling disheveled and sleepy, but pleased beyond words to see him. He'd been up late wondering if Declan would show, largely because the boy had always seemed like a recluse, hidden away in his bedroom, avoiding the light of the sun. He wasn't sure the lure of architecture was enough.

"I was about to come kidnap you!"

Dex shaded his eyes and made a face. "Did you sleep up there?"

"I like it. It's cozy, and it reminds me of Layla."

Declan shuffled in place. "Okay . . . guess she really did a number on you."

"She's an amazing person, but it's cool. Let's not talk about her."

Carter dropped down the ladder, pretending not to notice Declan's glance flick over his naked torso and ragged shorts. He fluffed Declan's hair and made his way around the base of the tree to the lowest level, where the plans were weighted down with rocks.

"I wanna put up the roof on this segment today." He pointed. "It's the last piece of major construction, and it needs to be finished before we add all the bells and whistles."

Declan seemed to acclimate to the complicated plans almost immediately, leaning over them with his glasses down on the tip of his nose. "Whatever you say, boss man."

"Think you're up to it?"

Declan shot him an adorable sidelong glare that was probably meant to be scathing. "I've been known to use power tools."

"Were they plugged in at the time?"

"Do I need to punch you? Just get it over with so we can move on?"

Grinning, Carter danced backward and headed for the workshop. As they gathered materials, he found himself thinking about Layla and how easily he'd entertained her with stupid jokes and ridiculous antics. He'd make some comment about his own capabilities, and she'd shake her head indulgently, that pretty smile pressed tight on the secret she carried but never begrudged—that men were really foolish boys, as much in need of play as passion.

Perhaps that was what he had liked about Layla the most: that she was immune to the universe, unfazed by childishness. She had been more comfortable and confident in her skin than any teenager Carter had ever met, which made her unbelievably beautiful in every respect.

Dex, on the other hand, apparently had fortified his entire persona against the world and everyone in it, even if they wore cat ears. As Carter pondered it, he knew it had to have something to do with the bullying he'd been through at his stuck-up private school. It was a hell of a way to reward excellence—putting an exceptional human being in a hostile environment of competition, conservative ideology, and puritanical morals.

He remembered the time Delia had once come over crying because Declan had been attacked on his way home, his eye so swollen they had to take him to the hospital to have it drained. It always seemed that Dee was crushed, not merely because Dex had refused her help, but because he no longer seemed to trust her or have any hope that things could be different. As children, he knew Delia and Declan had always been best friends, and suddenly her brother had become a whipping post, while she had been promoted to the ranks of popularity.

It was incredible that Dex had escaped that hell with his personality intact. To do that must have taken a kind of strength that Carter certainly didn't have. His strategy was always to avoid hardship, to morph into whatever personality would get him out of the situation. But Dex had a quiet certainty, as if he knew some greater truth and didn't accept that anything around him mattered.

That was a talent that was unique, in his experience. Most of the kids he knew couldn't put what they liked into words without parroting some commercial or commonly held opinion, or looking to each other for guidance or support.

Carter was beginning to feel better and better in the wake of Layla's disappearance, as if things might actually work out. He wanted very much to prove himself to her. He wanted to look that person—whoever she was—in the eye and see certainty looking back at him, faith and trust that he was the man she wanted, needed, even respected. If there was one person who could keep him honest and focused on that goal, it was Dex.

"What?"

"Nothing. You know, Goat's been talking about your debut on the paintball range all week."

"He really hates Spencer Barrett."

"Singer Valley won the last two Homecoming games. It's a huge bummer."

"I assume we're speaking of *the football*. That's the one with innings, right?"

Laughing, Carter dropped his armful of beams into a pile and began laying them out sequentially. "Football is about strategy."

"If I want that, I'll play *Warcraft*."

"Huh. Seems like having *real* people to predict would appeal to your genius."

Declan rolled his eyes and knelt down, stacking the shingles carefully. "I'm not a genius."

"See, that's not how this works."

"How what works?"

Carter sighed laboriously. "You're supposed to say something like 'My genius hasn't got the time for childish games,' or something."

Declan had his eyebrow raised. "Why?"

"Because! Be the confidence you wish to have against the world."

The boy's mouth fell open in awe. "You just paraphrased *Gandhi* . . . to justify your egotism."

"I'm shameless, but it really is effective as a confidence-building tool."

"That's because after you've said something like that, there's no other *possible* way to sound more full of yourself."

Carter pulled a face. "Don't cage me! I'm all about overcoming limitations."

Dex had a thousand clearly framed thoughts moving behind his hazel eyes, but gave voice to none of them. It made Carter nervous, trying to account for what he could be thinking as he took note of every detail.

"How about this?" Declan broached. "I'm not enough of a dick to exercise my genius on poor, confused teenagers for the sake of some trophy."

"What if it's a trophy *they* want to win?"

Declan frowned. "Okay. Valid point. I'll be sure to keep that in mind when I line up Barrett's face in my crosshairs."

They worked in silence for a long while, cutting the miters on the first centering rafters. After those were fixed in place, like two little points on either side of the box, the ridge for the gable could rest across them. This simple structure created a spine that all the other rafters could adhere to like ribs. As the sheet lumber went across them, the roof was essentially finished, and the many cedar shingles were added for waterproofing.

It only took a few hours, but the platform was transformed into a little barn amidst the branches, with a different means of ingress on either side. Declan ate his lunch inside it, looking like a bird with his skinny legs dangling down, his jeans rolled up to his calves and his feet bare.

"So tell me about this boy of yours."

Coughing, Declan blinked down at him. "What boy?"

"The one you like."

"I never said I liked a boy. I admitted I like *boys*. As in the *type* of human."

Carter stretched out on the grass and shoveled a few more chips into his mouth. "Are you kidding? You're like a ... prime target. There's gotta be a boy."

Declan rolled his eyes. "You make it sound like I'm being poached by pedophiles."

"Well . . . actually, but come on, he'd have to be older. I can't see you having patience for kids your own age. You're too mature."

"Most people just think I'm a freak." Declan kicked his feet and leaned his tousled head against the opening. It was a charming image that flew in the face of his words. "Including any boys I might be interested in."

Smiling widely, Carter swiped the sky with his hands as if to paint a vista of romantic infatuation. "Oh, so this is unrequited love we're talking about! The unattainable boy you stare at *longingly* while secretly despising the girls who *flock* to him. He *barely* knows you're alive, maybe he sometimes relies upon you, but that is your *one* contribution to his otherwise *perfect* life. You want to reveal your *feelings*, but *loathe* the idea of upsetting him—"

Declan made a hacking sound. "Your mental theater defaults to melodrama, doesn't it?"

He ignored the jibe. Declan's face was glowing a rosy shade of pink. Carter realized then that it was just as fun, if not more so, to tease him the way he would any girl. There was no manual for how this conversation could go, no convenient biological cues as to who was the pursuer and who the pursued. It was liberating, in a way. Though he would have to be careful, because this boy had an Army-certified paintball gun and knew how to use it.

"Seriously, there *is* a guy, right?"

Declan picked at an invisible spot on his shirt and was clearly trying to come up with an answer that would shut Carter up. As the pause stretched and Carter remained steadfastly fixated on the point, smiling up persuasively, Declan surrendered in a huff.

"Yeah, okay. There's a guy."

"*Ha!*" Carter threw his fist in the air. "I knew it! High school kids are *easy* to read."

Declan scoffed at him, the expression on his face dripping with condemnation. "You are so full of shit. You have no idea what's going on in my head."

"Of course I do." Carter jumped up and attached himself to the end of a rope they'd used to drag the rafters up to the platform. He dangled there, watching the spectacled face surreptitiously. "Doesn't matter what you like or how you like it, you're still a horny teenager who lost his mind at the age of twelve, like the rest of us."

Declan looked away dismissively. "So?"

"So, there's only one way a kid with as much currency as you isn't out flirting with every guy he finds the least bit attractive. You had to already have a guy in mind."

He'd made his little speech, albeit over top of continual sounds of annoyance and disbelief. Declan had fallen backward and was thrashing around on the floor of the treehouse. "What the hell does that mean? 'Currency'?"

"You're cute! With the nerdy charisma thing, and the face. I miss your shaggy hair, but the new look is catchy. There are, like, five freshman girls in love with you."

Declan was a knotted ball on the floor of the enclosed platform, groaning in metaphysical agony. "No, there aren't!"

"There are! I've seen them making goofy eyes at you. I'll bet there's at least one boy who finds you alluring."

"Why are guys so *awkward*?" Declan moaned.

"You're a guy, aren't you?"

"I never asked to be."

Carter laughed, noting that Declan's legs had stopped kicking, as if he'd finally given up on trying to control the conversation. "So tell me about this unattainable boy! Is he handsome?"

"Aren't they always in the fairy tales?"

"Usually, unless they're cursed."

Declan snorted. "A curse would glance off him. He'd somehow manage to convince the universe an unfair mistake had been made, and that it really didn't mean him any harm."

Chuckling, Carter shook his head. "Sounds like my kind of guy! Smart?"

"Too smart for his own good."

"Hmm, I like him more and more. Funny?"

"Sometimes," Declan mumbled. "When he isn't posturing."

"Posturing?" Carter swung from the tree, his arms hooked through a loop. "What does that mean?"

"You should know. You're an expert."

His brows shot up, but Declan began putting all his tools away and vanished back into the birdhouse. Tugging arm over arm, Carter gained the end of the platform and ducked inside. That word bothered him, because to him, it sounded an awful lot like *fake*.

"I'm serious, Dex. What's that mean?"

Declan didn't look around. Shoving the drill into the toolbox, he set his shoulders. "It means you're constantly putting up a front, playing to or with people's expectations. You almost never just confront a person or a situation honestly."

He thought of Taggert's slimy face and again felt the urge to punch it. "That's not true! I'm always honest."

"That's like saying a samurai is just a dude. He's a dude, sure, but he's a dude wearing a crap-load of serious armor, and a helmet he's perfumed so his severed head won't stink."

"Are you saying I wear armor?"

Carter stared at him, knowing in a deep way that Declan was right, but not sure how it could be changed. Without armor, every day would be excruciating, every situation the emotional equivalent of a burning building.

Declan lowered the box to the ground and hit him with a disbelieving glance. "That bragging bullshit you pull is armor. Every time there's an opportunity to deflect something difficult, you do it. You make some joke, and instantly the issue isn't so horrible, because it's just ricocheted off the side of your ego like a bullet. You trick people into thinking you can handle everything and that they should trust you. Even when you can't."

Mouth hanging open, Carter's brain stalled and rebooted. Hearing it explained that way made it so obvious. He'd always done it as a reflex, a way of making other people feel better, because they would laugh at him or with him, and forget to be upset. And then the difficulty, whatever it was, was his to handle. For some reason, he'd always assumed that no one was really paying any attention to his bluster. Then Layla had appeared, resistant to his coping mechanisms but still attracted to him, and now there was this kid.

"Why should it matter? People like to feel better—"

"But not at your expense, Carter! You don't need to run ahead of everyone like a shield! You don't need to make everyone's life level and plumb. Sometimes you have to look them in the eye and say, 'I don't know what to do.' People *need* to do things for themselves."

He took in Declan's determined expression, his hands on his narrow hips, and found himself glad he had such friends. This boy had tremendous insight, incredible understanding, and he refused to allow Carter to hide.

"That's what Layla said," he whispered.

"Well . . . it's the truth."

"My mom too."

"She's right."

Carter smiled, leaning against the wall in the breeze, feeling refreshed and somehow better for the scolding. "You really are a genius."

Declan deflected the compliment with a wave. "It's so obvious, I could be blind and have the IQ of a muppet and I'm pretty sure I'd see it."

Carter eyed him. "And now we see your armor. It's a nice set. Don't notice it unless you compliment the person wearing it. Camouflaged."

Declan refused to look at him, his eyes fixed on the leafy canopy that surrounded them. "Whatever."

"Turnabout is fair play. Whenever there's a chance you might stand out, whenever anyone hints that you're exceptional, you slam down that visor like you're about to take on a dragon. Why, Dex?"

He swallowed and shook his head. "Won't make sense to someone like you."

That stung. Carter took a deep breath. "Kids are better at seeing *different*. Better than adults. So when your parents see a normal boy who does normal things, the kids at school see a gay nerd. That's two separate weaknesses they can target. Your family doesn't understand why anyone would want to use you as a human punching bag, and even if they're supportive, it doesn't help anything, because the torture goes on and you still can't change who you are. And if you could, they wouldn't let you."

Declan's fingers snaked up behind his glasses and poked at the tears forming there. "You're pretty smart."

"I'm a politician."

"Good at spotting weaknesses, huh?"

Carter shrugged, but it was true. He encountered the world as a series of measurements, and people were usually easily quantified. But Declan defied that, and it was important that Carter make him understand.

"You're more than those labels, Dex. I know you know that, because you're starting to come out of your shell. Those kids that picked on you, they were looking for flaws in the armor. You can't have flaws if you don't have armor. If you *own* everything that you are, I mean *really* own it . . . no one will be able to find a way to use it *against* you. Then it's a weapon, and you're on the offensive."

Declan looked up at him, and there was a moment when they were two people enjoying a perfect instant of truth, when they were neither more nor less than they should be. A skinny arm lifted, presenting Carter with a fist. Without a word, he bumped it, and counted himself one moment closer to his goal.

Chapter 20
The Hero

Carter glanced at Declan in the passenger seat and wondered what he was thinking. He had a face that went utterly still anytime he was uncomfortable or preoccupied. He would suddenly become a porcelain statue, irises hardening to little slate chips behind his glasses. The only clue he was ever going to open his mouth on one of his profound little asides was a slight twitch of his upper lip. Carter found himself looking for those often, with the result that conversations were like a sparring match of feints and parries.

Declan sat there, staring straight ahead, absorbing his plan. Carter would have to prod to get a reaction.

"They have to give me five minutes. It's in the bylaws. If she can get me enough signatures, I might be able to make the case."

The Goat leaned forward and chewed over his answer. "Aren't there *real* laws? I mean, they can't actually do this, can they?"

"They can unless someone challenges them."

Hunter was ambivalent as usual. "I don't see why it's your problem. It's like *two* people in the whole school."

Declan's mouth finally twitched. "Some people would say that the suffering of one person is enough of a reason."

"Those people have lots of time on their hands."

"There were almost twenty people in the club. A rational person might assume that there may be a larger number of LGBTQ+ people and supporters on campus who *don't* come out because they see this kind of discrimination."

"We all have problems."

Declan's mask began to slip. "Do your problems include being beaten and dehumanized because you *love* someone? Love is supposed to be a happy thing."

"So tell them to fuck off."

"There's no peace even if you do. Any relationship a gay person has in that kind of environment is doomed to fail because of constant stress! Hatred is toxic for everyone."

"Maybe I'm missing something," Andre interrupted, diffusing the argument in his characteristically humorous tone, "but isn't religion separated from public schools?"

"Theoretically," Declan mumbled. "That's what was on the brochure."

"So why is Bambi Weatherton's God-club okay, but the Rainbow Corps isn't?"

Carter passed Andre a sardonic glance in the rearview. "Good question."

"Last week she wore a T-shirt with a rainbow on it that had been crossed out. The shirt was okay because she was exercising free speech, but the thing she was saying was just 'Hey, those other people shouldn't have free speech.' But queer people are the problem because they might teach us to accept one another for who we are?"

Shaking his head, Carter remembered the superior look on Bambi's face. That girl had problems. "We should start a hypocrisy club and take note of how *few* people join. That'd be the club's one contribution to the academic dynamic."

Declan snorted into his hand, his elbow propped against the doorframe.

"It's fucked up. And all that aside, why does the school get to tell us what clubs we can't have? It's our class, isn't it?" The Goat punched Carter's shoulder with a fist. "I say you do it. Get the petition thing and go call 'em out."

Carter parked the Charger and opened the trunk. Declan retrieved his rifle with a stern expression carved into his effeminate features. Carter could tell from the homicidal glare in his eye that somebody was going to get shot in the faceplate before the end of the day.

"You look like you want to chow down on some calamari."

Declan shrugged. "It's got five grams of protein per ounce."

"I did *not* know that." Carter chuckled. "You play with your food, Cat-boy?"

Declan gave him a sultry smirk. "Meow."

The Squid Army was already at the gate in matching gear, little eight-limbed paintballers patched onto their shoulders like insignia.

Carter had encountered Spencer Barrett before, and shared the Goat's distaste. It was one thing to win, another thing to win with a shitty attitude, and Spencer was the walking definition of bad sportsmanship. Carter felt somewhat enthusiastic about the prospect of kicking his ass, if only for bragging rights. It'd be all over both campuses inside of a day.

A battle was taking place on the obstacle course, running up against the maximum time limit before a draw was called by the range master. They would have to wait in sight of their adversaries for at least a while. Carter found Declan at a picnic table, generally looking skinny and unassuming but for the ferocious look in his eyes. He tousled Declan's hair and watched him react as stiffly as usual, with a glance of annoyance.

"Don't mess with me, I'm psyching myself up."

"Yeah. Let's face it, you're about as terrifying as Grumpy Cat, and you probably purr too."

"I tried purring once. I hated it."

"Nobody likes to purr alone. You're supposed to have help with that." He poked Declan's protected ribs.

"You're gonna get decked right in the pucker."

Carter leaned close and brushed Declan's ear with his mouth. "That just means it's working."

He flinched. "What's working? Your rejection beam?"

"My supernatural charm. You'll punch me, sure. You'll be okay for a week, maybe two, sure. But then a month later, you'll dream about me, and then it's all over."

Declan dropped his goggles into place. "Are you trying to make me lust after you as a testament to your own virility, or are you brave enough to actually *follow through*? Because I'm dangerous when I want something and can't have it."

The edge to Declan's voice caught his rough emotions and wore through. The honesty and promise there reminded Carter it was not a game, and there were consequences to toying with affections. Lesson learned, eyebrows in his hairline, he was made bashful.

It couldn't have had worse timing.

"Goat, right?" Spencer slithered over. "They call you that because you smell like one?"

"Shit." Declan slid down from the table and leaned against it, his rifle already prepped for combat. His eyes darted around the staging area as if getting the lay of the terrain in anticipation of a fight.

As would be expected, the Goat stood up to his formidable height and met the quarterback in a macho standoff. "At least they don't call me a douchebag."

Spencer had a weapon similar to Declan's, and judging by the look on Declan's face, it was just as formidable. Carter watched in confusion as the boy unclipped his utility belt and bipod, and laid them out on the table beside him.

"Are you one of those fainting goats?" Barrett continued. "When it starts to get loud are you gonna curl up your toes?"

Declan unslung the rifle and shoved his hands in his pockets. With a resolute huff, he was away from the table and in the vicinity of the confrontation. "Goat has a nickname as a term of endearment, because he has these things called *friends*, which incidentally, only laugh when your jokes are funny, instead of howling when you sound like a fourth grader."

The rest of the Squids fell silent. Barrett's ire was redirected. He looked down at the diminutive junior and made a face. "Who the fuck are you?"

"The team captain."

"You chose a middle schooler as your team captain?"

The peanut gallery went back to their merriment at his expense, but Declan was unfazed. He waited in uncanny silence for them to finish their little laugh and then tilted his head. When he finally spoke, it was in a voice Carter didn't recognize, so self-possessed and precise it gave him goose bumps.

"Maybe you should ask yourself why they did, before you antagonize me."

Barrett abandoned the Goat for what appeared to be a weaker opponent. Spotting the wicked smile, Carter shifted uncomfortably, certain this was going to get out of hand quickly.

"Dex—"

"I'm fine, Carter."

"But—"

"I suggest you leave my team alone, Spencer."

Barrett had a cruel gleam in his eye. "What are you going to do about it, you pathetic midget? You're built like a girl and probably a faggot."

Even Hunter pulled free of his customary dispassion as their group stood up in a body. Accusations like that, while ridiculous out of context, were the kind of incendiary that got people hurt. But Declan put them at ease with a chuckle.

"Are you flirting with me? Stick to that sidearm of yours when we tangle. It's probably more reliable."

"Burn." Andre snorted.

A weird rage was building behind Spencer's eyes. He invaded Declan's bubble. "You think I won't fuck you up, you little piece of shit?"

Carter looked on admiringly as Declan shrugged.

"You gonna do that before or after foreplay? Because I have needs."

Several things happened simultaneously, so quickly Carter barely had enough time to react. He was grinning proudly, and then all of a sudden, Barrett had punched Declan squarely across the face. Declan staggered, the Goat and Hunter jumped in alarm, and the Squid captain's fancy paintball gun clattered to the ground. He rushed Declan again, but before Carter could tap in, Declan stood up into the second punch and performed some kind of magic trick.

It looked as if he'd simply taken the charging boy's hand and guided him in a lazy arc. Then Spencer was on the ground looking up at the sky. Cussing, he scrabbled to his feet and took another swing. This time, Declan ducked and gave two sharp jabs to his ribs, immediately behind the breastplate. When Spencer folded in half, the boy cut him down to size with an elbow to the face. He bashed his boot up between Spencer's legs, and sent him to the ground in agony.

"Don't worry about those." Declan spat. A fat dollop of blood splattered the ground. "You weren't using 'em anyway."

"I'm gonna . . . fucking kill you," Spencer rasped, dragging himself up, covered in dirt and bleeding from a cut above his eye.

"Give it a shot, sweetness."

He staggered forward like some kind of zombie, egged on by shouts from his cohorts, but as soon as he was within range, Dex's fist caught him right in the nose and put him down. It had ended as most fistfights did, anticlimactically, with the spectators staring at each other and wondering who was supposed to look after whom.

The victor let out a dramatic sigh. "Why do people always assume that because I'm gay, I can't kick their asses? See, this is why prejudice is dangerous."

Carter's fears vanquished, he stood there in amazement as the larger, stronger pugilist slowly pulled free of unconsciousness. Andre was laughing like a hyena. The Goat had his drunken grin in place. Declan, however, had his hands on his knees and was still spitting blood. Catching him by the collar, Carter tilted his face. Red goop was oozing from the boy's chin to the front of his armor. A huge gash had split his lower lip on the left side, turning the girlish mouth into pulp.

"We better clean you up."

Declan jerked his head away. "It's just blood."

"It'll get infected."

He shot Carter a look. "Yeah, okay, Mom."

But when he dragged Declan to the bathroom and propped him against the sink, there was no protest. Declan was shaking with adrenaline and was patient as Carter mopped up the red slime. His breathing was slow and controlled, and he seemed to be gritting his teeth.

Carter cleared his throat. "Where'd you learn to fight like that?"

The expression darkened. "When you get picked on your whole life you either run or fight."

"It's fucked up that you had to do either."

"I wouldn't be who I am if I hadn't, and I like who I am. Or I'm starting to."

Carter shook his head in amusement. "You're too tiny to go into every situation with a death wish!"

Declan's eyes rolled. "Size has nothing to do with ferocity. Small people have the right to defend themselves too."

"Yeah, but it won't work out well if the brains don't compensate for brawn."

Carter took advantage of his open mouth and captured his lower jaw. Probing behind the gash with a tentative thumb, he jiggled each tooth. Declan's stony eyes were watching his face closely, his tongue conspicuously tucked up in his mouth as if denying this moment had *any* eroticism to it *whatsoever*.

"Well, he didn't knock out any teeth."

"That's because he's a weak-wristed fuck who fights with his mouth."

Declan tipped away and spat more blood into the sink, only to have his face stolen from him again. His breath smelled like bubble gum and tin. As Carter pressed a thumb on either side of the split skin to staunch the flow, he became acutely aware of how close they were, the feel of Declan's skin beneath his hands, that his mouth was right there. A tugging warmth was spreading down through his belly, toward his legs.

Carter cleared his throat. "You lack the instinct of self-preservation."

"Please! The only way that kid could scare me is if he asked me out on a date."

"You could have gotten hurt much worse."

"Maybe . . . but I've been hurt before. It's nothing new. Remember strategy? You wanted to crush Squid. Well, trust me, okay?"

The bathroom door opened before he could confront the impish wink, and the range master stepped in.

"Sorry about that, Scott," Declan greeted.

The man shrugged. "You had your hands in your pockets when he hit you. Pretty obvious how that shit went down."

"He okay?"

"Don't give a good goddamn. They only started coming here a couple months ago, and I've already given them numerous warnings about range etiquette. I have a no-tolerance policy for off-range aggression. So . . . they're permanently banned."

Declan flicked a knowing look his way. "So what do we do about the stats?"

"As far as I'm concerned, they forfeited. You guys are facing off with the champions three weeks from now. Come over to the target line, and your team can have a couple comp hours to blow off some steam. Sorry about the bullshit."

"No problem!"

The man vanished, and Carter blinked at Declan in surprise. "You know him?"

"I'm here a lot. Sometimes help out."

There was just no anticipating this kid. Declan had to be the quickest-witted and most perplexing individual Carter had ever encountered. He'd come out of nowhere, as if he'd been hiding behind his mop of hair for years, gathering intelligence and formulating a plan to infiltrate Carter's group and become indispensable.

"You knew that asshole was going to hit you!" he whispered.

Declan smiled lopsidedly, and didn't pull away when Carter cupped his face and plugged the cut with a dry towel. "He's a prick. That's generally what they do."

"You didn't have to let him."

"Carter, he was packing a Tiberius Arms T9.1 First Strike."

"That's bad, I'm assuming."

"It's a seven-hundred-dollar piece of hardware with a *minimum* F-P-S of three hundred, accurate at more than forty yards because it has a rifled barrel and proprietary ammo! They're barely range-legal. If we'd gone on against him, Andre would be missing an ear by the time we were finished!"

Carter's mouth fell open. "You cheated! You provoked him! So they'd forfeit!"

"'To fight and conquer in all your battles is not supreme excellence; supreme excellence consists in breaking the enemy's resistance without fighting.' Sun Tzu. I let Spencer be a fuck-wad. If he was smart, he'd learn not to be so good at it."

Declan finally tired of Carter's ministrations and wrenched free, marching out to meet his soldiers with a sly look in his eye. Bracing himself against the sink, Carter glanced from the pool of blood to the mirror. The young man staring back at him had a haunted look in his cobalt eyes, because he recognized this feeling too.

It felt like taking a punch, right in the pit of the stomach.

Chapter 21
The King

Carter appeared beside Declan's locker wearing a royal blue T-shirt and a black bow tie. The cat ears Yuki had given him had reappeared, and though Carter looked ridiculous, not a single person seemed to care. In fact, he got several thumbs-ups and choruses of approval as Declan stared on in shock.

"What fresh hell is this?" He slammed his locker closed.

Carter reached up and tweaked the bow tie around Declan's neck. He'd gotten rather good at tying them since Delia had convinced him to keep them as a signature element, but it always seemed to need straightening.

"Bow ties are cool," Carter said.

"Since when?"

"Since Andre Parker told the entire school that you knocked Spencer Barrett on his ass."

"Oh, Glob."

Declan froze as Carter took his face in hand and carefully examined the busted lip. It still stung, keeping him up most of the night, but as long as he didn't play with it, it would heal. Carter appeared to agree, and released him just as several students began to throw suggestive glances. Declan's heart fluttered, and he felt as if the hallway had suddenly gotten much warmer, but he busied himself with his bag.

"The story has been told and retold, embellished and embroidered." Carter was grinning his most adorable smile, and though Declan wanted to be angry or self-conscious, he could not.

"You're the official school mascot at this point, with the Homecoming game so close."

A contingent of the basketball team swept by in a flurry at that exact moment. Declan's carefully mussed hair got tamped down by at least five hands, and it felt like he might get whiplash. Carter scattered them with a bevy of enthusiastic high fives.

"See? Cat-boy is King! Or whatever kind of leader you'd prefer."

Declan rolled his eyes, but secretly enjoyed a moment of pride. "Did he tell everyone *why* I did it?"

Carter's sidelong glance was like an electric arc. "Yup. You may take some shit for it, but Chloe's cause went from the back burner to the talk of the school because, apparently, gay people get stereotyped. Imagine that."

With a shrug, he slung his bag over his shoulder. "Always play the long game."

The bell rang. Carter fretted with Declan's hair, carefully reworking the little spikes, then split. He got more compliments for his costume as he sauntered to class, leaving a confused and frustrated Declan in his wake.

He had assumed that when he stopped trying to pass as female, it would get easier to deal with Carter. He would say hello occasionally, maybe share a few secrets about a video game, adore Carter in silence. Carter would ignore him, forget about Layla, and move on to college. That was how it was supposed to go, but it was quickly being proven wrong. He felt more and more as if the young man missed the honesty of being with Layla, and was searching for a way to recover it. Perhaps Declan was in some way standing in for his own girlish alter ego.

It was getting seriously confusing.

Declan walked into his first class, shaking his head in wonder, and was greeted by an explosive round of applause. As he slid into his seat, smiling in spite of himself, a boy leaned over.

"Did you really knock Singer Valley's quarterback unconscious because he called you a fag?"

He'd been sure this would happen. Confusion was certain to abound when rumor hit the high school telephonic landscape. It was time to fish or cut bait. Bravery was about what a person said or did in the times when it might be hardest to stay strong.

Declan leaned back, his voice clear and concise. "No. This *fag* beat the shit out of Singer Valley's quarterback because he was an arrogant bully. This *fag* hates bullies. And B-T-dubs, he also hates the word *fag*."

The class was called to order. Declan endured the looks and whispers, flicking his battle wound with his tongue any time he needed a reminder. He was done being picked on. He was finished being a joke. And because he was, it seemed like everyone else was too.

By the end of second period, Declan counted at least seven more bow ties, two made of paper, and one a sticker. By lunch, Chloe was wearing one that matched her suspenders and was having tremendous success with her petition. She sat at Yuki's lunch table and leafed through the three full pages of signatures she'd managed to acquire.

"The school has about five hundred students. Carter says that if I can get the signatures of at least one hundred and fifty of them, he'll go to the school board himself. There are eighty here!"

His glowing reply was stifled by a sudden blanket of warmth as Carter's arms wrapped around him and took hold of Chloe's clipboard.

"Eighty-one! I haven't signed yet!" he said, plumbing the depths of Declan's ear with his playful voice.

"Get off me, Carter!"

"Aw, but why? You're so cuddly when your claws aren't out!"

He finished signing, but remained draped across Declan's shoulders like an exhausted sloth. Yuki's weeby fangirls giggled at the obvious flirtation, but knowing he had an audience would only bolster Carter's silliness. Declan jabbed him hard in the ribs and gave him a sharp look.

"People will talk."

Carter shrugged and stole a bite of his chocolate cake. "Let 'em. I'll sic my vicious Cat-boy on 'em."

"I'm not *your* Cat-boy."

"Then whose are you? I call dibs. I'll need a bodyguard for the Homecoming game, once this gets around Singer Valley."

Declan made noises, but there was no way to dissuade him. He was glued to Declan's side for the rest of lunch, and even walked him to his next class, all smiles and thinly veiled flirtation. By the time he was sealed up in his classroom, Declan was so red in the face and breathless, the teacher asked if he was feeling okay.

More bow ties began to manifest on kids he'd never met. Hands flew out of nowhere to slap his back or fluff his hair. He'd flinched so many times he was starting to think he had PTSD, and every time he glanced at his reflection, he looked as if he'd stuck his finger in a light socket while huffing glue. He was beginning to understand why Carter hated popularity. It *was* soul-sucking.

His library period was a dream come true. Declan took a deep breath and perched himself on his stool behind the counter, bathing in the scent of old bindings. Then his sister's literature class waltzed in to work on their first research papers and ruined it.

The teacher had to whistle to get attention, because so many of his students were meowing and ostentatiously fingering their bow ties. Delia had on a pink one, whispering to her mixed bag of friends that she was his sister.

The Goat approached as soon as the students were turned loose, and hopped up on the counter to present his tie. "Dude, like my Superman?"

Sighing, Declan buried his face in his arms. "It's lovely."

"Haven't worn it since second grade. Had to pin it to my shirt."

"Why did you bring it?"

"Carter called me last night. He's great at this school spirit stuff."

Declan let out a long sigh. "Where are theirs coming from?"

"Student Council room. Brown paper bag inside the door."

His head snapped up. The Goat was grinning effusively.

It was as if that charming young man was trying to drag him out of obscurity and into the limelight. Was he lonely? Could Carter be orchestrating some large-scale manipulation to make him the face of Chloe's rebellion? If so, Declan wasn't sure he wanted the acclaim. But the more he thought about their conversation in the treehouse, the more he became certain that this was Carter's way of refusing to let him hide inside his own weaknesses. This was Carter pushing him to live up to his potential, probably with Delia's fashion help. This smacked of her thrift store savvy.

The teacher and Ms. Folger disappeared into the recesses of the library, helping several students find research books on obscure topics. The noise volume around the front tables slowly grew as more joking and gossiping was done than studying.

As if she'd been awaiting the chance to cause trouble, Bambi lifted her voice above the others. "I told her I wouldn't sign that piece of garbage, and that I plan on circulating a petition against the Rainbow Corps or whatever they're calling it."

A hush descended. Declan's pulse kicked into high gear. Most of the students glanced his way.

His mom had once compared teenagers to shipwreck victims floating in the ocean. Most of them would glom onto anything that floated by. Apparently, the politics of high school depended upon being able to recognize this fact and capitalize on it.

One of her minions let out a derisive noise. "Is Carter really going to protest the school board's decision?"

"Probably." Bambi shrugged her shoulder haughtily. "Everyone knows he's only doing it to stay popular with the freaks, because there's so many of them around here."

Delia's head cocked toward the sickly sweet voice, her face raging. Her eyes locked with Declan's and he knew she was about to go postal. There was one thing a person should never do in front of Delia, and that was disrespect her friends.

"If he does," Bambi was saying, "I plan on bringing my own sign in support of the board."

Delia's mouth fell open, but Declan beat her to it. Chloe wanted a poster child? The other kids wanted to know whom they should follow? Well, he already had a split lip. And he was fierce in a bow tie.

"Why don't you nail together a giant crucifix and drag that around, Bambi, so that everyone gets the message loud and clear?"

If anyone had walked into the library at that exact moment, they would have sworn this was the best behaved group of students in history. Not the whisper of breathing was heard. It could have been a class of mannequins psychically writing a paper on petrification for all the life they exhibited.

"Excuse me?" That Bambi managed to make two words sound like an entire dictionary of insults being read in one breath was pretty amazing.

"You heard me."

She turned in her seat and fixed him with a menacing stare. "Just because you punched out a football player, doesn't mean God will forgive—"

"Aren't you *so* pious because you hate an entire group of people!" Declan flipped a few pages in his textbook and tried to look bored, though his body was surging with adrenaline. This was the kind of battle Carter had been talking about, and it was time to turn his armor into a weapon. "Maybe a teenager shouldn't try to decide what an omniscient deity will forgive."

Her face flushed, and her arms pressed to her sides as she gained her feet and turned on him. "The Bible forbids men to lie down with men—"

"It also forbids pants and pork. Noticed you crammed yourself into skinny jeans this morning so that you could deep-throat Oscar Mayer over lunch."

The room snickered as a body. Bambi searched the faces around her, glancing from scorn to amusement at her expense, desperate to find a life raft. But the majority was against her, and the few drifting minds must have taken in the bow ties and known not to say a damn thing.

One of her friends spoke up. "Eating pork is hardly the same thing—"

"As loving someone in spite of all the prejudice, hostility, and degradation society hurls at you? You're right, they're not the same thing at all." Declan removed his glasses and pinched his nose. "You either believe what the Bible says or you don't. Religion isn't a salad bar."

The Goat's low laugh peppered the shelves around them like a machine gun. "Salad bar . . . nice."

Bambi looked two seconds away from meltdown. "I hope you know you're going to hell."

But Declan had had enough. He stood up on one of the stool rungs and settled his glasses back in place. He had the psychological high ground of the library check-out desk and an annoyed Goat haunting the edge of it like a gargoyle.

"I'll see you there."

"Oh yeah—"

"Bambi, your outfits are right out of magazines, your makeup is put on with a straight edge, your hair makes NASA jealous in its precision."

"Well . . ." She fell silent, apparently unsure how to argue with someone who was evidently complimenting her.

"Makes me wonder what you're hiding."

The Goat hopped down off the counter. "Well, that's obvious! She worries she doesn't have any other valuable qualities, so she makes fun of people who do, and tries to make sure they can't say anything back. It's kind of stupid, really."

Declan smirked, hearing Layla's conditioning in that reply. Bambi's eyes were liquefying, and she'd lost her voice. This was a moment of weakness for her, and all she needed was a final blow. There was something to be said for killing people with kindness.

"You have many . . . wonderful traits . . . I'm sure, Bambi. The *least* of which are your looks. If you spent half as much time on your personality as you do in the mirror, people might actually *like* you as a person instead of using you as a powder-pink battering ram to popularity."

With a single whimper, Bambi flew out of the library as if chased. Her gaggle of idiots were smart enough to let her go alone. They sat at the table, looking at each other in embarrassment as Declan commanded his pulse back to a normal pace.

It was the finest irony that bullies thought they were winning at life, when all they were doing was training their targets to be stronger and more ferocious. The more he faced them, the more Declan learned how to recognize their tricks and turn them around with a little mental martial skill.

The rest of the period saw the class working quietly and wishing him a good day as they left the library. But as he walked toward the locker room for PE, Declan found himself nursing a wicked case of dread. What would the other boys say? Would they get awkward about dressing with him there? He stood outside the door, shifting from foot to foot and wondering how Carter would handle the situation. Something told Declan that he would do just fine.

As the clock ticked toward the tardy bell, Declan took a huge breath and ducked inside. Making a beeline for his locker, he raced along the aisle. As anticipated, the silence crept behind him until the entire room was a living, breathing hush. Declan closed his eyes, certain someone was about to make a disparaging comment, but not a word was spoken.

It wasn't enough to pretend like nothing would bother him. They could see through that defense. He couldn't very well face an entire class of combatants, either. The only way to fix the problem was to confront it honestly and take what came. Then, at least, the enemies were known and could be handled. With a nod to himself, hands shaking and stomach lurching, he turned and found a group of boys all wearing PE clothes and decorative bow ties.

Relieved, Declan fell against the lockers. What would Carter do? That was easy.

"I know it's on your minds, so let me get it over with. I'm not the least bit attracted to any of you. In fact, even if I had harbored some small crush, being in this room every day pretty much cured me of it."

Hunter was stretched out on a bench, throwing a volleyball up in the air and catching it. To Declan's surprise, he, too, was wearing a bow tie. "What? You mean our sweaty pits and athletes foot don't do it for you?"

"Not hardly. It's something I suffer through for people I care about."

"Well, I guess being gay really isn't a choice, because who the fuck would choose that?"

An explosive laugh echoed off the tile, and Declan breathed a shaky sigh. It probably wasn't the last word on it; he'd likely get picked on at some point in the future when the gossip about his fisticuffs with Barrett passed from memory, and not all of the boys in his class seemed keen or comfortable, but . . . he'd take it. It was almost like a miracle, because at St. Cat's, PE was like the designated "flirt with the gay boy through aggression and hate speech" hour. And the last period of the day was usually the "Dex sits in the office and hears why he's to blame for how others treat him" hour.

As they filed out to join the girls on the volleyball green, Hunter fell in beside him. "I don't usually care about all this school-spirit shit."

"You know, I couldn't tell that about you, Hunter."

The boy chuckled. "I'm not wearing this stupid tie because you busted Barrett's nose."

"No?"

"I'm wearing it for my friend Drey. She went to Singer Valley, until she got picked on so much by his crew that she finally had to go on homeschooling."

"Is she a lesbian?"

Hunter shrugged. "I'm not sure if she knows what she is. I think she wants to be a boy."

Declan's heart tugged. He felt that plight deep down in his soul. "She was one of the *two* people at her school, huh, Hunter?"

He gave a sheepish kick at the grass. "Sorry about that. I guess I thought there wasn't really anything we could do."

"So why bother?"

"Yeah."

Declan got into the line to serve. "Sure we *might* lose. But if you never fight, you *definitely* lose. And then cocky quarterbacks get to keep their good looks."

"That'd be a damn travesty." Hunter laughed and tossed the ball into the game.

Chapter 22
The Announcement

Carter looked at the clock. Each second felt like an eternity, but it was essential that he wait for the exact moment. Jose glanced at him, his hand hovering above the controls. The sound booth was like a mechanically enhanced cocoon, and the air was getting close.

"You sure you know what you're doing?"

He reassured the junior with a firm grip on his shoulder, but inside, Carter was writhing in anxiety. He would have precisely three minutes, if Taggert ran at top speed, but that paunch he was nursing might buy spare seconds. He pictured Chloe's face as she collapsed on the floor of the restroom, her girlfriend Anne clutching her. He pictured Declan's blood in the sink. The rage returned. He needed to hold on to those images if he was going to make this count.

"Thanks, dude. You're gonna want to bounce."

Jose got to his feet and looked back at him from the door. "Aren't you scared?"

"Sure. But being brave doesn't mean not being scared. It means doing what's right even when you are."

"Good luck, man."

"See you at the meeting?"

"Yeah. I'll come."

He took a seat and leaned toward the mic. One last deep breath to carry him through. As the door closed on the sound booth, Carter started the stopwatch.

"Good afternoon, fellow students!" He paused so that the teachers could halt their lectures for his unplanned interruption. "This is the fantastic Carter Aadenson, your duly elected Student

Council President! As many of you may be aware, the council met today to begin organizing this year's Homecoming Ball! I'd like to announce our chosen theme and the finalists for Homecoming King and Queen!"

So far so good. Chances were Taggert was standing out by the football bleachers, bemusedly listening to the speakers and wondering if he'd okayed Carter to use the PA.

His memory was again flooded by Chloe's tears, and a grim smile spread across his lips.

"First, the nominees! It's really no surprise I was nominated, so I'll leave myself off the list for the sake of modesty."

He allowed three seconds for the joke to drop, and then launched into the list of names. Delia's featured prominently among the girls; she'd been nominated by three separate clubs, and the Senior Class Rep. She was a shoo-in, really. Everyone loved her. She was friendly, fearless, feminine. It was a shame he had to cast a shadow over her well-deserved spotlight. But he was positive she'd understand.

"I think we all know that our athletic match-up with Singer Valley has ended badly for us the last couple of years, but thanks to a prizefighter Cat-boy in the junior class, I'm fairly certain this year's game will have a happy ending. Therefore, the theme for this year's ball is 'Fairy Tales!' Tickets go on sale this week! Come as your favorite princess! Wear a coat and tails! Arrive in a pumpkin coach if you're feeling fancy!"

He paused and made a leap of faith.

"Enjoy Singer Valley's imminent defeat, and do so in the comfortable knowledge that your school district has banned same-sex couples from participating."

A four-count nailed the severity of the issue. He glanced at the clock. Not much time left. Taggert would have launched into action, running like a sweaty bat out of hell for the PA room. Carter did a triumphant little spin in the chair, because even if he was caught now, the seed had been planted.

"Yes, that's right, my friends. Principal Taggert called several students into his office today and formally *uninvited* them, adding their names to a list formerly occupied exclusively by students with disciplinary problems. Your school district has singled out some of our best, and informed them that they are prohibited from setting foot on the premises, even if they should come stag. Why, you ask? Because they are openly gay and may end up dancing with someone of whom Principal Taggert disapproves."

He nodded. He'd remembered to pick up the dreaded prepositional phrase. That book on rhetoric he'd read in AP Government class had really paid off.

"I'm sure many of you have heard by now that the LGBTQ+ club, affectionately called the Rainbow Corps, was disbanded, and that I had planned to petition the school board for the right to have the club reinstated. Unfortunately, this devastating display of discrimination has reared its ugly head, so as you can imagine, I am tabling that petition. Which was probably part of the reason they did it."

He had anywhere from thirty seconds to a minute, depending on when Taggert took to his heels. Carter leaned over the microphone and gave his voice over to his true anger.

"I will be attending the board meeting tomorrow evening at six, and I hope I can count upon those of you touched by this issue to have my back. Help me tell the district that we are a united student body, and we will not tolerate this. You cannot treat sexuality as if it is a crime. We won't allow it. Principal Taggert, if you're listening, and I know you are . . . It isn't personal, sir. It's just politics."

He flipped the off switch and left the chair spinning as he sped out of the room and down the hall. At the main corridor, he collided with a small shape hurtling over the linoleum. Catching his breath, he held the person out at arm's length. It was the fetching Cat-boy, his horn-rimmed glasses askew. Without a word, Carter snatched his hand and raced toward the parking lot. The bell rang right as they reached the car, their escape covered by the hordes of teenagers spilling out the doors.

He didn't breathe easy until they sat at a red light almost two miles from campus. Pressing his forehead to the steering wheel, he let out a whoosh. Declan was a porcelain statue of resolve. When the light turned green, he settled a delicate hand on Carter's back.

"I cannot believe you did that. It was amazing."

Carter flexed his fingers over the wheel and glanced in the rearview with paranoia. "I guess I needed to get angry enough to hulk out."

"Yeah but . . . that joke about politics. That was . . ."

"Never condescend to me," he said darkly. "The outcome is not a good one."

Declan smiled, but there was something forlorn about it. Carter glanced at him and reclined back into his heated seat. He wasn't driving anywhere in particular and, in that moment, decided they needed a break. He steered the Charger to Declan's driveway. Delia's Beetle had not yet arrived, and if their schedules were the same as they'd always been, Declan's parents were still at work.

"I need my Cat-boy fix. Get your gear. Leave a note."

Declan blinked at him but didn't argue. He was back in moments, rifle slung over his shoulder. The drive was free of conversation, as Declan spun tunes from his phone, synced with the stereo. When they reached the range, Carter nearly leapt from the car, his energy was so wound up. He retrieved his weapons from the trunk and led the way to the entrance as if wearing springs on his shoes.

It wasn't until he was stretched out on the sniper platform beside Declan, his sights trained on a target, that calm returned.

"I'm going to get suspended for this."

Dex nailed a flag and glanced at him. "Yeah."

"I was iffy on that last line, but damn it that guy pisses me off."

Declan took another flawless shot, knocking a can off a rail. If he ever joined the military, their collective average would skyrocket. As would their fabulousness quotient.

"What's the point of school, Carter? Is it to keep us busy, or is it to give us the opportunity and logic skills to decide who we want to be?"

"I get you. What's that got to do with this?"

"It's the difference between staying pretty and winning a fight."

His third shot spun a swiveling arm so swiftly that a nearby target got spattered with paint. Carter smiled; going to the range was really an excuse to enjoy Dex's unbelievable talent in action.

He forgot his gun and rolled onto his back to stare at the boy's lip. It was still swollen, but the edges had knitted shut. In a few days, his mouth would be perfectly kissable. He closed his eyes on the thought.

If Layla could hear his mind at this moment, he wondered what she would say. Would she be happy or would she feel betrayed?

She had told him there was no hope for them as a couple, but Carter couldn't decide if that had been because of her own difficulties, or because she thought him incapable of understanding how to make a real relationship work. Either her mantra of "It's not you, it's me" was literal, or she really didn't want to kick this poor lost puppy. Either way, she had vanished, and the boy sitting next to him was a different challenge.

Carter swiped a hand over his face. "You're right. Let's not talk about this anymore."

"What then?"

"I need a distraction."

"I'm game." Declan took a fourth shot. This one made a loud pop as it ricocheted. "Pick a subject."

"Layla."

Declan's rifle went fully auto for a moment as he knocked down a line of targets. "Wondering if you've impressed her?"

"Not at all." He put his arms behind his head and stared up at the carefully trimmed branches swaying in the breeze. "Something she said to me about love. I've been thinking about it a lot lately, what with everything that's been going on."

Declan set the safety and sat up, leaning against the plywood wall. "What did she say?"

"That there was love, and there was chemistry, and that for a romance to grow, you had to have both. At the time, I agreed with her."

"But not anymore?"

He shook his head. He could still feel that strange absence, like losing a limb upon which he'd relied. "I think love is something you can only have if someone shares it with you. Like a handshake. I can hold my hand out, and so can you, but unless you take mine, it's not a shake."

Declan was mute, with the intensity of an army awaiting instructions.

"She talked about loving someone from a distance, without them knowing, kind of the way you deal with your unattainable. But that's not love. It's adoration, or desperation, and it doesn't go anywhere." Carter looked his way. Declan was staring into the distance as if assessing his accuracy. "She made it sound like it was noble, like a person was selfless by not bothering the other with their feelings ... but I really can't get my head around that ... Sorry. Maybe I'm rambling."

"I want to know what you think." Declan's voice had a soft touch. "I think I get what she was saying."

"Yeah, but don't you think your unattainable boy would want to know what he was leaving behind him? Don't you think he'd want to know if he was hurting someone like that? I would."

"You sure about that? If there was nothing you could do to change their mind? Would you really want to spend every day looking at that person and thinking, 'I can't help them,' or 'I can't be free of them'?"

"You sound like my dad." Carter sat up, fixing him with a stare, beneath which Declan began to wither. "I told Layla I loved her, and I don't regret it."

"Even if it scared her off?"

"Yes! To have romance, you have to have chemistry and love, but to have love, I think there has to be affection both ways. It all starts with *mutual affection*. I gave her mine in hopes she would give hers back and we could go from there. I took a chance that was worth it. I was brave for her. Silence never makes things better. It only ever leads to regret, regret leads to suffering, suffering leads to anger ... and that is the path to the dark side."

Declan smiled in approval. "Right."

"I think that by staring at this boy of yours from far away, you're just hurting yourself. There's no resolution. It's like being on pause. When I met Layla, I grew, and when Layla left, I didn't really stop. She made everything ... better. *Because* we got things out."

"Did you move on?"

"I have perspective now."

"Happy for you."

"Look, I realize I'm using your situation with your boy to try and prove my own hypothesis, but I really think you need to tell him. I wanted to set up the dance for you, but I underestimated my enemy. Taggert was a giant bag of dicks, and I didn't have a clue he'd move so quickly. Sorry."

Declan made a noise in his throat and face-palmed. "You're sorry I didn't get the opportunity to be dissed in public? That's okay! Now I'm glad Taggert went Nazi."

Dex was playing it up, but Carter could see the deep wound he was nursing. It couldn't have been easy to get called into the office and belittled for his identity as a person. Especially when there was absolutely nothing about that identity that was anything less than exceptional.

He reached out and fluffed Declan's hair. "It's okay, you know."

"What?"

"To be upset. What Taggert did was despicable. I wish there was a way . . ."

"A way?"

"To show you that the rest of the world isn't that shitty."

"It is, but *you're* pretty okay."

"What . . . you're surprised?"

Declan managed a husky chuckle, but soon fell into a silence punctuated by sniffles. Carter pulled him close and petted him for a while, feeling surer with each touch.

Chapter 23
The Resignation

Delia parked next to Carter's Charger and craned her neck. The pack of dissenters had congealed beside the wheelchair ramp in their purposefully drab color pallet. Declan shared her confusion, wondering why they hadn't already gone inside the boardroom.

"Chloe's pissed." Dee shook her head. "I would be too. I can't believe they're doing this, in the modern era."

"I can, but I'm pessimistic."

She pinched his nose. "On you it's adorbs."

Rolling his eyes, he got out of the car. Chloe and Anne were wearing identical black suits, their twenty-odd cohorts dressed as if for a funeral. There was one banner that read *Discrimination is DEATH.* Delia gave Declan a tight hug and tweaked his black bow tie.

"Have you seen Carter?"

He shook his head. "Does he have to do some kind of check-in with the board?"

Anne still looked miserable, her pretty face pale and withdrawn. "He went ahead and informed the trustees that he'll be taking his five minutes. I saw him like twenty minutes ago. He didn't look optimistic."

Declan's blood ran cold. "That's . . . impossible for me to imagine."

But it really wasn't. It was how he'd appeared after Layla had vanished. Until that day in the library when he'd come to apologize, Carter had had the complexion of a mushroom and an expression so blank it bordered on creepy.

"There was always a chance they'd honor his time as a formality." Delia shoved up her cardigan sleeves. "What do we do in case they refuse to change their minds?"

Priah and Brianna stepped forward, looking positively gothic. They shared a glance.

"We have a plan, but beyond that, I don't know," Brianna replied with a shrug.

"This is fucking stupid!" someone said. "There's nothing we can do!"

Declan looked over the hopeless faces and felt a surge of outrage. There had been a time in his life when he'd been sure that there was no more ground to be gained in this town, but that had changed. If there was one thing he'd learned in the last few weeks, it was that things didn't just get better at some later date. They got better as soon as you made them get better.

Carter was the general, but adoring him as he did, Declan knew a pep talk could only help. He jumped up onto the retainer wall and got everyone's attention with a wave. They turned, depression so obvious it might as well have been written on their banner.

"Think back to that first time, maybe as recent as tonight, when you looked in the mirror and knew who you were. We all remember it, because it's a moment that never fades. You see your face, your body, your dorky smile, or your crooked nose. You see all of that, and then suddenly, you see past it."

Chloe nodded subtly and clasped Anne's hand. Delia took a deep breath.

"That's the difference between us and them. There's no guarantee they've ever in their life looked in the mirror and *known* that they were different, and what that truly meant. But *I know*, by the simple fact that you are all standing here, that you have. We are strong, even when they are cruel and stupid. It's not about age. We are strong because we've had that moment. Think back on it. Remember that no matter what happens tonight, it's still yours. No one can ever take that from you. And no one has the power to undo it."

Heads perked up. Smiles and hugs were exchanged. His spirits lifted as he pulled a leaf from Carter's book.

"What they say tonight cannot dim our fabulousness. It does not change us in any way. So if it all goes wrong, take a deep breath, close your eyes, find that moment. Meet me there. Because if it takes me the next two years of my life . . . I'm not going to let this drop. I can't. That's who I saw in the mirror. Who did you see?"

He hopped down from the soapbox. Delia drew him into a headlock and gave his hair an unholy fluffing. "I love you, kid. When did you get so smart?"

"Always was, just didn't want to rain on your parade."

She snorted and shoved him away. He tumbled into a tall shape and looked up. A blue-eyed gaze blinked down on him affectionately, and a hand reached up and tangled in his curls.

"Nice speech, Cat-boy."

Declan stood up straight and tilted his chin. "Better than yours, I bet."

Carter's smile was taut. "I don't know. I've been working on my big words."

"That part of your 'anti-fake' mission statement?" He crossed his arms.

Carter looked back at the entrance to the boardroom. The community members who had decided to attend were straggling in. It was time to go.

Suddenly, Carter had Declan trussed up in an embrace that bordered on fatal. It was only a few seconds, but it was warm and fierce, and took Declan's breath away. Then he was set back on his feet to trail drunkenly in the young man's wake.

They lined the front-most rows like mourners, their banner stretched out across their laps, their faces masklike. It was an entirely more dignified protest than the situation deserved, but he knew that Carter had a reason. He, too, wore black from head to toe, eyes trained like azure lasers to the president of the board.

As business got under way, Declan snuck little glances at their leader, but Carter did not fidget or leaf through his book of bylaws. He appeared calm, but Declan knew better; in all their stolen moments together, when he'd been a girl in a blue dress, he'd learned Carter's body. The boy was a stiff machine for turning anger into purpose, waiting for his five minutes with his teeth gritted and his fists clenched.

Smiling, Declan tipped back into his seat and uncurled. He should feel nervous, but he couldn't. For the first time in his life, he was truly confident, in a way that relied upon no one. He had everything he needed, and no confirmation or affirmation mattered. No such thing as a permanent record. No more armor.

Only offense.

He pulled his bottom lip into his mouth and ran his tongue over the scab, feeling that sickening sweet pain like a tether to all those past beatings that turned him into this soldier for a cause.

Principal Taggert began the conflict by preempting any statement Carter would have made. The trustees sat through his monologue of platitudes with bobbing heads. Some debate went back and forth about the "concerns" held by the invisible members of the community who wanted their children to be raised in wholesome environments. Mockery was made of Carter's commandeering of the PA system, and a veiled threat manifested that he might face disciplinary action. Carter took it all in complete silence, his gaze flicking to the clock on the wall.

At last, they welcomed him to the podium. He pulled the microphone from its stand, but hesitated. Turning, his eyes met Declan's, and he spared one precious second to flash his cocky grin.

"Good evening, ladies and gentlemen. Thank you for taking the time to hear me out."

The board president nodded dismissively. "You have five minutes, Mr. Aadenson."

"Then let's get right to it without all the flattering fancy talk." He held his smile, but there was a sly look to his eye. "When Principal Taggert made the decision to ban the LGBTQ+ club put forward by Chloe Shannon, I was appalled. I have to admit I was completely shocked that a group organizing itself beneath the auspices of *education* could possibly behave in such a backward or, frankly, disgusting way. I did some research, and I learned some interesting facts."

The trustees shifted in their seats, but their faces were guarded. Declan knew why, and knew that Carter knew too: they had no reason to be defensive of their indefensible position. They had the high ground, their decision final.

Carter turned to his true audience. "I found out that according to the state constitution the school board 'must provide for the education of its pupils without discrimination as to religion, creed, race, color, or national origin.' There is absolutely *no* mention of sexual orientation. In other words, this educational body is within its legal rights to put the mental health of its dependents in jeopardy, create divisive environments in schools, teach children to be hateful and exclude their fellow students. It's all apparently legal! It would be surprising, if not for the fact that this state constitution they hide behind dates from the Cretaceous period."

There was a chuckle.

"The federal government, however, recognizes sexuality as a protected freedom. There's a disparity there, right? But it won't be corrected here, obviously. No matter how much we would appeal to better nature, common sense, or this district's desire to be on the right side of history, it's not going to be solved, because it's not their problem. They're just doing the job the community gave them."

Chloe was shaking, but when Declan wrapped an arm around her narrow shoulders, she grinned.

"What am I trying to say? Really, I'm not sure. I came here with the naive optimism of a child, one of those things you're supposed to be turning into an adult, and realized almost instantly that if this is what adulthood means, I'd rather not. Thanks."

His humor echoed, but the board was clearly losing patience, and Carter was losing time. Declan caught him glance at the clock, ticking away without mercy.

"The truth is, we all know my speech here tonight was pointless. You've made your decision, mostly founded on thinly justified, outdated prejudice, and if there's one thing this kid knows, it's that bullies don't suddenly come to grips with their damage in five minutes of rational conversation."

Delia sucked down a sharp breath, but Declan was wiggling in his seat like a fool. It was the jab behind the armor. Carter was trying to get a rise, so that they would make a fatal mistake, captured forever in their clerk-kept minutes.

"The decision you've made is horrifying, and if it didn't impact the lives of people I care about, I would treat it with exactly the reverence it deserves, and completely ignore it—"

The president of the board interrupted him. "Mr. Aadenson, I think we've heard—"

"The gentleman will yield. The bylaws afford me five uninterrupted minutes, and I intend to take every last second."

The protestors were shivering with pent-up fury, but not a catcall was uttered. There was no time for gavels and angry words, and if there were jibes to be hurled, let it be done by the adults in the room. Carter didn't need their help. He leaned on the podium with a face full of mischievous gallantry, and to Declan's eye looked every inch the handsome prince.

"Being Student Council President, well . . . it's a joke. I knew that when I won the election. I saw it as a nice addition to my portfolio of achievements. It has no teeth, no purpose, and having it makes me nothing more than your ally on paper. Let's be honest, I can put it to better use if I get rid of it, since standing up to institutionalized intolerance looks just as good on a college application. Makes for a fantastic personal statement too, incidentally."

He turned, and five bodies rose amidst the protestors. Priah's chin tilted upward. Brianna squared off with a thumbs-up.

"I, Carter Aadenson, Student Council President, do hereby resign in protest of the board's decision to discriminate against same-sex couples, and I'm taking the rest of the student government with me. We want no part in this."

And turning his back, Carter swaggered down the aisle, the rest of his cabinet falling in behind him. That was when Declan saw the phone being held like a camera by a boy he knew to be a junior from the AV club. It dropped into his black-clad lap, and the fingers flew.

For the rest of the board meeting, their rain cloud clot sat in complete silence, like a panel of judgment. When the mic was opened to the community, Chloe got to her feet and gave a very short speech about what her life had been like before she met Anne. By the time she finished recounting her fear and self-loathing, her thoughts of suicide, and her isolation, there were few dry eyes in the building.

"Anne saved me from that by loving me for who I am. I didn't tell you that story so that you could give me your sympathy or pity. I told you so that you would understand what I would have celebrated, had I been able to ask Anne to that dance. That's what you took from me, and I won't ever forgive you for it."

Declan looked back as she and Anne escaped the building. Carter was standing beside the door and put his arms around her. Declan stepped to the microphone as if pulled by an invisible cord and scratched his head.

"Everything I want to say has been said. I just wanted to tell you that you should be ashamed of yourselves. I really thought that being an adult meant you had to overlook your personal vision for the fate of the world, and sort of . . . I don't know . . . maybe realize that there are billions of people on the planet and that compromise is important, instead of being selfish and threatened that other people have different ways of pursuing happiness." He retreated a pace, and then thought better of it. If this was going in the record, best to make sure his little jab counted. "So . . . really, the only education you've imparted to me thus far is a counterexample. I really don't want to be like any of you. I guess you've done *some* good."

He stepped back from the podium with a shrug and joined the rest of his group. Carter took hold of him possessively when he attempted to get into Delia's Beetle. With a wide-eyed glance to his sister, Declan got in the Charger and buckled up.

"You know I have to go home, right?"

"No, you don't. We're going out to celebrate."

"Celebrate?" Declan let out a much-needed laugh. "You abdicated your throne! What are we celebrating?"

Carter relaxed in the seat beside him, looking sexy and surprisingly content. "Well, let's say I know a guy who has posted pics and footage of my little speech on every school website, Facebook page, Tumblr dash, and Instagram feed from here to Chicago."

Declan poked Carter's forehead and was pleased beyond words when he didn't shy away. "You're playing the long game, huh?"

"Going for supreme excellence."

"You might already be there!"

Carter winked slowly in the dim light from the gauges. "Careful, Dex. Your fanboy is showing."

Chapter 24
The Spell

Yuki was behind his locker door when he shut it, wearing an adorable rainbow tie-dye dress in support of Carter's protest. She had the look of a disapproving mother on her face and slowed his progress to the auditorium like a chain. The rest of his class filed in, whispering that the unscheduled assembly had to have something to do with the student council's challenge.

"*Dō natte iru no ka*? You've been awfully chummy with a certain hottie the last few days. Cassidy said that she saw you come to school with Carter every day this week, and every time I call you, you're at his house! I feel like there is something you're not telling me!"

"There are a few things." Letting out a sigh, he leaned against the drinking fountain.

He'd been living the last week in a cloud of happiness. The entire school was buzzing with the viral video of Carter taking the adults to task. It didn't seem to matter why he'd protested, just that he had. Kids began making way for one another in the hallway by saying "The gentleman will yield," and the council hadn't taken a single ounce of flack for tossing aside the titles bestowed upon them. In addition to all this, Carter had been appearing on Declan's doorstep every morning and following him around like a puppy, his usual bravado dimmed as if he had no reason to play to a crowd.

It had to be a magical spell, and though Declan wanted to tell Yuki everything, he didn't want to jinx it. But if he didn't tell her, he'd explode.

"Do you remember when you went to Carter's party this summer and you met a girl named Layla?"

"*Hai*. Your cousin. She went toe to toe with that bitch Bambi."

"Right."

He stared at her hard, until her dark eyes flew wide in understanding. She gasped and threw a hand across her mouth.

"Well, she sort of also ended up dating Carter for the rest of summer."

Yuki's squeal rang down the hallway; her hands flapped as if fending off bees. "*Maji de?*"

He gave a sheepish smile.

"*Damasarechatta!*" Surrounding conversations had come to a violent halt at her fit. She judiciously dropped her voice to a whisper. "Tell me everything! Does he know?"

"No! Layla disappeared when things got too intense, and Dee and I have kept our mouths shut."

"That's what that argument was about!"

He kept the yarn short, strung with intermingled gems of Japanese and English, and tied it off with Carter's latest behavior. Yuki listened to the whole thing as if transfixed, her ponytail of jet-black hair swishing slowly from side to side. "I was gonna ask if you guys were going out! He seems so into you!"

"Carter will flirt with anything with legs."

"Sure, but not the way he flirts with you."

Before he could weigh in, Yuki's mouth snapped shut and the cloud of warmth descended.

"What are we whispering about?" Carter's chin came to rest on his shoulder. "Is it me?"

"Because you're *so* fascinating?"

Carter pinched his ribs. "You wouldn't be the first to say that . . . today, even."

Declan changed the subject, keenly aware that his entire body was reacting to Carter, a tuning fork keyed to his voice that shivered with the slightest chime. "Do you think this assembly is to take back the board's decision?"

Carter's face had lately worn a constant sleepy expression. He shrugged and stared across the crowd through hooded eyes. "No. Taggert doesn't think that way. It'll be his next move."

"Do we have a plan for that?"

Carter's wry look was a shadow of its former self. "Who are you talking to? Come home with me today, okay? We need to finish that platform before we can hang the hammock."

Declan nodded as Carter floated to his seat amongst the seniors. His official chair on stage was symbolically vacant. Taggert waited impatiently, his knee jiggling.

Declan sat with Yuki and finished answering her questions, hissed in his ear with the insane fervor of the enthusiast. She insisted that he needed to reveal his secret to Carter, and took a firm stance when he gave her his reasons for not doing so.

"Who cares what you want? You are deceiving a great guy! You have to tell him!"

"I've gone through all of that in my head, Yuki. I agree with you, okay? I feel like shit. I have to wait till the moment is right."

"And exactly when is the right moment to admit you've lied to someone? When it hurts you least?"

"When it hurts *them* least."

"Uh-huh. That's why you didn't tell me about Layla until right now! I see."

She was upset with him. He had known she would be. Taggert interrupted his attempt to apologize with a weak cough that sent the mic whistling.

"I'm going to be quick about this, ladies and gentlemen."

Yuki stuck out her tongue. "*Yada*. He's such a—"

"Gummy-faced cock."

Taggert pulled a sheet of paper out of his pocket. "I'm sure you all know that the student council made the decision to resign, putting their own feelings above the needs of the student body and the school—"

His voice was overpowered by the swell of chaos from the audience. His hands went up to silence them. Declan found Carter and Priah, sitting side by side and soaking up the energy like stoic ferns. As the sound faded, a deep voice he immediately recognized as the Goat shouted that the gentleman on stage should yield. The crowd exploded in laughter. Taggert waved at the backstage area and one of the coaches appeared, carrying a whistle that the principal sent out over the airwaves like the trumpet of Jericho. Eardrums stinging, the kids fell back into quiet groans.

"I will *not* debate the board's decision with you! What I will do is inform you that a new election must be held. There are many things that were in the process of being organized, like the Homecoming Ball, and those were abandoned! Since Mr. Aadenson and his cabinet have given up their positions, we will be defaulting back to those students who ran against them, as well as a few inclusions from a list of candidates carefully selected by the faculty. We will have to rerun the entire election, including class reps, and because of its proximity, will be combining this with Homecoming Court elections. Voting will be held all day Friday. The candidate lists have been distributed to your teachers. Ballots will be handed out in second period, just before break, which will be ten minutes longer than usual. Ballot boxes will be in the gym."

The response was loud enough to drown out even the whistle. Taggert stood impassive. When the dissent at last died down, he gestured to the aisle where Ms. Folger was standing with a secondary microphone.

"We will now take questions, *only*—and I repeat, *only*—applicable to the election."

Several people called for the floor, but when Carter rose, the entire auditorium was stricken mute. Taggert was plainly raging behind his pallid mask, but allowed the mic to be passed to Carter.

"I recently had occasion to familiarize myself with the bylaws, Mr. Taggert." A small laugh tittered away from him in a ripple. "All school elections require a mandatory two-week campaigning period. As I'm sure you're aware, a few days is not enough time to get any idea of how a candidate will handle all of the *difficult* choices he or she will have to make while in office. There's been little time for the students to consider their Homecoming Court picks either. I really think this is a bad idea."

He was smirking, but the principal's face was slowly going blotchy. The audience again went berserk as they seemed to realize that all the rules were being broken under the guise of doing them a favor. It took nearly five minutes for them to calm down and hear Taggert's answer.

"The bylaws do not account for the situation at hand, Mr. Aadenson, as you well know. We have a need for a council. I could simply appoint one, but I am affording the student body the courtesy of expressing their opinions."

Carter looked around at the waving arms, rude hand gestures, and shouting mouths. "I'm pretty sure they're doing that now, sir."

"I think we've heard enough from you."

"I have a secondary question. Will the ballot conform to previous election standards?"

"Of course it will."

Carter relinquished the mic. Halfway down the aisle someone made a disgusting noise into it. Taggert took a few more questions, but not a single person besides him appeared to be listening. Declan fled the assembly as soon as the door was opened, and dashed out to the Charger. Carter was waylaid by admirers. When he finally arrived, he looked like he'd been dragged out to sea by an undertow or caught in a tornado. The sleepy smile was back. He reminded Declan of a Siamese cat.

"Giving your unattainable boy a run for his money, huh?"

Declan rolled his eyes. "That again?"

"Just saying." He unlocked the car.

Declan waited until they were out of the parking lot to wonder, "Why did you ask that second question?"

"It'll make sense Friday."

"Tell me!"

"No. I happen to know you've been nominated as the Junior Class Representative. Wouldn't be kosher."

"Me?" Declan looked around and caught sight of his bow tie in the side-view mirror. "Goddamn it."

"One step closer to being a fake asshole."

"Shut up."

As they worked on the final treehouse platform, Declan watched Carter. He appeared to be invested in his measurements, bearing not the slightest trace that he suffered any ill effects from Taggert's campaign of prejudice. When the last plank was affixed, they stretched out and relaxed.

Carter had a satisfied smile on his face. "I think you'll make a great class rep. It's the realest job on the council, since you're basically a mouthpiece for your grade."

Declan muttered.

"You're doing it again," Carter warned. "Your armor is so shiny! Do you polish it with Q-tips?"

Ignoring him, Declan rolled onto his side and looked at Carter's pile of sleeping bags and pillows. "You're not still sleeping out here, are you?"

"I've outgrown my room."

"You mean your ego needs more space?"

Chuckling, Carter poked him between the shoulder blades. "I mean I'm tired of being told what to do. I want to live in the house I build with my own two hands."

That gave him pause. For the millionth time, Declan felt the deep certainty that there was no one like Carter on this earth. "You have so much talent for this. Have you ever thought of turning it into a charity?"

"What?"

"Building treehouses for kids in need, like as a nonprofit? You could do it while you're in school. It's a tax write-off; it could be a really awesome project and therapeutic too, since I know you deal with stress by bending the universe to your will."

That aura of heat filled the narrow space between them. Carter's arm brushed his back.

"That's a fantastic idea," the young man replied in a mystified whisper. "You're a damn genius."

"I'll own that one. Yes, I am."

"I could kiss you!"

"Stop flirting with me."

Carter's bodyweight fell over him as he shifted positions, his head resting on the soft spot between rib and hip. "Why? I know you enjoy it. Can't see why you wouldn't! Besides, somebody should, and I don't see your boy doing it."

"Because I have currency . . . right?"

"He's a giant fuck-wad, by the way, if he doesn't notice you."

Declan's body ached. He considered pulling away, but the magnetism was too strong. He rolled so that Carter's head fell onto his stomach, and flicked the perfect nose.

"Don't be mean. He's just not gay."

A lazy blue eye swiveled to him. "Is *that* why you won't tell him you like him?"

Declan laid his head down and stared up at the patch of sky above him. The days were becoming overcast. Soon, they'd be knee-deep in snow. He wondered if this year, Carter would wear an ugly sweater to come see him, on purpose.

"Yeah, that's one reason."

"Since when are you afraid of failure, huh? Hypocrisy in this, there is."

Snorting at Carter's Yoda impression, Declan put his hands behind his head. "Having someone tell you why they can never love you is not failure, Carter, it's torture. Of the worst kind. Because there's not a damn thing you can do about it."

"I don't think that's what will happen."

"I'm not magical."

"Someday I'm going to teach you how to speak properly." He sat up and graced Declan with a gorgeous, full-wattage grin. "You're supposed to say something like 'Well, I *am* the physical manifestation of cute, so . . .' Got it?"

Declan shook his head and for the moment, let the boy's humor rule his mood. "Sure, Carter, whatever you say."

"Damn right, Cat-boy."

Chapter 25
The President

Carter flipped through the ballot packet and looked around the classroom. Several other students were doing the same, and as they reached the last page, turned to make faces at him. Delia tilted his direction in her desk with a sly smirk.

"How'd you pull this off?"

He gave a characteristically suave shrug. "I know some guys."

"You know everyone, but how did you get it *in* the ballot?"

"Very few assholes are diligent. If they were, they wouldn't be assholes. It's the kind of thing you fall into because you're too lazy to give a shit."

She rolled her eyes. "That doesn't answer my question."

He dropped his voice; this was the sort of plan that could only work if certain professional educators were not tipped off to look at the packets. "The ballots were being assembled all day yesterday. I found out from the vice principal's TA that they were being stored in the library till second period. Ms. Folger hides out. Everyone knows that. We had a staff of like a dozen kids with bathroom passes come in and out, doing twenty or thirty each before going back to class."

"Was Declan in on this?"

He took in her sharp expression and vowed to never come between her and her brother, which was a weird thing to think, given he'd dated one of them and flirted shamelessly with the other. "I wouldn't do that to him. He's on the junior ballot."

"Are you sure? You two have been spending an awful lot of time together."

A few more students noticed the extra sheet at the back of their packets and began showing them around. The Goat gave him a thumbs-up without looking his way and tore the sheet off the ballot.

"Because if he was in on this—"

"Dee, I promise he wasn't. Same as you. None of the other council members did it either. *I* didn't even go into the library. Chloe and Anne handled everything."

The bell rang. She got to her feet and led the way to the gym, twisting her arm through his as they wove through the chaos. The message had been disseminated efficiently; the hallways were packed with students who refused to look at him. Except for Bambi, who was looking as if she seriously wanted to rat him out. As they entered the voting area, he snagged her shoulder and backed her into a corner.

"Don't bother saying what you're about to say," he whispered.

Her perfectly painted lips drew up. She crossed her arms.

"I get that you're all jacked over this idea that gay and trans people exist, but you know what? They do. They always have, or the several-thousand-year-old Bible wouldn't have to talk about them. They're my friends." He let her go and smoothed a hand over his face. "Leave them alone. We graduate this year. You'll never be in high school again, Bambi. Let them go."

"You cheated," she hissed. "It's cheating to—"

"Is it? I'm pretty sure it isn't. What Taggert did is cheating. He stole the process by appointing a list of candidates. *I'm* not asking anyone to change their vote. I want you to vote however you think is best. But I'm asking you to let me do this thing and keep your mouth shut."

She scowled, all puckered vim and prissy vinegar. "Why should I?"

He took a deep breath. If there was ever a time to play on her crush, it was now. "Because it's important to me, and when you like someone, or you're friends with someone, you let them enjoy things. Can you do that? Or does God have a problem with just letting people have their lives?"

"He does, actually. Some things are abominations."

Carter blinked at her. He'd known her as long as he'd known Dee, and still couldn't figure out when and where she went off the deep end. "Bambi . . . do you hear yourself? Didn't God make everything in existence?"

She looked away, petulantly. "I'm not going to—"

He stepped as close as he dared with so many people nearby. "Listen to what you're saying. It makes no sense. You used to be cool. You used to be fun. Now all of a sudden it's like you're trying to control everyone around you. Does it make you feel better to do that?"

Her mouth fell open on a noiseless complaint as she stared at him. "What happened to you?"

She blinked. "N-nothing happened to me! I love—"

"Really? Are you sure? Do you need my help with something? Because if you did, I'd help you, but I'm not going to let you hurt anyone else to make yourself feel superior or fluff up your self-esteem. There's a bit in that book about casting stones. You remember? I looked it up. I read all the verses having to do with being gay. Aren't many, but Jesus—he's the dude from the New Testament, the one that makes it the reason it's called Christianity—he has all this stuff about loving each other and being kind. Something had to have happened to you to make you so angry and hateful that you'd forget an entire *half* of your sacred book."

"I don't hate anyone," she snapped, leaning in. She seemed about two breaths away from shouting at him, but he was almost to the point that he no longer had the energy. Energy was a precious commodity. It needed to have proper direction and not be wasted on one stupid person with a grudge.

With a look around, he realized that even if she did tell someone about the inserts, it wouldn't matter. Taggert would suspend him and call for another reelection, which would mean that he could have enough time and enough ground laid to accomplish the same task again.

"Sure seems like you do. What a strange way to show love— through control and revenge. Let me put it to you this way: if we're blown and they find out, everyone in school is going to know *exactly* who did it. And they're all going to be gunning for you."

Her chemically tinted face went pale all of a sudden. "How would they know?"

"Because I'd tell them. So, you'd better make sure no one tells, or your last year will be very lonely. See? That's how it feels when someone uses peer pressure to intimidate you!" He gave her a fake smile and walked to the ballot boxes.

Teachers stood guard. Taggert frowned his way as Carter dropped his vote though the slot. "Sir."

"Mr. Aadenson. What did you think of my selections for the council seats?"

He replaced a smart-assed remark with a charitable bow. "Well, I'm not sure if they'll have all the leadership skills they'll need, but they'll definitely keep their heads down and get things done quietly."

The principal's smile bordered on a sneer, but Carter didn't mind it. Taggert was clearly the sort of guy who had it rough as a kid, was still bitter about it, and probably instinctively despised anyone who managed to have fun in high school. He had all the charm of an infectious disease. He took pleasure in making kids miserable, like mono.

"When will the ballots be counted?"

"Mrs. Donovan will be tabulating the votes during sixth period and announcing it before the end of the day."

That was good. She was a no-nonsense woman with a penchant for liberal rants that burst forth from her American History classroom like old-timey socialist recordings. He tried not to seem too satisfied as he sauntered away, skewered Bambi with a glare, and then hooked Dee on her way out.

"I *really* hate that guy."

She grinned. "I couldn't tell."

"I'll see you in fourth."

She frowned at him as he slipped into the crowd. "Where are you going?"

"Off to get my Cat-boy fix!"

Before he could turn the corner, his phone buzzed. It was a text from Delia. He read it with a smile and sent her a heart.

You'd better not mess him up, she replied.

In a bad way, I assume. Good way's still on the table, right?

Her final message was an emoji with its tongue hanging out in disgust. He shook his head.

Dex was where he usually could be found, next to Yuki's locker, surrounded by his retinue of weebs, gamers, and cosplayers. It was clear that they all really admired him and were his peers. They all shared experiences and secrets, and suddenly, Carter was jealous in a way he'd never been before. It was so acute and forceful that when he'd crushed it back down into the pit of his stomach, he still felt the impression it had made.

Namely, that Dex was fucking amazing.

Carter captured him around the waist and gave his ear an affectionate nuzzle. Predictably, Declan hissed at him and turned beet red.

"Come on, tell me how wonderful I am."

Declan rolled his eyes, but there was the ghost of a smile on his pretty mouth. "But break is only *twice* as long. There won't be enough time."

He squeezed. "I think we should have 'Carter Aadenson Day.' I'll be sure to suggest that to the next president."

Declan face-palmed. "Do you ever get tired of stroking your own ego?"

"Absolutely. Wanna stroke it for me?"

A howl of earsplitting laughter erupted from the girls as Carter hoisted Declan over his shoulder kicking and spitting. With a wink, he carried Declan bodily toward his next class, unsettling a flock of scene-kids who took off in different directions, squawking about having found the ballot inserts. Carter blessed them with his free hand and then finally heeded Declan's protests, depositing him at the door. The room beyond was empty, except for three students at the back. Declan went right to his desk and slumped down, burying his face in his hands.

"Why do you do shit like that?" he moaned.

Carter straddled the desk in front of his and grinned. "At least it wasn't a trash can."

"You're so—"

"Attractive? Charismatic? Shockingly brilliant? I'll take any of the above."

Declan tugged on his own hair. "*Enervating* was what I was going to say."

"There's one of those big words again."

"I mean it, Carter. Don't do that."

"Again I say, why?"

Declan stared hard at him for a long time before he finally replied, his voice controlled. "Because it gives people the opportunity to turn my sexuality into their entertainment, and I'm not down with that. Okay?"

Mouth suddenly full of cotton, Carter looked sheepishly at the desk. "Sorry for pulling your hair. I won't do it again."

Declan swallowed hard and, after an instant of seeming confusion, stammered out his "What?"

"Never mind. It's a thing . . . with Layla, about boys picking on girls. I promise I won't do that kind of stuff."

For a moment, there was silence and understanding. Until Carter stole Declan's glasses. The boy yipped and accused Carter of not listening, but he was too busy not listening. He'd always wondered how bad Declan's eyesight could actually be when he shot with such aptitude. When Carter settled the spectacles on his nose, he was instantly seasick; Dex was apparently nauseatingly farsighted.

"Can you walk without these?"

"Not if I want to keep breathing through my nose."

That was good to know. "Do you ever wear contacts?"

"Sometimes."

Carter smiled at his blur. "Something tells me these don't look as cute on me as they do on you."

He pulled them off, cringing as his vision refocused. Declan was still pink in the face, like he'd been scarfing down chilies. He grabbed the glasses and shoved them back onto his nose as if donning a disguise. "Yuki emailed me this morning. And there were tweets."

"Oh, good! Glad the club presidents came through."

"The CIA should recruit you for espionage."

"Because I resemble James Bond?"

Declan overlooked his bravado and took out his textbook. A few more students had assembled and were needling him with surreptitious glances. He rested his chin on his hands and made eyes at the boy.

"Did you fill out your ballot?"

Declan nodded. "I'm dropping it in at lunch."

"I'll expect my good-luck kiss at that time."

"I'll let Bambi know," the boy replied blithely.

"Umm . . ." someone interrupted.

Carter glanced up, still gagging.

A boy with a face full of zits was shifting from foot to foot. "You're in my seat, Carter."

"Josh!"

"You . . . you know my name?"

"Of course I do! You won third place at the science fair last year, and if I remember correctly, you had a great booth. It was about refraction, right?"

"That's right! Wow. You have a good memory."

Josh's mouth hung open as he blushed. Unable to resist, Carter shot Dex a loaded glance that clearly advertised how exceptionally he managed people. The Cat-boy rolled his eyes.

"You voted yet, Josh?"

The craggy visage split into a knowing grin. "Yeah."

"Fantastic." He got up out of the seat and patted the usurping junior on the shoulder. "You must really like sitting here, huh? I think I'd rather sit here than anywhere else in the school. Declan, here, happens to be one of the smartest people in this school. He's also the best gamer I know. He's Saint Cat, from St. Cat's. They probably really miss him. I'm jealous—"

Declan scowled. "Go bother someone else, will you!"

"Okay, but we both know you're just playing hard to get. Come over after school, okay?"

Declan's slate stare melted to honeyed mercury as he looked up in gloom. When he murmured, "You're not taking me home?" Carter's heart suffered a mild palpitation.

"I'm pretty sure there's going to be hell on earth when the election is called, so I'm gonna make good on my escape. You'll come over though, right?"

Declan looked down at his desk and nodded shyly. The class was now full. The teacher had reappeared and was shoving him out the door with a stare. He slid out just as the first bell rang and winked from the door, delighted when Declan sank into his seat with a pained expression.

The rest of the day people barely spoke to him. There were many veiled glances and passed notes, high fives and little chin dips.

Gay rights issues had become the topic in several lectures. Faculty went from greeting him with tolerant smiles to calling him Mr. Aadenson. Mr. Eisman, the civics teacher, even made a "gentleman will yield" joke.

He did his homework at Yuki's lunch table, leaning his head against Declan's skinny back. He wanted the evening to be completely clear so that the hammock could take precedent. It was the finishing touch on the tree-castle, and he wanted to savor it and his company.

Declan would occasionally feed him bites of pizza and push a straw over his shoulder, saying very little, but radiating affection in a way that was so comfortable to Carter it felt magical. He was nervous, and must have looked it, because as soon as the bell rang, the boy took hold of his collar and then smooshed his face.

"Remember *the* moment?"

Carter closed his eyes and nodded. "It actually wasn't that long ago."

"Good. It'll still be fresh in your mind."

Kids were filing out of the room like a mob going somewhere to play drums. Declan seemed unaware of them, his hands warm on Carter's cheeks. In a sudden tilt, he pecked Carter's forehead with a kiss and disappeared. Carter stayed past the bell, staring after him. His walk to the student council room was an introspective one.

He and the other defunct council members sat around and continued to make the last few plans for the rally, football game, and dance. They were still assigned to Student Government until their schedules could be shifted, and the other committee members were still slated to be there. Despite what Taggert had told the rest of the school, they remained at their posts, doing their duty even though they no longer had the authority. No one seemed to mind. Mr. Eisman popped his head in to smile and ask how things were going.

Carter sketched out the decorations for the dancehall they were renting while the others looked on approvingly. The venue sat on the square, facing the bronze man on a horse, butting up against an Elks lodge and a fenced area for outdoor parties. It had once been a gallows, he'd read somewhere, but it would make an excellent place for Chloe to hold her leg of the protest. She could set up all the tables, the food, the speakers, and there wouldn't be a damned thing Taggert could do about it.

He thought about Layla, and how lovely she would be in a ball gown. He thought of Declan and the nicely healed lower lip. As his hand moved over the page, he found himself thinking in blueprints and plans.

"You look like you're in love," Priah whispered suggestively.

"How can you tell?"

"It's a cross between sleepy and drugged."

"So not altogether flattering, eh?"

Her glance slid away. "I didn't say that. Who's the lucky recipient?"

"Not sure yet."

Brianna lifted her head from her arms. "What do you think is going to happen? Do you think they'll—"

The door banged open. A TA smelling of nervous sweat handed him a note with an apologetic blink.

"Fuck." Leaning back, Carter searched desperately through his mind for the moment, finding it after a few steadying breaths. The chipped mirror, the trough sink, the trees swaying through the narrow window, the smell of bubble gum, the blood diffusing into water like ink. Peace came. He'd expected a suspension for the PA stunt, but Taggert had done nothing. Perhaps it was time to accept consequences.

He gathered his things without a word and walked calmly to Mrs. Donovan's classroom. The door was open. The bulletin boards were decorated in her trademark neon colors. She sat at one of the long tables in her orange dress, shifting stacks of ballots from one side to the other. Principal Taggert was nowhere to be found. Carter relaxed a little.

"You called, Madame Donovan?"

Her crimson lips were pressed down on a smile. She had deep brown eyes and golden-brown skin, but her warm appearance belied a voice like an ordained opera singer that could strip flesh off the unabashed.

"Sit down, Mr. Aadenson."

He collapsed into one of the bucket chairs, his bag falling to the floor. A sneaking suspicion was overtaking him that he was about to suffer permanent hearing loss.

A paper slid across the table. It was one of the inserts someone hadn't removed, though the instructions to remove them were clear. He stared at the list of names and shook his head. "It was all me. No one helped."

"Helped what?" she asked solemnly. "Helped you run a solid campaign on a few days' notice? Helped you organize your peers in a way this school has never seen? Helped you stand up to villainy of the most devious kind? Carter, if the school board needed any indication that the student body agrees with you about LGBTQ rights, you've given them one that is inarguable."

He'd always liked her flare for the dramatic. It brought history to life. That and the M&M's she'd deposit on the table if a group came up with the right answer. He tried to smile, but his face had grown tired of it. "How did we do?"

She lifted up her notebook and flipped the page as if calculating a derivative. "Well, let's just say I've never encountered so few check marks in all my years of vote tabulation."

He dared to hope, his fingers crossed beneath the table.

"I'd say the write-ins were a thirty-seventy split between a Mr. Deez Nuts," she articulated carefully, looking over her nose at him, "and you."

"We wanted to give people options," he said with a shrug, his mojo back in a flash.

"You can imagine how very shocked I was to learn that Mr. Nuts is not a student in this institution."

Carter couldn't help himself; he let out a chuckle and slid his hand down his face. "And the others?"

"It was a landslide, Mr. Aadenson. There's no way anyone else can pull ahead at this point. Congratulations on winning the election . . . again."

Chapter 26
The Unattainable

Declan looped the final square knot and looked across the seven-foot gap. Carter was on his belly, dangling courageously over the edge with the drill in hand. A finger of light had found exposed skin on his lower back, and was skipping over every rise and sinking into every valley as if teasing Declan.

Anguish thrashed in his chest. He dismissed it for the piece of selfishness that it was. This boy he'd coveted from a distance was so much more than an attractive bit of fun. He was way out of Declan's league. A champion, an architect, a man who was going to make someone simpler than Declan very happy someday, *that* was Carter Aadenson.

Carter whistled to get his attention. "You got it?"

Clearing his thoughts with a nod, he smiled. "All set."

Carter tossed a rope over a branch above their heads and tied it to the drill. The tool swung toward him. Declan sank the final few screws and stared out over their handiwork. The hammock was about the width of a queen-sized mattress, but was fully a dozen feet off the ground.

The young man was wearing his goofy smirk. "You're smaller."

"You're the designer!"

"You're a class rep."

"You're the prez!"

"You're scrappier."

Declan crossed his arms. "What's that supposed to mean?"

"If it collapses, you'd probably be able to stick it."

"I *am* braver than you."

"It's true." Carter nodded. "I'm a giant wuss."

Declan grimaced at the potentially life-threatening feat and made up his mind. If he died, then he wouldn't have to do anything about Layla. It would all be revealed at his funeral. That'd be some party; Yuki and Delia would make sure of it.

"Yippee-ki-yay."

He pitched into a forward tuck, somersaulting into place as if landing on the trampoline. The soft ropes cradled him, swaying only slightly against the force. Emboldened, he wiggled and stared up at Carter's handsome face. "Suck it up, pansy."

Carter was much more cautious, gripping the edge of the platform as he wriggled out into space. The taut mesh bowed with his weight, and sent him reeling into the center where they met in a pile.

"Sorry!" Declan blushed from his head to his naval. He tugged at the knots, trying to pull free of the sagging center, but Carter caught his shirt back.

"Stay. We need to test the load-bearing capacity. Can't have this thing collapsing when my mom sells the place."

Declan forgot his embarrassment. "She's selling? But—"

"She's been threatening it since the divorce. She'll probably wait till I graduate."

Silenced, he lay there, his fingers toying with the knots beneath him, feeling a new sense of loss. It really was going to be erased, like none of it had ever happened. Carter was going to move on, then their little kingdom would pass to a new family, and he'd be stuck, outed in high school with a principal who hated queer people.

"This is cozy." Carter shifted, his arm slipping out above Declan's head. Suddenly he was resting against the length of Carter's body, and the warmth was overwhelming. Declan sat up and rubbed beneath his glasses. It was as good a time as any.

"Carter—"

Carter interrupted his thoughts with a voice so tentative, it unsettled him. "I wanna ask you a question."

Declan looked to the ground below. It wasn't too far away. He could drag his body over the edge and swing downward like they did on *American Ninja Warrior*, escaping in the nick of time. But that would be the coward's way out.

"Go for it."

A hand grabbed him by the scruff of his neck and dragged him back into repose. Declan longed for the layers of padding Layla had given him as skin rubbed against skin and the friction became unbearable.

"Promise me you'll answer with the first thing that comes to mind. You won't think about it."

"I promise."

The knowing smile hovered in his periphery. "I'm *him*, right?"

Declan's heart took a flying leap into open air, every cell in his body grasping at his soul in fear of the fall. "Him?"

The chuckle rasped along the skin behind his ear. "The Unattainable Boy. It's me, isn't it? You could try denying it, but I think we both know I'm pretty irresistible."

Petrified, his lungs could barely gain enough oxygen to reply. "Yes, you are."

Humor was forgotten in a solemn whisper. "How long?"

"Since you dated Dee," Declan murmured.

"I dated Dee for two years."

"Yeah."

Carter bolted up, his hands raking through his hair in exasperation. "Shit, Dex! Shit!"

The world swam, its edges blurring in a watercolor of yellows and greens. He smiled vaguely at the kaleidoscope and wondered if sawing through this tie would take long, if it would hurt like this forever, or if the pain would dim.

"I should have let her answer the door," he whispered.

The shimmering pool that was Carter turned and watched him. "What?"

"When you picked her up the first time."

His throat swelled shut on the words, but he wanted to tell Carter everything. He'd felt in that first glance the shock of sudden awareness, the pang of longing, the pitch of pride as it hit the ground and shattered to pieces. All in one instant, while a handsome boy stood on the doorstep and made some joke about kidnapping his sister. For Declan, it had begun there in that moment.

"You were what?" Carter's voice caught. "Fourteen?"

"Thirteen and a half."

He let out a hiss of air. "Declan—"

"It's okay, Carter. I don't have any illusions. I've been hanging out with you because you asked me to. Nothing more than that. So you don't have to say it."

He squeezed his eyes shut, tears spilling from his face to the tree roots below. In a breath, he was rocking, and Carter's weight had settled over him. When he dared to look, Carter had a hand braced on either side of his head and was regarding him from a few inches away.

"Say what? That I can't believe I'm the person you'd pick?"

Declan snorted and made to roll away, but Carter wouldn't be moved. He snagged his knee in the netting between Declan's legs and held him there as if savoring the chance to tease him. "Where are you going?"

"Anywhere but here."

"I thought you liked me. Now you're running away?"

"We both know—"

"Stop!" As the young man took hold of his chin and stared down his resistance, Declan swallowed whatever he'd been about to say. "You're probably the smartest person I've ever met, Declan. I don't understand it, but I see how you think, how you pick problems apart. I know you get who I am, so please stop complicating things. Just tell me you like me."

"There's no point in that!"

"Why is there no point?"

"Because of *her*!" Declan sat up, pressing Carter back on the hammock. "You love Layla, don't you?"

Carter looked away and was slow to reply. "Yes."

"She's your red two-by-four block, not me!"

He flailed to get up, until Carter tipped over him and pressed his mouth to Declan's ear.

"Stay put and listen!" The command was husky.

Declan stopped struggling.

Flushed and overwrought, Carter sat back, his jaw clenched on some frustrated emotion seeking liberty. "She fit, it's true, but that place she occupies . . . it's not as important as I thought. I mean . . . I suppose in a way it is, because if not for her, I wouldn't have noticed you, but everything that came after her, everything I've built . . . it's all because of you. You're the one who helped me stand up to Taggert and part of my reason for doing it. You're the person I've been trying to impress. Not her."

In the silence, Declan found it difficult to make sense of this moment. Was *he* confessing? Was Carter? His skin was delighting in the bite of the ropes. His ears were pricked to the susurrus of the wind. He could taste the sawdust and smell Carter's shampoo. Every sense was awake and hungry, and his pulse was tripping over itself.

"I'm messing it up . . ." Carter whispered to himself. He rubbed his eyes and took a shaky breath. "Calm down."

Uncertain and self-conscious, Declan worked at the webbing around him, but the pressure of their bodies kept tension in the lines. Like a spider sensing his attempt to flee, Carter pounced, snatching Declan's glasses off his face. They ended up hooked over a knot, while their owner sucked down air.

"I said stay! Damn it, Cat-boy!"

The roughened edge of Carter's index finger curved behind his jaw and the thumb pressed against his chin. As if asking permission, the nose nudged at his cheek. Unanswered, the lips brushed his in a more insistent plea, but Declan's addled mind had finally fallen silent. With a stroke of Carter's tongue to the deepest part of his mouth, Declan's whole body lurched. His feet kicked out and stuck in the hammock as his hips bucked. Carter's hand slid up his side, pulling his shirt with it. Fingertips played over his shoulder, down his chest, along the angle of his abdomen, while lips held him captive. Each caress tested his strength, and soon every muscle vibrated. He moaned, but it was a feeble attempt to gain freedom.

Carter scolded him with a shove of his hips. "Say it."

Declan gasped and tossed his head back when Carter found the button of his jeans. His thoughts scattered. Every rhythm in his body fused, and his will rested in the palm of Carter's hand.

"Carter—"

Before he could beg, Carter silenced him. Declan's tongue lapped at that generous mouth as if desperate for moisture, while Carter mercilessly dragged him toward the precipice. His skin ran cold and hot, his whole torso ached with the ferocity of his heartbeat, and he thrashed without control. Declan braced himself as the sensation bowled him over, and then collapsed in its wake.

"That's what I thought," Carter murmured.

Snared, the wind playing havoc on his bare skin, Declan breathed his first free breath and drowsed in peace. This inexplicable miracle washed over him, delighting and horrifying all at once. If he had been honest with Carter from the start, could he have avoided all this heartache? It had to be too good to be true, but then again, it was Carter, a boy full of surprises. How strange to think that Layla had once been his refuge, and now she was standing in his way.

After some time, Carter climbed out of their roost and retrieved a blanket. Declan was released, and he was wound back up in a fluffy sack. Carter's voice thrummed against his eardrum, lazily sketching the timeline of their relationship with a litany of compliments and sweet nothings. He was so much kinder than Declan had been to him.

"I'm the first, right? First crush . . . first kiss?"

Carter Aadenson, he thought, *first.*

"Yes."

"I hoped so. I wanted to be."

Such a sweet thing to say, something that should have been wonderful and made him blush with the acknowledgment, but instead it stung like acid as it worked through his mind and then his heart. It did no good for Carter to be fond of him if Layla still existed. Even if Carter became tired of chasing her, he'd always wonder. And if, by some amazing turn of events, this meant that Carter could be with him, there was no way Declan could lie anymore.

He had to tell Carter the truth, for once and for all.

"Layla wants to see you."

He felt Carter's brow furrow against his shoulder. "You're telling me this now?"

"Sue me."

"You're jealous of her, aren't you? You don't have to be."

"No . . . it just would have been nice . . . if you'd noticed I was here without her."

Carter let out a long sigh and squeezed him around the waist. "What do you want me to do?"

"She said she'd meet you by the statue before the protest."

Declan tumbled onto his back as Carter lifted up and looked down at him in consternation. "Tell me not to go, and I won't."

"What will you do when you see her?"

Carter looked away, his mouth slack. "I don't know."

"Then you need to go."

"You just . . ." He chuckled insanely. "You never stop, do you?"

"Stop what?"

"Pushing me!" Carter's normally level voice broke as he turned away. "I have no idea how to deal with you! I have a few weeks to your two and a half years! I don't know what I'm supposed to do, and you know that, and it's like you're trying to . . . test me."

"Me? Test you?" Declan squirmed in his chrysalis, tugging his disheveled clothes back into place. He patted the hammock for his glasses. "You drive me crazy! First you're obsessed with Layla and now you're all over me? Are you straight, or gay, or bi, or what?"

"I like you. That's what I am."

"That's not . . . it's not a thing!"

"I'm saying it is! I like you! Why can't you be happy about that? Why are you so sure that I can't?"

"Because reasons! Okay?" Declan rolled away. "Gah!"

"Don't go."

But Declan was already on his way. He pulled his upper body over the edge and grasped the net beneath, flipping himself over like a trapeze artist. When he hit the ground, he felt surprisingly sturdy. His skateboard was still propped against a deck chair. He kicked it up and slung it over his shoulder.

He needed to leave before he broke down, before Carter stormed the gates of his mind-palace and demanded answers. But as he turned to go, he looked back. The young man was not pursuing. He was still huddled in his little nest, looking pathetic.

Declan's resolve faltered. Emotions and chemicals still clanging around his skull like wind chimes, he stepped beneath the hammock and cast his eyes upward. Carter was lying on his stomach, staring at the ground as if traumatized. Their eyes met.

"Go on . . . I'm used to being abandoned every time I kiss someone. I'm beginning to think there's something wrong with me."

The ignominy twisted in his guts as Declan considered how badly he had used this poor, well-meaning creature. How he had the nerve to run away instead of receiving his punishment in all its irony, he couldn't imagine.

Propping the skateboard against the tree, he clambered up the rope ladder. Sliding down the net, he landed in Carter's lap. The boy said nothing, but clutched him tightly.

"I adore you." Carter accepted the confession silently. "I wish I were a simpler person. I wish I didn't have to be this way. If I were—"

"I get bored easily, Dex. Don't wish to be anything but what you are."

The leaves picked up in a sudden autumn flurry. The blanket was fluffed and tucked around him. He closed his eyes and finally allowed himself to enjoy the moment. Maybe everything would end in a happily ever after. Maybe, but those were rare, and he wasn't exactly lucky.

"Are you going to meet Layla?"

"Yes."

It was finished then. "Okay."

"If I meet her and end things, will you be with me?"

Declan pressed the tears back. "You're pretty easy to be with."

"She didn't think so."

"Yes, she did. It's why she left."

Carter twined around him in a tidy little knot, their noses almost touching. "You're not planning on disappearing in the middle of the night are you?"

Declan shook his head shyly, and let his hands toy with the hem of Carter's shirt. The skin beneath was smooth, but damp with sweat. He found the spine, his fingers hopscotching up each vertebrae. "If you still want me to stay, I will."

Because that was all he would get. These few brief moments until Layla was unmasked, and then there'd be nothing but misery.

"So I have to deal with her."

He wanted so much from Carter, with a selfish lust he hadn't entertained until the first kiss. He had fought it back for weeks now, worked to keep some distance between them so that Carter would avoid the careless cruelty of vicious children. But now, with this sweet boy staring him in the face, willing and waiting, Declan felt a surge of bravery and dared to kiss him. With a slow, sensual meter, he stoked Carter's passions and then warmed himself in the glow.

"She's in love with me, you know. You're asking a lot. I may have to break her heart," Carter teased.

"How do you know she won't break yours?"

Carter chuckled and poked him in the sternum. "That's easy. I'll let you hang on to it for me."

"And what if she wants you? Can you really say no to her?"

"I guess we'll find out. She's pretty hot. You know where we'll be if you wanna scratch her eyes out, Cat-boy. I'd pay to see that, I think."

"I'd win." Carter's shirt came up over his head and found a place amidst the branches. His skin was hot to the touch and salty as Declan kissed below his ear. "She worries too much about her makeup."

"And we both know how much you like a good fight."

"She doesn't stand a chance."

Chapter 27
The Art of War

There was still a photo of them as a family sitting on the imposing desk. As a kid when Carter had come into this office, he'd felt out of place, unimportant. He'd always imagined that at the front door, his dad switched identities, becoming whoever he needed to be to handle the situation. That ran in the family, it seemed.

They hadn't really hung out in years, at least not since his questions had become more complicated than "Why do birds fly?" Carter wasn't sure they *could* talk about anything substantive, but now wasn't the time to hold back.

He pulled out his phone and opened his messenger. *I picked up my tux today.*

Declan replied in less than two seconds. *Ooohhh . . . send pics. Cat-boys need entertainment.*

For purring purposes.

Purring should never be done solo. I need a new wallpaper pic.

He had very nimble fingers. A memory of how nimble flashed through Carter's mind and made him even more uncomfortable. It had been three days since that cuddling session in the treehouse, and for some reason the boy wouldn't indulge, no matter how much he flirted at school. Declan was obviously worried about how it would go when he encountered Layla, but Carter wasn't. Not even a little.

Nope. You have to wait for the big reveal.

>_<

He pictured Declan's eyes squeezed shut and grinned. *I thought about getting one of those suits from the seventies that has the frilly shirt and the pointy lapels. A nice powder blue.*

You'd probably pull it off, actually.

Helps to be blindingly handsome. He chuckled. *Are you gonna wear your ears?*

No.

What then?

Wait and see.

The door opened and his father appeared, fresh out of a meeting. His sleeves were rolled up and his tie loosened, and he had a sharp look, like he wanted to tear someone's face off. When he saw Carter, it softened and melted into his features. There was only a moment of recovery, and then the man was at a small table in the corner, pouring two glasses of something the color of apple juice from a decanter.

He put one in front of Carter and sat down across from him on a matching leather and chrome armchair. "So . . . you're my three thirty. We're to the point where you have to schedule a meeting with me, instead of calling me on the phone and saying 'Hey, Dad, got a minute?' Or did you end up deleting me?"

"I'm not here as your son." He took the check his father had given him out of his pocket and smoothed it on the coffee table. "I want a consultation with you."

His dad looked at it for a long moment and then threw back half the drink. "Have you broken the law?"

"Not that I know of."

"Lay it on me."

Carter picked up his tumbler and sniffed. It was a Scotch. Apparently the laws about alcohol consumption weren't important to lawyers.

"This is private property and you're my son. It's legal," he said, as if reading Carter's face. "Don't drive home. I'll call you a car."

Taking a tiny sip, Carter decided he'd have to wait a bit on that front. It was interesting, but licking something that tasted like a leather sofa dipped in butterscotch was not his favorite pastime. He set the glass on the table.

"I want to sue my school district, the board, and most especially, Principal Taggert, for discrimination."

His father got up, poured another drink, and returned. He didn't laugh or ask condescending questions as Carter had expected. Instead, he took off his tie and perched on the edge of his seat.

"Okay . . . start at the beginning. And leave nothing out."

So he did, from the private conversation Taggert had had with Chloe, to the standoff with the school board, his parley in the principal's office, and the subterfuge surrounding the emergency Student Council election. By the time he had finished, the Scotch was gone and his father was staring at him in shock.

"Why am I only hearing about this now?"

"Because you're always such an asshole about everything I do that's the least bit off the track of graduating with honors and going to a good school. But you know what? None of that shit matters if I don't do something to help people when I have the ability to. So I don't want a lecture on why I should shut up and leave it alone. I'm your client. I want to know if there's something we can do."

The man across from him changed suddenly. He leaned back and looked Carter over with the most assessing glance Carter had ever received from anyone who wasn't of the Elliott clan. After a while, it broke into a wistful smile.

"Who are you and what have you done with my little boy?"

Carter watched the light filter through the prismatic glass in front of him. "I met someone and I figured some shit out."

"Is she pretty?"

His hands were trembling slightly. It surprised him to find that though he had been kinda sure he hated this man, he was actually terrified to meet his judgment. Now he fully understood what Delia had meant when she said that he had never been tested.

First time for everything.

He picked up the glass and took another sip. It burned his throat, but did the trick.

"*He's* very adorable, and a genius, and funny as hell, and complicated, and unbelievably interesting, and all the other things I've ever wanted for myself. I don't care what you have to say about it. I like him, and this directly affects me. I'd do it even if it didn't, but since it does, I'm more determined."

There was a long silence. His father got up and poured a third, nursing it from a lean against the bar. Secretly, beneath the anxiety, Carter wondered if he was getting his money's worth or if all legal advice was fueled with booze. Suddenly, his dad came to life.

He strode to the door and leaned out, having a quick conversation with the paralegal outside in jargon. Then he was back at the bookcase, pulling several volumes off the shelf.

"Is this boy out to his parents?"

"Declan."

His dad swiveled. "Declan *Elliott*? Delia's brother?"

He nodded and got to his feet. "Delia knows he's gay, but I don't know if his parents do. I don't want to force him to come out if he isn't."

"Is that why you two broke up?"

"No, and yes. I don't know. She dumped me, sort of."

"None of my business. But he's a year younger than you," his father said calmly, without looking up from the screen. "In another few months it'll be one thin legal definition away from statutory rape."

"One and a half, actually. I looked it up, though. Prior relationships don't count."

"In *this* state," his dad said quietly. "Across state lines things change. You're talking about college in California. At least tell me this isn't something casual. Do you actually feel that strongly about him?"

"Dad . . ." Carter crossed his arms and waited for the blue eyes to lift to his. They looked a lot alike, people said. He wondered if he was staring at an older version of himself, or if his father was trying to redeem the boy he'd once been by giving such advice. "We haven't spoken in anything but shouts for almost two years. I haven't been here since I was eight, and it's in the same damn town. I just asked you to sue my school. You tell me. Am I serious?"

The man folded his hands behind his head. "I met your mom in high school."

"I know."

"I don't want things to end for you like they did for us."

Carter took a deep breath and tried to make sure his father could see the sincerity in his features. "Please, have a little faith in me."

"That's one thing I've never lacked, Carter. I always knew you'd do well, once you found a reason. Glad to see there's a fire under your ass now. You've coasted for too long."

"That's what Declan says."

They shared a look. After a moment, his dad got to his feet and came around the desk. Carter was caught up in a giant papa-bear hug before he could back away. His dad patted his back ferociously for long enough to make Carter feel as if he had a sun burn.

"I love you, son. I do. You were the best thing to come out of our relationship, and I'm proud of you. And, if it's okay, I'd like to meet this boy of yours."

"He'll be at the protest outside the dance."

"Cases like this go better if there is more than one complainant. In this case, it's a civil rights matter. If Chloe's family and Declan's get on board, we may be able to put together a strong argument."

"Can you file the case and then add more complainants later?"

"To a point."

Carter crossed his arms. "How long does stuff like this usually take . . . to resolve, I mean?"

His father held him at arm's length. "Sometimes years."

That took Carter by surprise. A decade of watching *Law & Order* had not prepared him for the delays of a life lived outside the forty-five minute time limit. If it wasn't resolved by the end of the year, prom would be ruined.

"Isn't there something we can do to speed it up, like . . . say, if I could turn this into a huge deal. Like, get it on TV and stuff? Make it go viral?"

His dad stood back and chewed it over. "What do you want? What are your goals in suing?"

"I want them to reverse their decision and make the school a tolerance zone. And I want an apology for Chloe and Anne. I want them to stop being giant pricks."

His father chuckled. "That I can't do, but if we could get some press out of this, I might be able to force them into a settlement. Especially if you aren't seeking any monetary damages. This has happened before, and recently too. There's legal precedent."

"Yeah?"

"Media really helped the other cases. The schools came back with press statements and sealed settlements. I could get the ACLU involved. With this political climate, it's . . . a hot-button issue."

Carter thought it over. The protest was already organized, but it was possible that he might be able to inflate it some, with his particular flare for managing people. He thought over who would be at the dance, and how they'd responded to his parties. He thought of Declan. He thought of Delia's surefire win. He even thought about Layla.

And then he thought of Sun Tzu.

"'If you know your enemy and yourself, you need not fear the outcome of a hundred battles.'" He knew Taggert pretty well. Well enough to give him enough rope to hang himself. "What if I told you I have a plan?"

He laid it out like he would a schematic, which took a while, as he had to go back and forth, telling odd bits of disjointed stories, indicating how much help he could pull from other sources, and how much he would need.

"When is this dance of yours?"

"Day after tomorrow."

His dad slapped him on the back and practically shoved him out the door. "Go get it done. We don't have a spare moment."

From the lobby, he made a few calls, and then headed for the car, feeling accomplished and resolved. He was blocks from Chloe's house when he spotted a skinny body balanced precariously on a skateboard, navigating the sidewalk as if racing a tornado.

He pulled over and rolled down the window. "Hey there, Cat-boy. Going my way?"

Declan got into the Charger before Carter could ask him what was wrong. His face was red and he looked as if he'd spent the last hour stuffing Kleenexes up his nose. Instinctively, Carter reached for him, but the boy waved him off.

"Drive, please, anywhere! Just go!"

Mind spinning, Carter pulled back out into traffic. As he watched Declan sniffle and rub his face, he began to wonder if he was somehow to blame. "Do you want to come to my house?"

Declan shook his head and balled up in the seat, turning away to the window to finish his cry. Carter passed his house and kept heading west. Elevation shifted as they neared the national park, and insects began to pelt the windshield. Seeing a turnout, Carter parked the car and got out. He had to peel a whimpering boy off the seat. Wrapping him up, he set Declan on the warm hood.

"What's wrong, Dex?"

"Do you really like me?"

The sudden outburst caught Carter off guard. He tugged on Declan's hair until he could force the face up to his. "I told you I did."

"Yeah, but you're as confused as I am. What if you stop liking me and then I have to be alone again?"

He was back to gushing, his face so covered in snot, Carter had to dig out some napkins from the glove compartment just to find his features. Heart breaking, he stood there helplessly, aware at last of exactly how terrifying it must be to be not only different, but at odds with everyone. Declan had spent his entire childhood hiding, and now he was out in the open, stunningly brave, but desperate for any kind of support he could find. The promise of companionship, to most people, would be a beautiful thing, but for Declan, it was laden with pitfalls and risks.

Carter pulled him close, burying his face in the messy hair that smelled of apples. That anyone could hurt this boy infuriated him, and he'd be damned if he'd let it happen anymore.

"I'm not confused. I'm not going to stop liking you."

"How do you know?"

"Because I know myself, Declan. For the first time. I'm happy this way. I'm not going to stop liking you, because you're amazing, and you're the only person I haven't been able to read. You're strong and kind and brave. Why all of a sudden are you freaking out like this? I need you to keep me on point!"

Declan coughed, his head thrashing from side to side. "Principal Taggert called my mom. He told her that he was going to suspend me if I spent any more time on campus organizing the protest. He said I was inciting other students to be defiant."

Carter's head snapped up. "What?"

"She was angry! And there I was, staring at her, thinking that there was no way to explain my side of the story without coming out and—"

"Did you tell her?"

Declan nodded. "I didn't have a choice."

"And?"

"I don't know. I ran away!" His voice garbled, he went back to clutching Carter's chest. "He's gonna win. If he keeps doing this kind of shit . . . there's no way anyone will show up."

Carter rocked him back and forth and shushed him, but all the while his thoughts were raging. Taggert had taken note of every participant at the various encounters, and now he was picking them off one by one, forcing them to face their families days before the war was to begin. How many people would he be able to turn against their own interests with this kind of despicable maneuver?

Taggert had thrown the first punch, and really, it was completely expectable. He thought he could get away with it, because his opponents were children, but he thought wrong. What had Declan said about Spencer? Well, Taggert was also a "fuck-wad" who should learn to not be so good at it.

"Don't worry, Dex. I know in the past I wasn't the sort of guy you could rely on, but I have a plan, and I know it's going to work."

"I'm going to tell Layla not to come. It's too much right now and—"

"No! It's okay."

Declan looked up at him suspiciously. "You *want* to see her."

"Stop throwing shade, Cat-boy," he said with a kiss. "Meet me at the protest as planned. I'll be there, looking dashing."

Carter put the boy back in the car. At his front door, he handed Declan off to his mother with instructions that she should install him in the treehouse, jack in a game system, and keep sending snacks up the bucket dumbwaiter until he was calm enough to show his face again. Kissing Declan on the forehead, he went back out to the car and pounded the steering wheel.

There was no more time to waste. This was the moment in the movies when the general made his speech, rallying his troops in the face of daunting odds. He pulled out of the driveway and headed straight for Declan's house.

Chapter 28
The Parade

Carter wiped his hands down the front of his jeans and glanced at the clock for the tenth time in as many seconds. The pressure was building in his head. Layla, the dance, Declan, the plan, all the pieces herded into place according to design, and yet here he was, watching two groups of armored combatants chase a ball around.

His knee began to bounce up and down.

"If you look at that clock one more time, I swear I am going to have to break your legs," Delia muttered.

"I'm sorry. I'm nervous."

"I couldn't tell."

He let out a grunt. She waved her tiny flag and gave a whoop as a call was made in their favor, but Carter wasn't able to focus on any of it. He checked his phone. No texts from his dad or Declan calling the whole thing off. What was he doing that meant he couldn't be at the game? Delia was here, and she was wearing a pair of jeans. How long could it really take for Dex to get ready for a dance?

"You're sure I'm supposed to be beside the statue at eight exactly?"

She sighed. "Yes, Carter."

A few more seconds passed. Two boys collided a few feet from them in a sickening sound. Ignoring it, Carter turned to her. "Did you talk to Chloe about—"

"Oh my god, Carter will you chill out?!"

"I can't! Dee, I can't. Please. Just . . . I don't know . . . Help me."

Arms crossed, she surveyed his features as if trying to decide if she should scramble them. "I've literally never seen you like this."

He turned away. Singer Valley's red and gold was tumbled by a wave of blue and silver. Shrill whistles sounded. A loud blast of noise filled the stadium, marking the end of the quarter. Delia folded up in a wince with her ears covered as the cacophony sliced the air, but Carter's mind wandered through a thick fog of muted noise.

Layla or Declan? Was she going to appear in splendor and make sense of it all finally? If she did, he doubted life would get simpler. Then again, he wasn't sure it *should* be simpler.

He was in love with two people, but no matter how he looked at it, they really weren't that different. Layla excited one part of his mind and Declan another. The more he examined his own structured metaphor of blocks and carefully erected towers, the more he knew he'd been wrong. His heart wasn't built and cemented to another with precision and physics. It was fluid, evolving, a constant storm.

He imagined Layla standing there at the statue, her hands clasped in front of her. She could say *anything*. That she didn't want him, that she couldn't love him no matter who she was. She could tell him that Declan had nothing for him either, or that he wasn't worth the ache or the hardship of trying to fit into the world, the way humans had crafted it.

When the halftime music began, Dee hauled him to his feet and dragged him through the bleachers to the staging area at the far side of the track. The classic cars were already parked, gleaming in the brilliant white stadium lights, and a few of the other court contestants were gathered. Bambi had managed to arrange a perfect life-sized replica of Barbie's hot pink corvette.

Decorated with shimmering white bows and crowned with a silver pillow for her and her male counterpart to sit on, it drew a gag from Dee. "Wow, Kyle looks super stoked to be paired with her."

The boy in question was dressed in maroon plaid and was leaning against the car, tonguing his lip piercing and rolling his eyes every time Bambi touched up her makeup in the side mirror.

Carter accidentally caught her gaze as they swept by and regretted it as if it were a reflex.

"You are *not* serious," she snarled.

"Yes, Bambi, I'm here," he mumbled, making for the black convertible that was meant to be his float in the parade.

"Well . . ." she spat out, her invectives failing, "how come?"

"He was nominated, Darth Shopkins," Delia said, spinning in her tracks. "He deserves to be here, same as you."

Bambi crossed her arms, and there must have been something wrong with the nerves of her shoulder, because every time she did that, her head inevitably fell to one side. "I thought you guys broke up. Why is he riding with you?"

Dee was in rare form. "Probs because he doesn't want his obituary to read, 'was crushed under a doll car after avoiding sexual advances of sycophantic twit,' is my guess."

For a moment, she reminded him of both Layla and Declan, and it was just enough to pull him out of the funk he was in and remind him what he was doing.

The cheering crowd, the frenetic echoing band music, the announcers over the PA, all of it was clawing at Carter's mind. He didn't have time for Bambi. Finally he could see how it was that people like her functioned; she'd sense a disturbance in the force and pounce on people to glean whatever it was she was searching for. Was it superiority, comfort, to make people feel as lost as she already did? He couldn't say, and he didn't know how to stop it, but he had to do something. This moment needed to be protected, insulated, guarded. He needed to gather his thoughts and get his feet under him, or there was a chance everything in his life would shift.

All it would take was one delay, one missed step.

Turning on his heel, he strode up to her, took hold of her shoulders gently, and looked her in the eye. She was petrified in place, painted lips ajar, and not even the sound of breath escaped her.

"Bambi. Stop. Okay? I know you're trying to hurt me. I get it. I think I know why. There's nothing you can say that would surprise me anymore. So stop. I'm not your enemy. I want you to be happy. I want your life to turn out great. Okay? But I also want the same for myself, so let's . . . find a way to coexist, please."

Leaving her there, staring after him, he floated to the car and took his seat on the back dash, his legs dangling over the seat. When Delia appeared, she was eyeing him. He kept his face pointed at his shoes.

"Seriously . . . Carter . . . are you okay?"

"I love your sib."

She spluttered and flushed. "Uh . . . right. Yes. Sure! He, uh . . . Dex is really into you too."

"Do you think . . . Is it possible to be all these people at once? I feel like I'm split so many directions. For the last three years I've been turning all this bullshit into a game, so that it didn't hurt to stay ahead of things, be that guy who can talk to anyone. Be that asshole who tricks everyone into liking him."

She sighed. "I know."

"But that's just surviving. And now I have this moment to look up and to say who I am and . . . I don't know who I am. Do any of us know? Do you know who you are?"

Their driver hopped over the closed door and took his place behind the wheel. Delia stared into the distant crowd and the thumping rise of the halftime celebrations. As Taggert, the superintendent, and the school board president began to prepare the mobile stage for their parade, her features were stern and pensive.

He felt the stab of guilt. This wasn't the right time for this. Dee was going to miss out on all the fun if she sat here trying to play Dr. Phil. As he thought this, however, and their entrance music slammed into his ears, she appeared to have solved his problem and was wiggling on her perch.

"Remember back in biology, when we had to look at those slides of brain tissue?"

Carter blinked. "Yeah. The flattened squids."

"Yeah! Exactly! And remember every one of those, like, little *thingies* touches another cell's . . . *thingy*, and that's how the information gets passed from cell to cell. But, like, every cell has all these *thingies*, so it's touching all these other cells' . . . *thingies* . . ." Her manicured gestures were a flourish of mauve complete with wriggling dendrites. "Like a big storm!"

"What does that have to do with anything?"

"*Boy* . . . you're just a flat squid!"

"Don't say that too loudly or Spencer Barrett might hear you."

The car began to inch forward. She dipped forward to fasten the seat belt across her feet, her head rolling to reveal a huge grin. "You're many things, Carter, but all of them are good. You know how I know?"

"Not a clue."

"Because every single version of you has only ever tried to make things better for people, and never tried to hurt anyone. Well . . . maybe except for Spencer, but he totally had it coming."

"I didn't hurt him. That was Declan!"

"Yeah, but you're the one who brought him. I feel like you learned a valuable lesson in that one."

"Always bring a cat to a squid fight."

His heart began to slow, lazily dragged over the rubberized track by their chariot's easy pace. He felt like he could finally take a deep breath. If Delia told him he was good, then he could believe it. If she said it was all right to be complicated, to be a dozen versions of himself in one body, to love everything or anything no matter who or what it was, then he could calm himself down and enjoy the moment.

If things turned out wonky tonight, well . . . he would try harder the next time. He would learn and do better. If he didn't go through with it, everything was going to stay the same. That guaranteed defeat was unacceptable. It wouldn't get better until he made it better.

As the cars lined up and the fanfare swelled, cheerleaders tumbled across the field and flags shot into the white light. For the first time in his entire high school career, the score was tied at halftime. And the fans were going nuts.

"Ok, game faces." Delia nudged him. "Look like a handsome king."

"Are you going to do the beauty queen wave?"

She snorted. "Hell no. That's Bambi's gig. I'm gonna flap like an ostrich doing a sexy dance."

"What a mental image."

True to her word, as soon as the car commenced the parade down the track, Delia sprang to her feet and waved her arms like the ex-cheer captain she was. Decked out in all her school pride, her face painted like a silver cat, her comedic oversized bow tie in place, she stoked up a chant so thunderous he couldn't hear Taggert announce the nominees.

Laughing in her shadow, he felt lucky to have known Delia. When she threw her sparkly pom-pom at him, they made the car's suspension creak with a tiny bit of borrowed choreography, and Carter didn't think twice about whether or not it was the politic thing to do.

They dismounted the car by leaping out of it and mounted the stage just in time to see Bambi's inelegant slide off the top of her carriage, skirt flying up over her head. When she joined them on stage, the befuddled mess was close to embarrassed tears. Delia glanced pointedly at him and then put her arm around the girl, patting her shoulder with the usual magnanimous grace.

The crowd was on its feet, the sound so loud as to be confusing. Declan might not have been there, but everywhere he scanned, all Carter saw were the trademarked ears and neck decoration. Even the mascot, the Wildcat, was out shaking its tail on the field in a silver bow tie.

Some things were universal, foundational truths of reality. Gravity worked and what people believed didn't matter. It existed and couldn't be argued with in any sensible way. Positivity, and every emotion that came from it—like love, or charity, or compassion—was like gravity. A law that no one could mess with, even if they didn't get it.

Carter smiled.

He'd played the conversation again and again for the last three days, changing little things here and there. He would say this and then Layla would say that, and on and on, but suddenly that was silent. All his feelings and thoughts, filtered through all this light and color and sound, refined themselves, and settled into place.

Calm overtook him as the last of the contestants arrived and completed the formation on stage. There was pomp, there was circumstance, there were a hell of a lot of blinding flashes and squeals as the mic dealt with feedback, and then it was over, and he could finally move on to the important things.

Delia looped her arm through his and danced him off the stage. Singer Valley's football team was preparing to retake the field, as the royal court performed its way off, obeying few of their instructions. Like oil and water, the two groups collided.

For a split second, Carter's mind awoke from its peace. "Hey, Barrett!"

The figure in the number ten turned with as much machismo as it could likely manage while wearing a bucket and crotch armor. Carter was glad to see through the helmet grate that the nose was still misshapen. He cleared his throat and raised his voice as much as he could without ruining the joke. "How's the face?"

Everyone within earshot yowled with laughter, and a few of Spencer's teammates had to hold him back, but it was worth it to crush their morale and watch the asshole choke on his own sportsmanship.

The echo of a hundred meows bounced all around them. The Goat slid out of their formation to rejoin the real army, slapping everyone with painful-looking high fives. He meowed right in the opposing quarterback's face, though it sounded more like the kind of sound a tiger might make. As if summoned, the Wildcat had appeared and was shadowboxing the Singer Valley's wide receivers. By the time he reached the fence line, Barrett looked like a haunted man.

Chuckling, Carter knew at least one battle had been won.

Chapter 29
The Princess

Declan's pulse was moving like a ballerina on speed, bouncing behind his rib cage as if falling downstairs. His skin felt on fire, but his hands were like ice. He hadn't thought to bring a coat, though the season was changing rapidly, and he was wearing a backless dress. He wished he hadn't been so focused on sneaking out, and had paid more attention to the weather report.

How he could have let Dee and Yuki talk him into this, he wasn't sure. It was hard enough to see the dress hanging in his room and talk to Carter on the phone, let alone fend him off in the hallways at school. He had to be insane.

He leaned against the statue, paced in his fashionable shoes, and checked his wig repeatedly. Every time Declan peeked, the beautiful girl in the mirror was still there, looking as if she was about to throw up. But it had to be done. Carter needed it. *He* needed it. If he was ever to move on, to keep building who he wanted to be, he had to get rid of this one gap in his Lego palace.

He watched Chloe and her protestors set up, wondering if he would have the fortitude to stand with them and their colorful signs when this was all over. A few limos were parked along the scenic drive and well-dressed boys and girls were spilling out. They were going to have a wonderful, fairy-tale night, get their pictures taken, dance to stupid songs. He was going to be curled up in a ball nursing a black eye with a pint of Everything But The . . .

"Here she is," Carter said quietly. "I forgot how gorgeous you are."

Declan's body went numb from toe to scalp. He took some deep breaths and turned to face his reckoning. Carter was leaning against the foot of the statue, wearing a tuxedo with a patterned vest in pastel shades. There was a smile there, and an adoring look in his eye.

Here was the thing Carter had been chasing, about to unmask itself and break his heart, and the poor boy had no idea.

"You look handsome," Declan managed, though he sounded like he had a sore throat. "But you probably knew that."

The eyes were relentless, following his every move. "You know, I thought I was the prince in this story. That I had to rescue you. It took me a long time to realize that you didn't need it."

"So who are you, then?"

"I know I don't want to be the thing you dread. Who are you?"

He looked down at his feet. "None of this is your fault."

"None of what, Layla?"

The shame was crippling then, and he pressed his face into his hands. Best to spit it out, to rip off the Band-Aid as quickly as possible. Best to keep some distance there, so that when he pulled off the wig, Carter couldn't punch him without working for it.

Before he could lift his gaze, Carter's loafers clicked across the cobbles. Strong fingers wrapped around his wrists and forced him to look up. For his bravery, he received the sweetest punishment of all. Carter's tongue slid along his lower lip and found a way in. Declan's face was captured and his body pressed back against the statue. A feeble voice within told him to push Carter away, but it was overpowered. He needed this one last kiss, one final embrace.

Just one more.

Carter's palm slid down to the small of his back and yanked him close. For once, he didn't fight. There was no point. Tonight was the end anyway. There was no lie to protect. Instead, he threw his arms around Carter's neck and clung to him.

How was he ever going to be himself again? How was he going to be the person who had learned all his confidence from this charming prince? He wouldn't. This was the end.

Carter let out a groan and squeezed him tightly, his foot stepping between Declan's high heels. Declan's emotions warred, head screaming in danger, heart sighing happily. This stolen moment would make it so much worse, cause Carter even more pain. Caution finally won and he sent the boy backward with a shove.

They stood a few feet apart, both gasping.

"Fuck, I needed that!"

Finally able to stand upright, Declan looked up to the overcast sky. "Me too."

Carter stepped toward him.

"No. Please . . . let me do this right . . . the way I should've done the moment I realized—"

"What an impressive guy I am?"

His laugh shattered into sobs, but when Carter attempted to rescue him, he warded him off with a hand. "Don't. Just stay there!"

Carter's voice dropped to a whisper. "Whatever you want."

"I want to tell you the truth. I want to tell you *why* . . . before I tell you *what*. So that you know . . . so that you understand."

"So tell me!"

Finally the dam burst, and it all came tumbling out. "I love you! I really do. *So* much—"

"I know."

"You are *not* Han Solo, Carter Aadenson!"

He chuckled. "Yes, I am. No, you're right. I know a parsec is a unit of distance, not time."

"Stop trying to make me laugh, damn it!"

Carter's reaction was not the affected bravado he'd expected. The smile vanished instantly and the solemn look returned. "Okay, but please stop crying. You know I can't stand that."

"I can't stop!"

"Why?"

He fanned his face and fought for control, but the strength didn't materialize. "Because I didn't mean to lie to you! I only came to your party because Delia made me! She caught me, and then it was too late, and I just wanted one night to feel different, so I let her talk me into it, but I really shouldn't have—"

"Layla—"

"I went there and then you were so nice, and you had no idea I've had a crush on you for like ever, but there you were talking to me, and I really wanted to know what it felt like. And then you kissed me, and I thought it couldn't really get any worse, so what's the harm—"

"Layla—"

"So I came back to your house! I shouldn't have. I'm sorry I kept letting you talk me into it. You didn't know! How could you know? The only way you'd know was if I told you, and I couldn't tell you, because what if you were angry? Of course you'd be angry! Who wouldn't be angry?"

"He has two thumbs and dimples!"

Declan swiped his hand across his running nose, determined to see this through. "You don't even know what you're angry about. You don't know because I haven't told you yet. I had so many chances, but I was too afraid—"

"Layla—"

"I know that I pretended to be brave, but I wasn't before I spent time with you. I wasn't, but I think I'm getting braver. I wanted you to know it wasn't a joke, I swear it wasn't a joke. Please don't be angry with me! You don't have to love me, but please don't be angry—"

"Declan!"

The avalanche slammed into his frontal lobe and buried his voice. He choked on air, and gulped down tears. Carter was staring at him calmly, his hands up as if to pet the anxiety out of him.

"How . . . how did you—"

"I'm an unholy prodigy."

Declan shook his head fiercely. He hadn't told anyone but Yuki. The makeup had been perfect. The phone had been erased back to factory settings. There was only one way Carter could have found out, and his girls wouldn't do that to him. "How?"

Carter's crooked grin slid into place. He shrugged in his comfortably sexy way. "You erased the phone, sure, but there's this thing called *the cloud*. My text history was retrievable via my laptop. Imagine how surprised I was when I called the number I knew *had* to be Layla's and got your new voice mail. 'This is not Declan. Beep.' That felt like a punch to the gut, by the way."

Sniffling stupidly, Declan looked around. Couples were walking beneath the twinkle lights draped across the entrance of the hall. A local news van had pulled in and a camera was being set up. The protesting students were a small rainbow-colored knot inside the wrought-iron fence.

"Why aren't you angry?"

"I was"—Carter shrugged—"for about an hour. I was pissed as hell that you lied to me, that Delia lied to me. But mostly I was angry that Layla hadn't vanished at all. She was still right here, and you were going to let me be miserable when you could have told me the first night."

"You wouldn't have—"

"Give me some credit. You know me better than that. I don't leave puzzles alone. I would have found you brave and fascinating. I would have pestered you till you punched me, and then it would have been exactly the same."

Declan's lungs were slowly relaxing, allowing cold, nourishing air to find its way in. His heart was slowing down and the chill of adrenaline was running through his limbs like an arctic storm. He shook, and to his surprise, Carter finally braved the divide. He took off his coat and wrapped it over Declan's shoulders. He chafed Declan's arms and took his hands hostage.

"I knew I could fix it easily if I just told you I'd figured it out, but I wanted you to trust me. I wanted you to see that no matter who you showed yourself to be, I could be there for you the way you need. I've been working toward that. Now here we are."

"Carter—"

"My turn, Princess."

Dumbfounded and giddy, Declan allowed Carter to tug him close.

"At first, I thought it might have been revenge. That Dee was angry with me, and you helped her, but she wouldn't have talked me through it if she was really that pissed. I thought maybe you were pulling a cruel joke, but no." He traced Declan's neck with little kisses that plucked every nerve in his body. "I remember our last night together . . ."

His face flushed with the heat of a supernova. "Me too."

A soft laugh whispered down his back. "Nobody goes that far for a prank, do they?"

"No."

"That left me with only one possible answer, and damn, if I hated a beguiling little gay boy for wanting to wear a fancy dress and hit on me—this glorious specimen of masculinity—what an asshole I'd be."

"True." Declan laughed, snot dripping.

"So when I took into consideration what a compassionate person I am, I decided I couldn't possibly be angry. And then I wondered how much of her was you, and if you could kiss me like she did . . ."

A shudder wracked him, hitting so hard that Carter had to brace him, tangling him up in a full-body hug. "Calm down. Everything is okay."

"When? When did you find out?"

"The second day of school."

"What?" Declan shouted. "You knew all this time and you didn't say anything!"

"You dated me for a week and didn't say anything."

Declan's face fell. "Fair."

"Don't worry." He nuzzled Declan's ear, sending the sparkly earrings clattering. "I'm not the least bit angry that you didn't. I made you promise to protect yourself. I meant it."

"Carter . . . I don't know . . . what to say to you."

"I'll settle for 'I have exquisite taste, so this is really no surprise.' And then raise that eyebrow of yours and sashay your hips."

"Sashay my hips? I don't think I even know what that means."

"Sure you do," Carter murmured seductively. "I've seen you do it."

"Have I done it while wearing boy clothes?"

Carter stepped back suddenly, hooking Declan's chin with a gentle finger. The silence stretched, the look of longing grew.

"Declan, I don't care what you are as long as you're mine."

Fresh tears spilled down his face, making the situation worse. Words failed, but he knew it when he felt it. This was *the moment*. The most momentous moment of such moments, it put all other moments to shame. For the first time, he truly was himself. Not Layla, not Declan. He was Dex. Whatever else happened tonight, this moment was the beginning of forever.

"I need you to understand that. Completely. Just accept it as fact, okay? The most important item on the list of things Carter doesn't mind is what form the love of his life might take. Yes?"

He wanted to cry, to dance, to grab a sign from the protestor's table and run through the streets clobbering naysayers over the head. "I understand."

"Really?"

"Mm-hmm."

A peck landed on the tip of his nose. "Good. Dee?"

Declan looked around in surprise. Delia emerged from behind the statue, looking a vision in deep-green chiffon with roses woven into her hair.

"Hey, kid."

Declan shook his head, his smile so strong it wouldn't be moved. She had been acting strangely all night, insisting on waterproof cosmetics and being ridiculously precise about every detail of his costume. He'd wondered if she was trying to make it impossible for him to be honest, but no, she'd been preparing him for this.

"Hi, Deedee. You look like a woodland sprite."

"You look like Cinderella."

Carter presented him with a wave. "Fix this pretty face, please?"

Relinquished to his fairy godmother, the magic was reworked. Delia staunched the flow of tears and reapplied foundation. Whispering reassurances, she sharpened the eyeliner and made sure the eyelashes would stay in place. Lips were repouted and sealed. All the while, the boy he loved looked on in reverent curiosity, as if watching a temple being built.

He stepped around Declan and tugged a box from the coat pocket. "This is the final touch. See if you can get it to stay."

Delia untied the ribbon and revealed a tiara Declan recognized as the one Carter had fished from the bottom of the pool. Tucking it carefully in place, she pinned it down and gave a final nod. "Good as new."

"Thank you."

"My date's waiting. Have fun tonight."

"Good luck, Dee."

She kissed his cheek and walked toward the lights, leaving them alone together. Carter walked around him in a slow circle, regarding the completed effect.

"Stunning as always," he said, with his lips at the nape of Declan's neck.

"Prefer it this way?"

"No. The glasses are dorky, but cute. And your back is the same regardless."

"You're sure?"

Carter gave him a sardonic look. "No. I tackle-kissed you because I failed biology."

He held out his arm, and after a few moments of contemplation, Declan twisted his hand through.

"So are we going to protest?"

"In the best way possible." He grinned. "Tell me, Princess, how do you feel about crashing the ball?"

Chapter 30
The Ball

Carter waited nervously for an answer, shifting his feet on the uneven paving stones. Declan was staring at the entrance to the dance and smiling at the true magnificence of the plan. Which was good, since he was kind of the lynchpin. "I'm impressed."

"Sun Tzu said, 'All warfare is deception.'"

He snickered. "We'll get suspended, or worse."

"Know how many college apps ask if you've ever been suspended? Who gives a shit about that? What I care about is you."

The gaze was suddenly veiled. "Why?"

"Because I'm on my way out, but you have another year. If you do this . . . everyone will know. It won't be a secret anymore. You'll have to live with it for the rest of high school."

"Carter, some kids have to live with unplanned pregnancies, criminal records, their shitty families. On the list of things Declan does not care about—" he looked up and beamed "—is having to stand up to bullies. If that is what I have to live with, it's worth it."

Carter couldn't help himself. He pressed his lips to Dex's forehead. "Well, when you have such a formidable boyfriend, it's easy, right?"

Declan was laughing, but when he nodded, Carter knew he meant it.

With a deep breath, he led his beautiful date toward the hall, sending Chloe a conspiratorial glance as they passed. He was pleased to see her wink at Declan. One of the others complimented his dress effusively.

Ms. Folger sat at the check-in table in the foyer. She scanned the guest list and her eyes flicked over Declan, apparently failing to recognize him. Carter breathed a sigh of relief and handed over the two tickets.

She seemed disappointed. "Mr. Aadenson, I thought sure you'd be outside leading the charge."

"Beware Greeks bearing gifts, Ms. Folger."

"A classical reference."

"Thought you'd like that."

She cocked her head. "Be careful. Taggert is on the warpath. Apparently the media have been tipped off."

"Who would do something like that?"

Her mouth pressed around a smirk. "He's been on the phone all night to find out if they are actually allowed to set up in the courtyard."

"Oh, they are. That area is a separate venue, with permits."

"I wonder how you know that."

"Probably because I got all of them."

"He'll be gunning for you. You could get expelled."

He freed Declan to wander and watched him slip gracefully inside. He really was breathtaking, though now it was different. Layla had been a very separate person from Declan, extroverted and insightful, while Declan hid inside of fantasy worlds and racked up statistics. Now Carter felt as if they had somehow meshed, balanced. Declan's resolve, Layla's sass. Layla's poise, Declan's snark. Carter had a feeling that no matter what happened now, this new, splendid creature would be able to handle anything.

He couldn't help a smile. "Some things are worth it. Is he planning on personally announcing the king and queen?"

"Yup."

"Perfect."

"Allen Cliff is on the sound system."

He grinned. "I'll be sure to say hi. You have a nice evening, and please feel free to come out later and have a go in the bouncy house."

"Bouncy house?"

He shrugged. "There's something about jumping up and down that makes people happy. Learned that a long time ago. And if you want people to take your side, you make them happy when the other guy can't."

"Playing politics, hmm?"

"It's what I'm good at."

Beyond the door, the hall had been transformed into a sparkling wonderland. Faux-marble arches decked with white floral garlands led from the door to the dance floor. On either side, tables were dressed with edible centerpieces from the local bakery, from magic candied apples to gingerbread houses. The ceiling was festooned with enough lights to create a brownout, and the castle on the stage was the perfect backdrop.

Carter found Declan beside a table of fresh-cut flowers for sale. He was trimming a small white rose and wrapping it with florist's tape. The pale, beaded dress made him shimmer like crystal, and the chain of diamonds that dangled down his naked back was a tempting lure. Carter fished out his phone and snapped a photo before he dared ruin the scene.

"Those are for the *boys* to buy the *girls*," he whispered in Declan's ear.

The princess trembled, and Carter's heart danced a jig.

"Fancy me ignoring gender norms."

"It makes sense."

Declan glanced over his shoulder coquettishly. "You can't wear a tux without a boutonniere. It's like a fashion crime, and you're much too charming to commit a crime."

"Well . . ."

"Defending the honor of a Cat-child is not a crime."

"I wouldn't wanna live in a world . . ."

Carter lost his voice. The enchantment of the setting, the soft music playing from the stage, the look in Declan's eye, and the line of his neck, it all combined at once and made him realize that he was Carter, and Carter was content. It did not matter what reaction the crowd would have, or what the principal or the school board said. They couldn't impact this moment. This moment was theirs for the rest of time.

"You okay?"

"Yeah. I'm just really ecstatically happy, and you are sexy as hell."

Declan fitted the flower to Carter's lapel and shook his head shyly. "Just so long as you're aware of what's underneath all this clothing."

Carter guided him into a shady corner and pressed him bodily against the wall. After a long, emphatic kiss, where he demonstrated how ineffectual said layers of padding would be, he waited for his blood to cool. It became clear, however, that the entire night would be a serious exercise in self-control.

It sounded like a blast.

"I am very aware," he murmured in Declan's ear. "In fact, I've been developing a whole catalog of fantasies."

"Another list to memorize? I'd very much like to hear this one."

"It's a bit X-rated for this crowd, but my drafting table is involved. It tilts."

Declan's mouth dropped open, releasing a hysterical giggle. "Wow! Okay. And once I've returned to my normal color, we can leave this corner."

"I plan on making you blush most of the evening."

Declan blinked at him as if stupefied. "What planet are you from?"

"Earth. Turns out there's hope for us yet."

The boy brushed his cheek, his chin, across his bottom lip. "I really can't believe this. You can't be real. I'm dreaming."

"I told you it'd happen."

"I love you."

Carter took the compliment with a grateful nuzzle. "I don't want you to worry, okay, about all this gender, sexuality stuff."

"No?"

"No. In architecture, there's this thing called the organic element. Like in the treehouse, the tree is that element, and it has to be in harmony with the man-made structure."

"Like a garden?"

"Yeah. I kind of think about this the same way."

"What do you mean?"

"Well, like, the relationship is the structure: that we are friends, that I can talk to you about anything, that we work well together and have shared interests, that we challenge each other. That's all the structure we build together. But this . . ." He trailed his hands down the curve of Declan's shoulders to his wrists, around his palms, and back up again to his exposed collarbones. "This is the organic element.

We shape it by the little things we notice about each other, by what feels good. It grows how it wants, but it grows into that structure, in balance. Like a vine up a trellis or ivy up a wall."

When Carter tried to step away, Declan refused him with a crushing embrace. "I really do have excellent taste."

"You are pretty perfect."

"Running out of things to tweak."

They meandered through the tables, posed for formal portraits, and danced to every slow song, leaning so close that a chaperone had to separate them more than once. Some of the kids shot him dirty looks, and whispers of his hypocrisy for attending a dance he'd told others to boycott rippled away from him occasionally. He ignored them easily, because he knew the truth, and he was brave enough to let that be enough.

Declan slipped off to the bathroom to touch up his makeup before the main event, and Carter took the moment to drop in at the sound booth.

"Allen."

The boy was dapper in a black-on-black suit and skinny tie. He had a Stetson cocked over his deep-brown skin and wore a red boutonniere. "Hey, man. I thought you weren't coming."

Carter made a noncommittal sound. "I thought I'd wait to see if I win. See if I get to make an acceptance speech."

Allen immediately understood. "You want me to play dumb?"

He extended a fist, and Allen tapped it. "I plan on dropping the mic. That okay with you?"

"Can't wait. I voted for you."

"Vote for Delia?"

"Yup."

Carter nodded and glanced at his phone. It was almost time. "Thanks for the support."

"Well, it was you, or Deez Nuts."

With a chuckle, he caught sight of a harassed Taggert and slipped away. Declan returned, but he had somehow acquired a new accessory. Bambi Weatherton, red-faced and a hair's breath away from sobbing, was draped over his arm as if drowning. Declan planted her in a chair with a few soft words, and cut through the crowd to get to him.

"Her boyfriend came with another girl and called her a harpy bitch. She's been hiding the whole night in one of the stalls, and no one bothered to ask if she was okay."

Carter made a face. "I could say something about reaping what you sow, but I'm pretty sure she knows the Bible better than I do."

Declan's wry look was his only reward. "We had a very productive talk. I need you to do me a favor."

"What?"

"Use that bountiful charm of yours for good and ask her to dance."

Groaning, Carter ran a hand over his face. "Seriously? Do you go around finding people to enlighten?"

"Be better than your enemy, Carter Aadenson," Declan scolded quietly, "or join them."

Marveling, Carter sighed. He really had no idea what he'd been doing with his life before Declan had materialized in it. If he ever managed to predict what Declan would say, it would probably unlock the wizard achievement. "I love you."

"You should know she has a crush on you too."

It was a difficulty that was oft-lamented, but he left his glittering princess behind and bought Bambi a rose. When she looked up, her eyes were swimming, and she clutched a handkerchief in her pastel-pink lap.

He gave her a winning grin. "I hear you followed a toad to the ball."

She brought the bloom to her nose. "No. I think maybe he was right. I *am* a harpy bitch."

"I don't even think that's a thing." Leading her to the dance floor, he swept her in an arc and spun her up. "But guess what?"

"What?" She was breathless, but the sorrow was forgotten.

"You're not dead yet!" He hooked an arm around her waist and dropped his face to her ear. "That means you still have the chance to set things right."

Bambi nodded. "Carter, I'm sorry. Thank you for bringing Layla tonight. She is really nice and made me feel a lot better, even though I was really . . . a jerk to her at your party. I'm sorry I've been so stupid about the gay thing. I've thought a lot about it. Declan was right."

"He usually is."

"Are you two . . . like, a couple? Like, are you together?"

Carter let her down with a gentle dip. "Sorry, babe. It's too bad you couldn't live up to your name."

Giggling, she curtsied her thanks as the music came to a halt. "I think I'm gonna go out to the protest. Do you think Chloe would be okay with it, or would she be angry?"

"The whole point of the club was acceptance, Bambi. She'd be a giant hypocrite if she didn't welcome you." Carter captured her hand and gave it a light kiss. Taggert was walking up on stage. In the spreading silence, the chants of the protesters became audible. "But you might wanna hold off on that, for a minute."

He winked, and watched a truly genuine smile spread across her face.

"I voted for you for king."

"Really? You're kidding."

Bambi shrugged and, beneath her defenses, she was actually quite pretty. "Couldn't help it."

Declan appeared beside him, shaking a bit. Carter took his hand and looped it over his arm, massaging the manicured fingers in encouragement.

Taggert tested the mic, and scowled at the main entrance as the chant rang out. "Welcome everyone to our little fairy-tale village! Thanks to the planning committee for organizing such a lovely ball, in spite of the recent difficulties." He stared daggers at Carter and adopted a self-satisfied tone. "It's nice to see such a *healthy* turnout!"

The crowd was impassive. The silence dragged. It was to Carter's advantage that no one liked the bastard anyway.

"Congratulations to our football team for their incredible win! I wasn't sure we could pull it off, but we did! And may I say that you all look wonderful! Our students really do clean up nice."

"I hate that guy," Declan whispered.

"Join the club."

"You mean he hasn't banned it yet?"

Taggert coughed. "Well, I suppose it's now the moment you've all been waiting for. The envelopes, please!"

A girl walked them out as a few participants took position. Carter had made certain both the winners and their dates would end up on stage. It turned out it was a good idea to be friends with every committee chair. His pulse picked up speed. Declan squeezed his biceps.

"Your Homecoming King is . . ." He tore open the envelope and took a full measure to absorb the results. His voice dissolved into acid. "Carter Aadenson."

The crowd cast around for him, the seething hush echoing as he and Declan swept toward the stage. An usher accepted Declan's hand, guiding him to the side stage. He spotted the Goat above the crowd giving him a reassuring salute, Sophia LeGrange at his side, looking like she was having fun. As he bowed to receive his crown, the committee chair winked.

Taggert apparently couldn't resist the chance to be a giant asshole. At least he was consistent. "Well, Mr. Aadenson, I am a bit surprised. After all the drama, I thought sure you'd turn up your nose at this honor."

"That's because you lack imagination, sir."

The man turned away on a muttered insult and took up the second envelope. "And now, the highlight of the evening. The contest for Homecoming Queen is not just about popularity. She should embody all those qualities that best describe who we are as a school; that is, after all, what Homecoming is about. Our list of nominees this year were all quite appropriate, every lady accomplished and amicable, active in sports, clubs, and academics. But enough from me! Your Homecoming Queen is . . ." His grin faded as he scanned the writing. "Delia Elliott."

A cheer went up. Carter found her in the crowd as she and her date made their way to the stage through a gauntlet of high fives and hugs. She really was a beautiful person, inside and out, with a kindness and integrity that was dauntless. Accepting her crown and bouquet with dignity, she glanced back at the lanky youth who'd won her hand to the ball. Camera flashes lit up the scene, as with a persuasive smile she coaxed the microphone from Taggert's death grip.

The chant outside was growing more insistent. Delia shot Carter a look. He gave the subtlest of nods.

"Thank you everyone who voted for me. And thank you to all the other girls up for this. After tonight, no one will care about the fact that I won some arbitrary pageant, and really the only record will be the yearbook, so I'd like to say something in my brief fifteen minutes, if I may."

Upturned smiles granted her permission as she reached up and took off her crown.

"There's been a lot of controversy over this dance. I want to put it to rest. We're kids, it's true, and we don't always know what's best for ourselves, but this school is our gateway to the world outside. This is where we decide who we want to be and make choices that establish our place. When I heard my name on the nomination list, I knew this was an opportunity, and I made myself a promise that if I won, I would accept the award on my terms."

Carter glanced at Taggert. Worry was slowly dragging down his mealy features.

"I'd like to introduce you to my date this evening," Delia continued. "I've had a wonderful time, and been treated like a queen from start to finish."

The boy stepped into the limelight, wearing his tuxedo and matching ascot with swagger. Delia gave him a sweet kiss on his cheek.

"Her name is Andrea Stanton, but you can call her Drey."

While the crowd erupted into gasps and whispers, Carter put his track skills to good use, snatching the tossed mic from midair before Taggert could traverse the distance. Dex appeared within reach, looking imperious in his gown that caught the light like a diamond.

"And my lovely date this evening is one Declan Elliott. Some of you may know him as Delia's brother; the Cat-boy; or that kid who punched out Spencer Barrett, demoralizing their team, and clinching us the Homecoming victory." Taggert grabbed for the mic, but Carter sidestepped and swept it over his head. "Incidentally, he's a fantastic kisser."

There was momentary confusion as he danced out of reach and the principal's shouts to the sound booth went unanswered. Allen was conspicuously absent.

"It's true that this ball is a chance to have fun, but as Delia said, fun is temporary and completely self-serving. We came, we danced to that same music we always do, we peacocked around a bit, but despite Mr. Taggert's protestations, this is not about who we are as a school unless we make it about that. I can't celebrate a school that segregates its students. Homecoming should be for all of us."

The educator dismounted the stage in a furious disarray, storming toward the sound booth with his fist raised. Carter would have only one more instant.

"If that's the kind of Homecoming you want to have, please join the rest of us outside on the lawn, where the party will continue, courtesy of some very kind local businesses who donated their time and supplies! There's a DJ, food, a bouncy house, and an army of news crews if you'd like to say hello to your moms!"

Taggert pulled at random wires in an apoplectic fit, his curses audible even at that distance. The mic went dead. With a grin, Carter stepped forward and dropped it center stage. To a chorus of shouts and thunderous applause, he wound his fingers through Declan's and led him triumphantly from the dance.

As they reached the door, the red-faced little man caught up to their righteous phalanx. Tied to them by his own rage, he followed them outside onto the steps, carrying on like a crazy person. Right where Carter wanted him.

"You are suspended!" he shouted, practically hopping. "All of you! And you'll be lucky, Mr. Aadenson if the board doesn't move for your immediate expulsion!"

Carter leveled him with a cool glare. "On what grounds? I'm the Homecoming King. I've been voted Class President twice. I'm up for valedictorian. On what grounds could an educational entity justify dismissing, arguably, its finest student? I sure hope you're not about to say it's because I'm queer."

"The district may not agree with your lifestyle, but you—"

Declan stepped regally between them, his lip already twitching. Behind Taggert, the cameras were rolling, and parabolic microphones caught every elegant word.

"*Agree*? The fact that you use that word demonstrates *exactly* why we are having this argument. It's like saying you don't agree that the sky is blue! Reality does not rely upon your opinions, Principal Taggert. Complex sexualities *exist*, whether or not you understand them, whether or not you possess one. What you're advocating is not education, it's conformity, and it's contrary to what this country represents. You can suspend us. Hell, you can expel us. Go right ahead! Because in that moment we will know exactly who and what you are, and that you have no idea what you're dealing with."

He reached up and yanked the wig off his head, so that his audience would get the full picture.

Taggert stuttered, his pea brain slowly becoming aware that the protestors had gone quiet, and that their numbers were swelling as kids spilled from the hall and out into the open space. Carter spotted his dad, and took note of the clerk trailing behind him.

"Mr. Paul Taggert?"

The principal turned, confused.

The clerk handed him an envelope the thickness of a newspaper. "You've been served."

Bewildered, Taggert stared at the paperwork. When his father presented the principal with a business card, he took it out of reflex.

"Mr. Taggert, I'd like to notify you that you've been named as a party in a civil lawsuit put forward by the families of Declan and Delia Elliott, Chloe Shannon, Anne Milton, and my son and client, Carter Aadenson. You have a nice evening."

Chapter 31
The Happily Ever After

Declan was lying in the treehouse in the hazy half-asleep state he'd occupied for most of the three-day suspension, when Carter planted a kiss on the back of his neck. It took root in his tailbone and sent shivers down his arms and legs. The diffuse gray light filtered through the clouds and transformed the world into a still palette of saturated color. It caught the beadwork of the pale dress, still hanging over the railing like a flag to hail the passing of his virginity. Beneath it, the silver shoes gleamed.

"I called the fire department. Told them there was a Cat-kid up my tree."

"Is that a dick joke?"

Carter grumbled disapprovingly. "Chloe's family just got here."

"A little longer, please?"

His ear was affectionately chewed in protest. "You can't spend forever here."

"I'm tired of answering the same questions again and again."

Phone calls had been streaming in from press agencies all over the country. Never had Declan hated cable news networks so much. He'd heard his own words repeated back to him so many times, they were burned in his brain. The dance had been a dream come true, the after-party a mind-freeing blast, and the wee hours of the morning . . . something out of a fantasy, but all that ever got played was the loop of him stripping off his wig, and the impromptu press conference Mr. Aadenson had given about Carter's achievements, his single-minded desire to attend an elite architecture program, and the unfairness of the predicament.

"You'd think they'd get their panties in a wad over every situation like this, but no . . . only when a few wealthy, white, honors kids get dinged."

Carter sighed and climbed on top of him, massaging his shoulders as a clear excuse to straddle his hips. "Take the win, Princess, or I'll get the Brasso for your armor."

"Meh."

After a few moments, Carter gave up and snuggled down into the mire of sleepiness with him, his hands roaming freely. Declan's mind swept backwards and forwards over their fairy tale. As Carter coaxed a moan from him, he wondered why it was that such stories focused solely on one brief period of time, bookending it with horrible understatements like "A long time ago," and "Happily ever after." People put the story of the meeting on a loop, repeating it like a mantra to some love god, but didn't they know that the rest was just as important?

He didn't want to talk about wearing fake boobs. He didn't want to ruminate on what it meant to be gender-fluid. He didn't want to talk about pronouns or what they meant to him. He didn't want to think about this intermission anymore. He wanted the boy and all the happy moments that came after the ending. He wanted to go on and explore forever. Only that, with Carter. Nothing more.

"You have to come inside."

"No, I don't."

"My dad will be back any minute."

"When he is, I'll come inside."

Carter rolled him over and took advantage of his nudity, nipping at his flesh with those perfect white teeth. "Everyone misses you!"

"I miss *you*. They're stealing my time away."

The back door opened. Carter's mother stuck her head out and called for him. He groaned, but pulled himself away, smacking Declan's backside as he left. "Put on your clothes and come inside! I don't want to do this alone!"

Declan shot him a look, but rolled around collecting garments like a snake shedding in reverse. With his feet on land, he felt unsteady, but he trudged into the house and waved at Delia nonetheless. She'd become a fixture at the bar, playing card games with her new best friend, Drey. The way the two of them were carrying on, it looked like his parents were going to have even more mental adjustments to make.

Chloe and Anne both embraced him and introduced their parents. Before they could find a place to sit, Carter's mother had produced a tray of drinks and was busy putting her son's hosting skills to shame.

The television was muted, but playing their featured MSNBC interviews on repeat.

Declan sank into the sofa and glanced at his dad. They hadn't really talked since he'd run out of the house the night Taggert had called. He'd sort of been dreading it. It was his father who'd taught him marksmanship, taken him out camping, insisted on reading him a brochure about condoms.

His dad sipped a beer and pointed it at Carter. "I was bummed when Dee dumped his ass."

"It was *mutual*!" Delia shouted.

He rolled his eyes. "Glad one of you pinned him down."

"You're only saying that because you like talking about baseball with him," Declan accused.

His father shrugged. "He knows his stats."

"He knows everything."

"Wrong tone of voice!" Carter corrected from the kitchen. "That almost sounded sarcastic."

"*No!*"

"That too."

His dad shook his head. "You looked . . . pretty . . . in the dress."

Declan thought his face might break if his forehead tugged any harder on his eyebrows. "Wow, take it easy, Pops. Don't want you to hurt anything at your age."

"Woulda fooled me."

His mother laid down her last hand of rummy and took up her cocktail. "Get him to tell you about when he dressed as a woman for Halloween and asked out his best friend."

Declan picked up a pillow and screamed into it, then set it down primly and returned to the conversation. "I'd rather not, thanks."

"Why not?" Carter appeared behind the sofa and draped himself over it languidly. "Sounds like a hilarious story."

Taking a few deep breaths, Declan tried to find his Zen center. All that came to mind were the crosshairs of his scope. "Because it's not a costume for me. It's not dress-up. It's not pretend. It's me, or part of me, an aspect of me that gets to be in that moment. I guess . . . like when you wear your uniform, or your wedding gown, or church clothes. I haven't figured it all out yet, but when you guys make those jokes—"

"I'm sorry, kid. You're right." His dad leaned forward and patted his knee. "Go easy on us. We're old."

But the room had gone quiet, the elephant transcribed in whispered breaths and uncomfortable sounds. Some people understood and some didn't. Then Declan felt it, or rather heard it, like a ringing bell, the tone within the silence that turned reckoning into music. These friends and family might not grasp what he was trying to say, or understand why Delia was flirting with Drey, or how Carter could prefer him, or even how Anne and Chloe had found each other, but they were all there regardless. Love really was a handshake, an agreement to always meet in the middle and *do*.

He smiled and let Carter's embrace warm his shoulders. "It's okay. Just don't shoot me if you get up in the middle of the night and see a swanky woman digging through the fridge for leftovers, okay?"

"This doesn't confuse you?" his dad said to Carter, who was wrapped around his neck like a boa.

Carter laughed in that way that took on the universe as if batting at a pesky fly. "Not really. I'm greedy by nature. Why pick one when I can have it all?"

When his dad blushed to his receding roots, Declan thanked Carter with a lecherous glance.

The front door opened. Mr. Aadenson dropped his briefcase and coat at the dining room table as if he still lived there, and brought his hands together in a loud clap. Every head snapped to, and every ear was bent.

"They went for it!"

With a leaping heart that brought him to his feet, Declan clutched himself. "The whole thing?"

Mr. Aadenson grinned like a schoolboy, looking so much like his son that it took Declan's breath away. Suddenly it was clear why his ex-wife had clung on so long. That charisma was a trap he knew the sting of all too well.

"The formal apology will be issued next week. You'll return to school tomorrow, and the suspensions will be wiped from your records."

Carter apparently wasn't buying it yet. His arms were crossed over his chest, fists flexing as if he wanted to rip someone's head off. "What about the tolerance policy?"

Mr. Aadenson swiped away his concerns. "It was the first thing we discussed. Apparently someone from the community who heard you speak at the board meeting circulated a petition among some friendly ranks. They didn't want to yield, but they didn't really have a choice. Those ACLU guys are on point! And the best news . . ." He grabbed a beer from the table and tugged off his tie. "Taggert resigned in protest."

A gasp escaped, so loud it sounded as if the house itself was breathing.

Carter's laugh had a dark tinge to it that gave Declan goose bumps. "Yeah, sorry, prick, that trick's been done to death."

"You did it best, babe."

Declan was wrangled into a group hug, where laughter turned to well-deserved tears of joy.

Chloe was hopping up and down. "Can we celebrate?"

Carter high-fived her. "The trampoline is out back if you really wanna jump."

The phone rang and the room emptied.

Within minutes adults were gathering around the fire pit and the barbecue and kids were jumping in elation and swinging from trees. Declan sat down at the dining room table and let out a sigh.

Finally, it could begin.

Carter's mother set the phone down after a few soft words and turned to him, her face pale. "Did he leave?"

"Carter? I think he's showing off his tree-castle."

She walked to the door like a zombie and called him back inside. Declan began to feel the creeping anxiety slither up his spine.

Carter came past her into the house and picked up the phone in a whirlwind of annoyance.

"Hello?"

Their eyes locked, but suddenly, Carter was far away, his mouth hanging open. Declan glanced outside; faces were beginning to turn toward the windows as his mother spread the word.

"Yes, sir." Carter broke away, running up the stairs like a high jumper. Declan heard the inner sanctum open and Carter's heavy footfalls thumping overhead.

Declan's mind went blank. He wondered if it was all about to be snatched away, like some kind of horrible joke, or like an enchantment being lifted. Maybe he would wake up in his bed, and this would all be a dream. The wait was interminable, and by the time Carter had returned, Declan had chewed off four acrylic fingernails.

Carter had his laptop in hand when he reemerged. His face was flushed, and an undying, crazy smile was affixed to his mouth. He thanked the mystery caller and collapsed into the chair beside Declan.

"I got in," he breathed.

"What?"

"That was the dean of the school I wanted to go to." Carter looked up, and for the first time, Declan watched his eyes well with tears. He was grateful it was in happiness, and hoped it always would be. "He saw the press conference. He's been following the situation. He asked to see my work. I got *invited* in."

Suddenly Declan understood. As the young man bounded to his feet and tore outside to shout the good news, he smiled into his hand. Carter Aadenson, probably the only boy who could get into a competitive university's architecture and engineering program without even applying. It was too perfect, and so of course it would happen.

He got up and drifted through Carter's house, up the stairs to the drafting room. Leafing carefully through the drawings, handling the models, Declan went back to the moment. This was where it had happened. This was where he had been when he knew that it wasn't enough to crush on Carter Aadenson. This place was where he'd known he could love him.

Sitting down, he pulled out a sheet of fresh paper. Gently displacing the current sketch, he clipped the page to the table, and drew a playful little picture for his boy.

"What are you doing up here?" Carter's good humor was bubbling up into every word.

He bounced into the room, but came to a sudden halt as he spotted Declan's artwork. Without a word, he plucked the sheet from the table and stuck it to the wall.

The composition really didn't mesh with the precision of the place, but Carter didn't seem to mind. He took in the darkly scrawled heart and elaborate penmanship with a grin.

"I was thinking about after . . ." Declan lay his head down on the table and looked out at the fire pit. "When you've gone away to school, and the rest of the world gets to view your loveliness. You won't need a silly little Cat-boy anymore."

Carter settled on the floor at Declan's feet and laid his head on Declan's lap. "A silly little Cat-boy, maybe not, but a vivacious warrior priestess . . . possibly. A gender-neutral sure-shot general . . . I hear they're all the rage."

"I was thinking you might learn to love someone else."

"There is no one else." He kissed Declan's charcoal-stained hand as if he were a princess. "No one on earth compares, I promise."

"Yeah . . . then I thought that, as I was drawing big hearts around your name."

Carter's chuckle turned to a laugh, and the supplication to a dance as he swept Declan off his feet and carried him down the stairs shouting, "Finally!"

Epilogue

Declan murmured an objection as Carter shifted beneath him. The leafy canopy overhead cast speckles on their bare legs.

It had been such a long time since they'd been able to cuddle amidst the branches, what with Carter's schoolwork and the nonprofit, Declan's own exams and upcoming graduation. There'd been a whole week of silence as he'd written his valedictorian speech and awaited the one acceptance letter that truly mattered. He pictured the drab black cap and gown and wondered if he could get away with wearing a dress beneath it. That would be an absolutely perfect way to say goodbye to this chapter of his life.

"I swear you've grown like two inches since I last held you."

Though Carter was now officially an adult, his voice still had its playful undertone. The softness of it tickled Declan's ear and lifted every hair. He wondered how it could be possible that in only a few short weeks, he'd be able to experience this happiness every day, as they built their "real life" together. His toes curled in anticipation.

"What does it matter? I'm still shorter than you."

Carter watched his languid stretch with a ravenous glint in his eye. "Not when you wear high heels."

Declan rolled onto his stomach as Carter climbed to the edge of the hammock. He was as handsome as ever, though there was an air of confidence about him that he'd never had before. He had taken to a short beard, and dressed like a contractor in blue jeans and steel-toed boots, but instead of convincing Declan he could wield a buzz saw, the look inspired lurid construction-worker fantasies. Carter had changed, but had never gone back on his word; they'd remained a pair through separation. Perhaps that was what happened when love was tested by adversity in its youngest days.

He looked down through the hammock at the ground below. "Where are you going?"

Carter flipped over the edge and landed. "Mom's found a buyer for the house. She's bringing—"

"No!" Declan bolted upright, his long rope of hair yanking at its tether. "She can't sell it! I won't let her!"

Carter looked up at him with an indulgent smile. "She can't stay here forever, Dex. It's too much house for one lady. Besides, you're about to graduate too, and there won't be anyone here to enjoy the treehouse!"

"This is *our* place!"

"Stop worrying. I promise you, we'll make a new place."

Pouting, Declan refused to look at Carter as he walked around the tree to a different platform. He lifted his chin in the haughty way that he knew Carter appreciated and huffed. "But where are *you* going? This is prime snuggling time you're eating up!"

With a low chuckle, Carter appeared at the base of the tree for an instant. "I told Mom I had one more project I wanted to get done here before she bails."

Picturing a new tier on their tree-castle, Declan wriggled over to the crow's nest and searched the lower platforms. Carter was squatting down on the north-facing balcony overlooking the yard.

"Can I help?"

"I sure hope so! See that toolbox there?"

Declan tipped backward lazily and found the toolbox, a shiny red gem at the edge of their little blanket-nest. "Yeah?"

"Open it and grab the chisel there on top."

Noises of protest worked their way out of him as he shifted around through the comfortable bedding and crawled free. Pushing his long hair from his face, he slipped his feet into his sandals and knelt down.

"Chisel . . ." Declan opened the toolbox. Everything in his body came to an abrupt halt. On the top shelf of the chest was a tiny velveteen clamshell. "Babe?"

"Yeah?"

"There's a jewelry box in here."

"Oh yeah?" And Declan heard it, that playful lilt in Carter's voice. It had charmed him so many times, and had never dimmed. "Well, you'd better open it, Princess."

Declan swallowed down the lump and ran his fingers over the soft blue case. His hands were shaking. When had that started? The lid came up with a pop, and sitting there quite happily was a thin metal band. Platinum branches wove together around a central diamond, as a leaf glimmered green with tiny emeralds.

"Oh my god," Declan breathed.

He snapped the box shut and nearly broke his neck tumbling over the rope bridges and several platforms between them. The young man was leaning casually against the tree trunk, cocky grin already in place. Captured as he came within reach, Declan's treasure was stolen from him. While he wiped furiously at his damp cheeks, Carter pulled the ring from its little cushion. There was a shimmer of writing around the inside curve as it slid onto his ready finger.

"Marry me."

"*Well...*"

"I'm extremely charming!"

"True, *but...*"

"I'm handsome, I have prospects, a company, a skill set. I'm funny, I'm smart, I'm charismatic." White teeth flashed as Carter pulled him close and tugged on his braid. "I'm pretty much the whole package."

"So now we're talking about your package?"

"We could, but I think we both know that's also an item in my favor."

Giddy, Declan wrapped his arms around his prince and tried to breathe. "Hmm... It's just..."

"What? You're killing me!"

"It's just you've *ruined* it!"

Carter was blinking, stunned and pale as they parted. "What?"

Declan dug into his pocket and retrieved something he'd been carrying since he'd picked Carter up from the airport. He'd worked all year at the paintball range to afford it. It deserved the appropriate words, timing, *moment*.

That moment was now.

"*My* proposal."

The blue eyes sparkled. Their owner swept a hand over them. "Well . . . Shit."

"I'm pretty sure you're going to say yes. Because I'm *devastatingly* persuasive."

Carter let out a sniff. "I knew I should have led with you proposing."

The gold band fit perfectly, looking warm and suited to the hand, calloused from building so many wonderful things. Declan lifted the fingers and brushed them with a kiss. Content, he rested his face against the throbbing pulse in Carter's throat.

"It's engraved," he whispered.

"Yours too."

"What's it say?"

Carter squeezed him and dragged their bodies to the floorboards. "'As long as you're mine.'"

Declan found his home, leaning against his favorite pillow, admiring the sparkle of their hands entwined. "Exactly."

"So, Princess, how do you feel about crashing a courthouse?"

"I have just the dress."

Dear Reader,

Thank you for reading Kristina Meister's *Cinderella Boy*!

We know your time is precious and you have many, many entertainment options, so it means a lot that you've chosen to spend your time reading. We really hope you enjoyed it.

We'd be honored if you'd consider posting a review—good or bad—on sites like **Amazon, Barnes & Noble, Kobo, Goodreads, Twitter, Facebook, Tumblr,** and your blog or website. We'd also be honored if you told your friends and family about this book. Word of mouth is a book's lifeblood!

For more information on upcoming releases, author interviews, blog tours, contests, giveaways, and more, please sign up for our weekly, spam-free newsletter and visit us around the web:

Newsletter: tritonya.com/newsletter.php
Twitter: twitter.com/TritonBooks
Tumblr: tritonbooks.tumblr.com

Thank you so much for Reading the Rainbow!

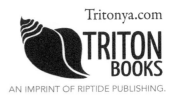

Tritonya.com

TRITON BOOKS

AN IMPRINT OF RIPTIDE PUBLISHING.

Acknowledgments

My thanks to my agent, Laurie McLean, for sticking with me and always entertaining my haphazard thoughts. Thanks to Tapas Media, for allowing me to build a great fan base and for being so flexible. My intense gratitude to my editor, May, who is boss and knows what I mean even when I don't. And finally for all my fans who beta read and supported me through this process. You guys are all awesome, and I couldn't be more pleased with this book. Thank you everyone!

About
the Author

Kristina Meister is an author of fiction that blurs genre. There's usually some myth, some mayhem, and some monsters. Kristina's fond of creative swearing and has an obsession with folklore and pop culture, adding humor and complexity to her work. Her story *Cinderella Boy* was the first book selected for RuPaul's Love Yourself Library.

She and her mad-scientist husband live in California with their poodles Khan and Lana, and their daughter Kira Stormageddon, where they hoard Nerf toys, books, and swords—in case of zombie apocalypse.

Follow her on Twitter @kristinameister and on Facebook at facebook.com/kristina.meister.

CPSIA information can be obtained
at www.ICGtesting.com
Printed in the USA
FSHW021633120820
72877FS